## Praise for *Bridesmaids Revisited*

"With its ancient setting, complicated story, mysterious old houses, hidden diaries, simmering passions, spooky emanations and love matches gone awry, the tale sometimes reads like *Wuthering Heights* on steroids. . . . Cannell's smooth narration and her appealing, smart-mouthed characters charm you into suspending disbelief. The result is a thoroughly delightful puzzle."
—*Publishers Weekly*

"Full of gothic touches and the ineffable sweetness of memory, this is clearly Cannell's best so far."
—*Booklist*

"[In her] eleventh witty mystery . . . Cannell fleshes out an entertaining gothic tale, old-fashioned in structure, sprinkled with . . . wacky humor."
—*Chicago Sun-Times*

A PENGUIN MYSTERY

# BRIDESMAIDS REVISITED

This is Dorothy Cannell's eleventh mystery. Her others include *The Trouble with Harriet*, *The Spring Cleaning Murders*, and *Down the Garden Path*. Her first mystery, *The Thin Woman*, was voted one of the 100 Best Mysteries of the Century by the Independent Mystery Booksellers Association. Born in England, Cannell now lives in Peoria, Illinois.

# *Bridesmaids Revisited*

## DOROTHY CANNELL

PENGUIN BOOKS

PENGUIN BOOKS

Published by the Penguin Group

Penguin Putnam Inc., 375 Hudson Street,
New York, New York 10014, U.S.A.
Penguin Books Ltd, 27 Wrights Lane,
London W8 5TZ, England
Penguin Books Australia Ltd, Ringwood,
Victoria, Australia
Penguin Books Canada Ltd, 10 Alcorn Avenue,
Toronto, Ontario, Canada M4V 3B2
Penguin Books (N.Z.) Ltd, 182–190 Wairau Road,
Auckland 10, New Zealand

Penguin Books Ltd, Registered Offices:
Harmondsworth, Middlesex, England

First published in the United States of America by Viking Penguin,
a member of Penguin Putnam Inc. 2000
Published in Penguin Books 2001

1   3   5   7   9   10   8   6   4   2

THE LIBRARY OF CONGRESS HAS CATALOGED THE HARDCOVER EDITION AS FOLLOWS:
Cannell, Dorothy.
Bridesmaids revisited / Dorothy Cannell.
p.   cm.
ISBN 0-670-89205-X (hc)
ISBN 014 10.0186 0 (pbk)
1. Haskell, Ellie (Fictitious character)—Fiction.   2. Women interior decorators—
Fiction.   3. England—Fiction.   I. Title.
PS3553.A499 B75 2000
813'.54—dc21                    00-038148

Printed in the United States of America
Set in Fairfield
Designed by M. Paul

To my daughter, Shana, for all the journeys taken together

# ACKNOWLEDGMENTS

Much love and appreciation to Barbara and Uncle John,
who are always there when needed.

And to my cousin Rosaleen, who is like a sister. Thank you for
going out in the middle of the night with your father to say
that last goodbye to your Auntie Charlotte. She loved you very much.

# CHAPTER ONE

I HADN'T THOUGHT about the bridesmaids in years. My only meeting with them occurred when I was about seven or eight years old and my mother took me to their house for the day. Their names had sounded to me like the start of a nursery rhyme: "Rosemary, Thora, and Jane." From a child's vantage point they had seemed middle-aged. But they could only have been in their forties. My memory of that day's visit was a little fuzzy around the edges. The house was old with a gate that creaked. There was a parrot in a cage by the fireplace and a dark red cloth with a balled fringe on the table, and a jug of lemon barley water on the sideboard. I vaguely remembered sitting on the edge of a hard chair when the one in the kitchen bent to give me a kiss.

Afterwards I asked Mother why she called them the bridesmaids. It was a long story, she said, best forgotten. So I stored that visit and my curiosity away like scraps of black-and-white photographs in some attic corner of my mind, where they gathered cobwebs along with other child-hood memories. But when I was seventeen my mother was dead, and so many things I might have asked her would be forever left unanswered.

Now on a wet and windy morning better suited to midwinter than June, I stood in the hall of my grown-up house, reading the letter that had just dropped onto the flagstone floor with the rest of the post. The handwriting was neat and precise. One sensed the ghost of a teacher, with ruler to hand, leaning over the shoulder of Rosemary Maywood, for that's whom the letter was from. In opening she said she hoped it reached me and found my family and me in good health. Then she went into a paragraph of detail about how she, Thora, and Jane had managed to track me down, by way of talking to someone who knew someone who had a friend who knew Astrid Fitzsimons, the widow of my mother's brother Wyndom. Why the bridesmaids had gone to such trouble was the burning question. I had to read page two to find out. Here Rosemary explained that her purpose in writing was to inform me that my maternal grandmother was anxious to get in touch with me. And, that she, Thora, and Jane would be pleased to arrange matters if I would come as soon as possible for a long-neglected reunion at the Old Rectory.

How peculiar! My grandmother had been no more than a name to me and I had never imagined having any sort of contact with her. My immediate reaction was to rush into my husband's study, where he was usually to be found at nine in the morning, already hard at work on his latest cookery book. Unfortunately I was out of luck today. Ben not sensing I was about to need him desperately had left at the crack of dawn for Norfolk. Even the children weren't available to me. He had taken our four-year-old twins, son Tam and daughter Abbey, and sixteen-month-old Rose on a fortnight's holiday so that I could finally finish my last bit of decorating. Therefore, I took the next best course of action, which was to head for the kitchen intent on confiding in my daily helper, Mrs. Roxie Malloy. Luckily she was just where I hoped to find her—seated at the kitchen table with a feather duster in one hand for appearance's sake and a cup of tea in the other.

"Make yourself at home, Mrs. H.," she proffered kindly. "If you're looking for Tobias, I just let him out into the garden. And don't go telling me it's not fit weather out there for man nor beast, because I already told him. If ever a cat had a mind of his own that one does. Meowed at me something dreadful he did until I just gave in." She shifted perfunctorily in her seat. "When all's said and done, there's only so much a woman can be expected to put up with in these enlightened times."

"Very true," I said.

Ours was not the typical employer–employee relationship. Mrs. Malloy and I had been through a lot together since the day I changed my name from Miss Ellie Simons to Mrs. Bentley T. Haskell, and she showed up to help hand round plates of mushroom caps on toast points at the wedding reception. Over the years she had come to behave as though Merlin's Court was her home and I was someone in the habit of dropping in unannounced in the hope that there might be a cup of tea and a piece of cake in the offing. She'd also made it clear that she didn't think much of how I'd decorated the place, despite the fact that I'd been in the interior-design business before I married and had been working part-time for the past year or so. According to her, the kitchen's quarry-tiled floor was hard on her feet, the glass-fronted cupboards looked silly with just a couple of eggcups sitting in them, and a fireplace in the kitchen was a nonsense. Nevertheless, as was the case this morning, she was usually the one to set a match to the logs at the first hint of a chill in the air.

There was no denying that I was fond of her, but Mrs. Malloy could be a royal pain at times. Presently she was looking even more long-suffering than usual. But I wasn't about to let her get started. Call me selfish, but I felt entitled for once to unload on her.

Fetching a cup and saucer from the Welsh dresser, I sat

down across from her and reached for the teapot. "Mrs. Malloy, I just received a rather disturbing letter."

"Well, if that isn't a coincidence, one came for me this morning." She nodded her jet-black head with the two inches of white roots. This was for her a fashion statement, along with the neon eye shadow, magenta lipstick, and the taffeta frocks. My cousin Freddy, who lived in the cottage at our gates, had once noted with an admiring grin that she managed to create the impression that life for her was one long cocktail party. Still, as she frequently informed me, there was a lot more to her than her glamour-puss image might lead one to suppose. "Don't let me go dwelling on my problems," she now continued magnanimously. "Just because my life is in ruins, there's no call for you to bottle up whatever's got you upset, Mrs. H.; you pour it all out, have a good snivel if it'll help."

"Oh, no! You first," I said, resolutely stuffing the envelope back in my skirt pocket. "It's not bad news about George, is it?"

"Who?" Mrs. Malloy frowned, putting a few more cracks in her makeup, which this morning appeared to have been applied with a trowel.

"Your son." We didn't often speak of George, who had been married briefly to my alluring cousin Vanessa, Aunt Astrid and Uncle Wyndom's daughter. Only to discover that the child he thought was his wasn't. This being how Ben and I had come to have Rose with us.

"That's right; me one and only—the pride and joy of his mother's heart. George is fine, thanks ever so for asking." Mrs. Malloy let the feather duster fall from her hand and sat exuding a most unnerving humility. "Course, I don't hear from him as often as I'd like, but it's not to be expected, is it? Not from a busy man like him. Quite the businessman is my George. Anyhow, you can ease your mind, Mrs. H., the letter weren't from him."

"But I wouldn't mind if he wanted to see Rose," I protested. "I understand how terribly hurt he was on finding out he wasn't her father."

"We all get a reminder once in a while that life isn't all it's cracked up to be; not for none of us it isn't." Mrs. Malloy passed me the sugar bowl. "Look at yourself, left all alone while Mr. H. goes bunking off with the kiddies for a fortnight's fun and games at that holiday camp place. Or so he says. Let a man off the lead for two minutes and there goes your marriage, you mark my words! It's the story of me third husband, Leonard, all over again." Her sigh created a whirlpool in her teacup. "Off he goes to the butcher's one Saturday morning for a pound and a half of stewing steak—I remember particularly I'd been fancying a nice meat pudding—and that's the last I sees or hears of him. Until this morning, some twenty years later, when he writes to say as how his reason for not coming home was the fault of a rare form of amnesia."

"Not the common or garden kind?" While sipping my tea I thought about the bridesmaids. They hadn't mentioned my mother, except in reference to that long-ago visit. Did they know she had died? Had they thought it in poor taste to mention the fact? Was the parrot still alive?

"There was never nothing common about Leonard." Mrs. Malloy's eyes took on a dreamy glow. "A gent through-and-through he was. Always went to a proper tailor he did; no buying his clothes down the market for him. Hair styled every week with a lovely deep wave in front. And you couldn't count the shoes in his wardrobe, polished the like you've never seen. Oh, yes, he was something to look at, was Leonard. Even when he was in the altogether, which is where most men come up short. Course"—her sigh would have done a whistling kettle proud—"he carried on with something terrible with other women, but on the bright side, they was all classy types."

"That counts for something," I conceded, wondering if I was right in thinking that Rosemary was the tallest of the bridesmaids.

"It certainly does, Mrs. H., seeing as one of me other husbands went off with a real cow that was got up like a streetwalker. I'll have you know, Mrs. H., that sort of thing takes a lot of living down for a woman like me that's always taken pride in presenting herself right." Mrs. Malloy pursed her butterfly lips, and pressed a hand to the cleavage revealed by her sequined neckline. "And when all is said and done, Leonard is my George's father."

"Really? I thought your second husband was his father."

"Well, maybe it was that way." She eyed me somewhat coldly. "It's easy to lose track when you've been married as often as I have. What it comes right down to is that Leonard had his good points. And now here he is writing to say he wants to come home to me."

"With or without the pound and a half of stewing steak?"

"There's no need to take that snippy tone, Mrs. H. Can't a man say he's sorry?"

"For keeping your meat pudding waiting twenty years?"

"Put like that, I would be a fool." Mrs. Malloy tottered to her feet, the very picture of tortured womanhood. Her black suede shoes had three-inch heels and were at least a couple of sizes too small for her. But I could tell that only a fraction of her anguish was physical.

Draining my second cup of tea, I forced myself to stop thinking about the bridesmaids. "Of course it would be a mistake to even consider taking him back," I told her. "I expect Leonard is down-and-out and needs somewhere to stay until he has another win at the dogs or whatever is his usual means of getting by. Try telling yourself how well you've done without him all these years and write back saying you've got amnesia. There's been a lot of it going around lately."

"That's easy enough to say." Mrs. M. retreated into the

pantry and emerged with a bottle of gin. For a moment I thought she was about to drown her sorrows by getting busy washing the windows. She was a great believer that gin was the best all-purpose household cleaner. Instead, she poured a good slosh into her teacup and sat back down at the table. "Leonard didn't put a return address on the letter. And I know what that means. He's going to show up on me doorstep in the next day or two and I won't have the heart to send him away, not once I get a whiff of that lovely cologne he always wore."

"It wasn't the hairspray that got to you?"

"I'll choose to ignore that crack, Mrs. H., seeing as how it's understandable you're down in the dumps." Mrs. Malloy could at times take the high road. "Clearly it don't need saying that I know better than most what it feels like having a husband bunk off to Greener Pastures. And what's worse in your case is that he took the kiddies with him."

"The holiday camp is called Memory Lanes," I corrected her.

"Well, it said a lot about greener pastures in the brochure. Sounded more like a nudist colony to me than a place for decent family fun. But if it really is about sitting around the campfire singing songs in the rain, I doubt Mr. H. will be having the time of his life. It's just another of the vicar's potty schemes, if you ask me."

The Reverend Mr. Ambleforth was indeed inclined to be eccentric but, to be strictly fair, Mrs. Malloy must have been thinking of another brochure; one she had herself picked up at the travel agency. Also, it was the Reverend's wife, Kathleen, who had organized the fortnight's holiday in Norfolk. There were now several of these Memory Lanes holiday camps scattered around England. The brainchild of a financial wizard named Sir Clifford Heath. At first, like Mrs. Malloy, I gained the wrong impression. I had imagined that Memory Lanes provided all the joys of sleeping in leaky tents and whiling away the afternoons making daisy chains or learning to play "Little Bo Peep" on the dulcimer. The concept didn't appeal to me much. I've never appreciated being organized into having a good time by a large woman with a badminton racket waiting to swat me if I failed to find a four-leaf clover, or whined about gnat bites. Initially I thought it said much for Kathleen's forceful personality that she had persuaded a dozen men at St. Anselm's parish that here was a thoroughly jolly way to spend quality time with their children. Leaving their wives at home to enjoy a relaxing couple of weeks turning out cupboards, repapering the kitchen, or whatever else gave them a sense of true domestic fulfillment. Ben, having always been a hands-on father, manfully assured me that he was genuinely excited about the trip. And after thumbing through the brochure provided by Memory Lanes, I began to think it wouldn't be so bad. It turned out that Sir Clifford Heath's vision incorporated village settings, complete with thatched cottages and cobbled streets, tearooms and haberdashery shops, duck ponds and bowling greens. The emphasis was on nostalgia, a return to a simpler way of life. Entertainment included poetry readings and musical evenings, nature walks, sketching and crocheting classes, cricket matches, and gatherings in the assembly hall listening to nineteen-forties–style programs on the wireless. To enable parents of very young children to participate fully in activities unsuited to their offspring, fully trained nannies were provided around the clock. Ben might well have the time of his life. It was selfish of me to wish he were here.

The grandfather clock in the alcove under the stairs struck the half hour—10:30. Was it possible he had been gone for two hours? It felt like the tail end of the fortnight, not the beginning. I pictured myself going into the study and perching on the edge of his desk while he sat pegging away at the old manual typewriter that he refused to abandon for an electric one, let alone a word processor. I would sit absorbing those little things about him that I loved. His crisply curling dark hair, the intent line of his jaw, the endearing way his glasses slid further down his nose every time he hit the carriage return. Very likely he wouldn't notice me at first. He would be in the thrall of his muse; totally absorbed in getting down on paper the ingredients and instructions for preparing Roasted Grouse with Prune and Walnut Dressing. I would wait until the keys slowed from a rapid clackety-clack to a tentative tap or two before interrupting him.

"Darling," I would say, very softly so as not to bring him back to reality with a jolt that would send his chair into a tailspin. "I've just received rather an odd letter from the bridesmaids."

"Who?" He would look perplexed; charmingly so—with a lift of an eyebrow and a slight tilt of the head. And instantly life would be sane and serene again. The feeling that a goose had gone waddling over my grave would become something for the two of us to laugh about.

"Rosemary, Thora, and Jane."

"Who?" Mrs. Malloy's voice came back at me from across the kitchen table.

"Oh, sorry!" I blinked and reached for my empty teacup. "I didn't realize I'd spoken out loud."

"It wasn't speaking." She could be a real stickler on some things. "It was more like singing. And not very good singing at that. The kind, like when you're a kiddie and out skipping rope on the pavement."

"It's a rhyme that popped into my head after I met them." I spoke to her from the attic inside my head, parting the cobwebs and lifting out the memory. "Rosemary, Thora, and Jane,/Lived at the end of the lane,/One was thin, one was fat,/And one was very plain."

"And you was how old when you wrote it?"

"Seven or eight."

Mrs. Malloy looked relieved. "Well, you've had time to grow out of it. Lots of kiddies go through a nasty stage. And now you'd better get what's troubling you off your chest. For it's clear to me, Mrs. H."—glancing regretfully down at the feather duster lying by her chair leg—"that I won't be able to get started working meself to death until you do. And to be fair, I do remember how just as I was drawing breath to tell you about Leonard, you started to tell me about some letter you'd got. It was from them, was it? These three women that I've never heard you mention in all the years I've worked for you?" She made a commendable effort not to sound overly miffed. "Now who exactly would they be, if it's not too much of an impertinence to ask?"

"Friends or they could be relatives of my grandmother. They live in a village called Knells, not far from Rilling. That's in Cambridgeshire. They live together, have done for years, in an old house."

"At the end of the lane?"

"Yes, it's called the Old Rectory. I hadn't heard from Rosemary, Thora, and Jane in years. Maybe they got in touch with Daddy when Mother died, but they didn't come to the funeral. And now they've asked me to come and see them right away."

"Today?"

"As soon as possible."

"All that distance, at a moment's notice!" Mrs. Malloy looked thoughtful as she graciously filled my cup, adjusted the spoon, and passed it back to me.

"It's not all that far. It shouldn't take me more than a couple of hours in the car if I stick to the motorway."

"Unless the weather continues as bad as it's been these last few days. And I doubt you're allowing for traffic. They all drive like maniacs down there, bound to with all those university kids out on larks." She handed me a plate of biscuits and encouraged me to take two. "You'd end up having to stay overnight; there's no sense in thinking otherwise."

"That's the idea," I said. "They want me to stay for a few days. They suggested a week, but I really couldn't. I've so much to do here; I promised Ben I'd finally finish Rose's room. I've got the walls to paper, her chest of drawers to strip and refinish, her little table and chairs to sponge-paint, and the floor to stencil to match the Mad Hatter's Tea Party design on her toy chest."

"We can't always think of ourselves first, Mrs. H.; from the sound of them, those three women have to be getting up in years. Poor old things! Maybe they want to talk to you about leaving you a little something in their will."

"That's not it."

"Then what's it all about?" Mrs. Malloy stopped looking soulful to shoot me a piercing glance. It was my moment to produce the letter but I found myself suddenly reluctant to do so. The kitchen was warm and cozy with the firelight gleaming on the copper pans hung around the Aga. It was the sound of the wind howling around the house, in an unlikely manner for June, that chilled me inside and out. For a moment I was a little girl again, feeling my hands grip the sides of my chair when a strange woman bent down to kiss me.

"Spit it out, Mrs. H.; why do these old girls want to see you?"

"Rosemary said my grandmother wants to get in touch with me."

"Well, I think that's nice, I do." Mrs. Malloy could be family-minded when she chose, but she quickly remembered to take umbrage. "Course it cuts me to the quick that I've never heard mention of her neither until now. What happened? Had a falling-out with your old gran, did you? Cut you off, did she, when you upped and married Mr. H. against her wishes?"

"No, nothing like that."

"Then what's the problem?"

"She's dead."

Mrs. Malloy paused to add a drop more gin to her tea. "Now that would tend to put a damper on things. Cuts down on the chances for a nice long chat, doesn't it? Been gone long, has she?"

"Since my mother was tiny. A baby in arms, I think. She didn't speak about it much."

"Funny that, her being so close on the subject. It causes me to wonder if maybe these old girls, Rosemary and the other two, haven't really come to grips with your gran being gone. Could be they've got it into their heads, wishful thinking like, that she's not really dead. Just popped out for a packet of biscuits and will be back any minute, the way I kept thinking about Leonard."

"But what if she truly isn't dead?" I asked. "What if the family made it up? To conceal a truth that they considered worse, such as her abandoning my mother to run off with a married man or pursue a career they considered unfit for a woman?"

"Or it could be"—Mrs. Malloy pursed her magenta lips—"that the old girls that live down the lane aren't quite with it mentally. Perhaps they haven't been eating right, not getting their three squares a day and forgetting to take their vitamins and minerals. An old auntie of mine started going around saying she was worried sick that she'd find herself in the family way. Well into her seventies she was at the time. But her doctor got her sorted out and she was back to being right as rain. It was her daughter, Ethel, as wasn't. She's the one that found herself in the family way, because Auntie had been sneaking her birth-control pills and replacing them with the iron tablets. Good for the baby, was how Ethel had to look at it. Forced herself to make the best of things, she did. And that's what you and me have got to do. It'll do me good to get away for a bit to this Knells place in Cambridgeshire. That way, when Leonard comes knocking on me door, I won't be there to fall in his arms, and you'll be glad of the company."

"You're a dear," I said, getting up and giving her a peck on the cheek. "But you're not coming, because I'm not going.

I'll find out what the scoop is by talking to Rosemary or one of the other bridesmaids over the phone."

"Okay, Mrs. H., spill the beans. Why don't you want to go?"

"I've told you! I've so much to do. Ben hasn't taken the children to Memory Lanes so I can go off gadding."

"Don't give me that." Mrs. Malloy tapped an impatient foot. "There's something going on inside your head that you're not telling me about, otherwise you'd be bursting with curiosity to find out about your gran."

"I am, but for some silly reason I'm afraid."

"And that's just why I'm not letting you go on your own." Mrs. Malloy spoke as though I were one of the twins, to be gently but firmly dissuaded from climbing into the laundry chute. "It's clear to me you don't know these women from the man in the moon. So who's to say that this business of your grandmother isn't something they've cooked up between the three of them for reasons nice people like you and me couldn't even begin to guess at?" She gave a nicely executed shudder. "Just standing here I can feel the spooky vibes all the way down to me toes."

And as she was fond of saying, those toes of hers didn't lie.

# CHAPTER TWO

I THOUGHT I WOULD have trouble falling asleep that night. I had been puzzling about the bridesmaids' reason for their invitation on and off throughout the day, although I can't say that I had allowed Mrs. Malloy and her toes to scare me. She was as partial to gothic romances as I was myself. The kind where any locked door concealed a diabolical secret. And every cup of tea was suspect. But when I got into bed it was to think how vast and empty it felt without Ben. Was he missing me, too? Were the twins and Rose? I tried to picture them at Memory Lanes, but even when images came they slid one into another and became fuzzier until I felt myself getting muffled up in sleep. Then I heard a bell ring, and keep ringing, and struggled up thinking that it must be Ben at the door with the children. They must have realized they could not stay away from me for more than a day and were at the door. By the time it took me to get my feet on the floor I was wondering why Ben hadn't used his key. And then I realized it wasn't the doorbell ringing, but the telephone. Heart hammering, I fumbled across the bedside table and picked up the receiver.

"Hello?" I stammered.

There was a pause, which seemed to go on forever before a voice spoke in my ear. "Don't come to the Old Rectory."

I was struggling to ask "Who is this?" when I dropped the phone and upon picking it up heard a buzzing in my ear. We had been disconnected.

It was several minutes before I was able to lie back down. I was so shaken I wasn't even sure whether the speaker had been a man or a woman. And now I doubted I would be able to close my eyes for the rest of the night. But after I stared at the ceiling for a while the phone call began to take on a dreamlike quality and the feeling of menace receded. Perhaps it was one of the bridesmaids calling. Probably if I hadn't dropped the phone she would have added the word "tomorrow" to her admonition. That it would better for me to delay my visit for a couple of days until the hole in the roof could be repaired. So that I wouldn't be tripping over buckets set out to collect the rain the weather forecaster had predicted. Or so that the silver could be polished, or the ironing finished. I would call them in the morning . . . I fell back asleep.

And the following morning I did call, to be assured that, no, neither Thora, nor Jane, nor Rosemary had phoned and that of course I was to come as planned. Perhaps I had dreamed the mysterious phone call? Putting my suspicions aside, I crept out of the house at the cockcrow, secure in the belief that Mrs. Malloy would still be safely tucked up in bed. But when I opened the doors to the stables, which now did duty as the garage, I was greeted by the self-appointed grand dame of Chitterton Fells hefting an enormous suitcase into the boot of the bottle-green Rover that Ben had given me for Christmas. Before I could finish converting a yawn (I am not by nature an early riser) into a gape, she had squeezed my modest-sized travel bag into the limited space remaining and climbed into the front passenger seat. Resisting the urge to slam down the boot lid with sufficient force to send the car into orbit, I got in beside her and gripped the steering wheel in what I hoped was a menacing manner.

"Nice of you to show up." Mrs. Malloy opened her fake alligator handbag and pulled out a map. She was wearing a raincoat, as was I, but unlike my sensible beige affair hers was a wild-cherry red. "I was afraid"—she contorted her purple lips into a grimace—"as I'd be forced to take the bus."

"Don't even think of it," I said, backing the car onto the drive in a series of hopefully sickening lurches. "I'm more than happy to take you straight back home. As I thought I made plain yesterday, you are not coming with me to Knells to visit the bridesmaids. This is a family matter which I intend to handle, or mishandle if you'd rather, all by myself."

"That's you all over." Mrs. Malloy was spreading the map across her cherry-red knees as I spun the car around in a shower of gravel and shot down the drive. "Selfish to the core you are some of the time. You're afraid one of those batty old women will bop me over the head in the dead of night just for the fun of it, and you'll be left to do your own housework for the rest of your days. All alike, you upper-class types are, just like my Leonard used to say."

"Me! Upper class!" I narrowly missed colliding with the copper beech to my left. "You're the one who's always harping on about how your ancestors came over with the Normans."

"So they did." Mrs. Malloy dug in her stiletto heels and belatedly fastened her seat belt. "Only if you'd been listening properly you'd have realized I was talking about the Normans of Bethnal Green. Alfie and Myrtle was the mum and dad. I lost count of the children. A lovely hardworking family of poachers from the sound of them."

"Poachers? In Bethnal Green?"

"Well, you don't think they wanted to put 'pickpocket' on them job application forms! And I don't see how it was their fault there aren't all that many rabbits hopping around bus stops or down around the train stations in London these days."

"No, I don't suppose so," I found myself saying as we passed my cousin Freddy's cottage at the end of the drive and went out through the iron gates onto the cliff road that wound down to our left towards the village of Chitterton Fells. That was the trouble with Mrs. Malloy. Few knew better than she how to divert a conversation until returning to the point of contention became more effort than it was worth. But in this instance I did manage to fumble my way back to Leonard.

"What about him?" she asked as I eased to my right to let a bus pass without either vehicle going over the cliff. Something which would have annoyed the people at the town hall who were tired of putting up new railings every six months.

"I'm wondering why Leonard's opinion on any subject under the sun should matter a grain of rice to you," I said.

"Now what are you going on about, Mrs. H.?" If Mrs. Malloy sounded snooty it may, in all fairness, have been due to the fact that she was sucking on a peppermint humbug.

"You just said something about his take on the upper classes."

"Did I?"

Even while keeping my eyes directly ahead in order to watch the approaching traffic light, I could tell she had gone all misty-eyed. So I bit my lip and waited for her to rally.

"Well, that goes to show, don't it? That man's right back inside my head, and if I wasn't to get away from home for a few days there's no saying what I'd do if he was to show up at me door doing the old sob-and-dance routine." She swallowed, from the sound of it the whole peppermint, and placed a tremulous hand on my knee. "I know it's hard for you to understand, Mrs. H., after what I told you about Leonard and his womanizing; but I only have to get thinking about him saying: 'Come on, Roxie old girl, lend me fifty quid for old times' sake' to go all weak at the knees.

That sort of sweet talk did it for me every time when we was together. What it all comes down to, Mrs. H., is that it'd be nothing short of wicked for you to drop me off back home to wait like a mouse with one leg in a sling for the cat to show up."

"We've already passed the turnoff for your house," I pointed out, stopping for another traffic light.

"So we have." Mrs. Malloy offered me a peppermint, which I stoically refused even though I was dying of hunger, having skipped breakfast in my haste to be off before she showed up. "Speaking of cats . . ."

"Were we?" I passed a lorry that didn't seem to know whether it was coming or going.

"Being the thoughtful sort I am, Mrs. H., I just wanted to say I hope you was able to make arrangements for Tobias. Poor little love," she added with all the insincerity at her disposal, having disliked my beloved cat from the word go. "It would just break me heart to think of him meowing his way around that house starving to death."

"Freddy's taken him down to the cottage."

"And there's a dear young man if ever there was one." Mrs. Malloy did not go so far as to dab at her eyes, but I got the picture. "A son any mother would give the earth for. All that lovely long hair and the earring. Of course"— adjusting the map on her knees—"from what I've seen he doesn't have any tattoos, but give him time; they all mature at different rates and the lad's not yet thirty when all is said and done. Truth is, I'm rather surprised, given his lovely nature and all, that Freddy didn't insist on going with you on this nice little visit to the wacky old ladies."

"There is absolutely no reason to think that Rosemary, Thora, and Jane aren't perfectly sane, sensible women." I kept a grip on my temper and a lookout for the entry onto the motorway that should be coming up shortly if I hadn't gone the wrong way around the roundabout two miles back.

"Well, if you say so, Mrs. H.," the woman who should have been looking at the map said in her most conciliatory voice. "How did they sound when you phoned them? You did ring them up, didn't you?"

"Yes, of course I did. Last evening." We were now on the A40 or it could have been the M16 for all I knew; anyway, there was a lot of traffic all moving purposefully along as if intent on arriving eventually at someplace or other, so it seemed best to keep going. Especially as I'm not particularly good at doing U-turns at a hundred kilometers an hour. "I spoke to Rosemary, told her that I could come today if that suited, and that was pretty much it. When I tried to talk to her about Grandma, she said it would be best to leave all that until I arrived and had had several cups of tea."

"And you thought that was all perfectly normal!" Mrs. Malloy scoffed.

"She was very likely thinking about my phone bill; older people are conscious of running up the charges." I knew I didn't sound very convincing. But that was only, I told myself, because like Mrs. Malloy, I was addicted to romance novels with a gothic twist. Having read about innumerable heroines being lured back to decaying houses under one preposterous pretext or another, it was pitifully easy for me to foresee a dark turret with bars on the windows and an iron key that went clang in the night as part of my immediate future.

What I couldn't hope for was to have my head turned by a dark, stormy-eyed hero ensconced in the drawing room, nursing a glass of Madeira along with his chagrin at having a mad wife in the attic. The only man for whom I would have risked life and limb was presently in Norfolk with our children. When he had telephoned at ten-thirty the previous evening I hadn't had the heart to put anything but a cheerful spin on the bridesmaids' invitation. Poor darling! He had sounded exhausted from a surfeit of fun listening to one woman playing the harp and another singing "There Is a Lady Sweet and Kind" for two hours straight, in the assembly hall. This treat had been followed by cocoa and biscuits, at which time, Reverend Ambleforth, our abstemious vicar, had been heard to whisper that he could have done with a stiff teaspoon of brandy.

Besides, had I sounded the least bit uneasy, Ben would have told me I was under no obligation to visit the bridesmaids. He might even have reminded me how I had promised to finish my redecorating. With all that in mind I had focused on what Ben had to say about Rose's antics. And how much Abbey had enjoyed the boat ride on the river that afternoon. And how Tam had even more enjoyed almost falling in. Afterwards I wasn't sure that I had said anything about my grandmother, other than that Rosemary, Thora, and Jane were girlhood friends of hers. And wasn't it rather sweet of them to get in touch with me after all this time? Ben wouldn't have thought the phone call I'd received later anything of the kind. But I was forgetting— that must have been a dream.

Mrs. Malloy broke into my thoughts. "I can see you're looking worried to death."

"I'm concentrating on the road." I smiled at her, because seeing that she was here it seemed silly not to be pleased she was coming with me. If the bridesmaids thought it peculiar, so be it. I could always say she had been poorly and needed a change of air. They were of the generation to believe in that sort of thing. Or I could say I couldn't risk leaving her with the silver for fear she would polish it down to the nub. No mention of the nefarious Leonard would pass my lips. He was entirely Mrs. Malloy's business, I was thinking self-righteously, when she nearly caused me to swerve off the road.

"I must say it was nice of Gwen to offer to put me up at short notice, but as I've always said, Mrs. H., there's no friends like old friends when all is said and done."

"Gwen? Who's Gwen?"

"She and me went to school together. A plain, spotty-faced kiddie she was, but no fault of hers is what I'd tell her. I used to help poor Gwen with her homework. She wasn't none too bright neither, especially when it came to doing her sums. Any rate, the long and the short of it, Mrs. H., is you made it more than clear I wasn't welcome to stay at the Old Vicarage, or whatever it's called, for fear of putting the old girls out. So I cast me mind back and remembered how when you said they lived near Rilling something rang a bell upstairs. And last night it came to me as how Gwen had got a job there after being sacked from Woolworth's for never being able to remember the price of licorice allsorts. Such a fuss her parents made when she finally took her thumb out of her mouth and told them she was going away to work."

"It must be hard to see your children go off on their own," I said.

"You're right, broke me heart to see George on his way. I could hardly stand watching him picking up the cases I'd tossed out the door after him. Mind you, Mrs. H., Gwen wasn't fifteen. Thirty-five if she was a day." Mrs. Malloy sucked on another humbug and continued talking out the side of her mouth. "But to be fair to her mum and dad, I had doubts meself as to how she'd cope getting herself up of a morning, let alone being a nanny to three little children. And them with a sick mother and a father that was helpless, as most men are if it don't have to do with work."

"I hope they treated Gwen well." I was eager to get to the outcome. Was Mrs. Malloy coming with me to the Old Rectory or wasn't she?

"Fiddler was the name and me luck being in I was able to get the number last night from Directory Inquiries."

"But surely the children are grown by now," I said, growing moment by moment more in dire need of a cup of coffee, to say nothing of bacon and eggs.

"The eldest must be forty, Mrs. H., and the other two well up in their thirties."

"Unless they're all extremely backward they can't still need a nanny. But from the sound of it Gwen stayed on in Rilling."

"She lives several miles outside. Closer to the village where you're going."

"Knells." On catching sight of a Little Chef, I had decided to pull off the motorway and was now stuck within view of the parking lot behind a lorry whose driver appeared to be taking a catnap.

"Where Gwen lives is called Upper Thaxstead."

"But surely she isn't still with the same family, after . . . how many years?"

Mrs. Malloy opened her mouth, then closed it. She wasn't about to give me a chance to do my sums and work out her age as a contemporary of Gwen's. "Course she's still there," she said as the lorry finally got moving and I was able to pull into a parking space close to the Little Chef entrance. Mrs. Malloy kept her patter going as we entered the restaurant. "Poor Mrs. Fiddler died from whatever ailed her—heart trouble I think it was—and after a decent interval Mr. F. married Gwen. I don't suppose he felt as how he could do anything else. If she'd stayed on at the house, tongues would have wagged. And letting her go would have been like putting a kitten out the door and telling it to bugger off and fend for itself.

"You'll have to remind me," she said piously as we sat down at a table and picked up our menus, "that I've to thank Mr. Fiddler for behaving like a true Christian gentleman. Not that I expect it's a real marriage, if you understand me. Separate bedrooms is my guess. Gwen couldn't never bear the mention of sex. Said just the thought of it put her off her dinner for a week."

"How long since you've seen her?" By now I could have eaten the menu and there wasn't a waitress in sight.

"Not since she went to Upper Thaxstead."

"Perhaps she's changed."

"You'll have to meet Gwen. Born a repressed spinster she was. As I've said, not meaning to be nasty, plain as a suet pudding." A smiling waitress had appeared at our table like a nymph rising out of the deep. Mrs. Malloy ordered bacon, eggs, tomatoes, and fried bread along with a pot of tea and, because the nymph looked as though she had already worn out the soles of her feet, I made things simple by saying I would have the same.

The restaurant was quite crowded, and subdued waves of conversation flowed around us as I unbuttoned my raincoat and slid it onto the back of my chair. Mrs. Malloy had done the same and I was stunned to see that she was wearing a sweatshirt. This woman who I wouldn't expect to be caught dead in anything less dressy than black taffeta and sequins. The sweatshirt was pale blue and read: I WENT TO CAMBRIDGE.

"Well, so I did." Her heavy makeup cracked in a couple of places as she caught my eye. "What if it was only for a day trip, on the coach last summer? When in Cambridgeshire, try and fit in is my way of thinking . . .

"All I'm asking, Mrs. H.," she said, gusting a weary sigh, "is a few days' peace and quiet where Leonard can't get his paws on me."

I poured us both a cup of tea from the pot the waitress had deposited in the center of the table and raised mine in salute. "Then here's to hoping that things will be delightfully dull at Gwen's. With any luck I'll have an equally boring time with the bridesmaids."

"You're not looking forward to a chin wag with your grandmother's ghost?"

Luckily my mouth was full with bacon and eggs and I couldn't respond. We ate for a while in silence. The fried bread was golden crisp and the tomatoes sent up little wisps of rosy steam. As I plied my knife and fork I wondered what

Ben and the children were doing. Had they already had breakfast? Were they wandering through sky-filled meadows picking buttercups and daisies with other happy Memory Laners? Was there a babbling brook for them to sit beside while birds trilled overhead and cottontailed bunnies in plush brown suits popped in and out of the hedgerows? My mind wandered round one green-shaded corner after another to a time and place I hadn't visited in a long time, until Mrs. Malloy brought me back to the table with a jolt.

"Thinking about Mr. H., aren't you?"

"What?"

"You've got that soppy, dreamy-eyed look on your face that only a man can put there." She clinked her teaspoon against her cup the better to call me to attention.

"Actually, I wasn't thinking about Ben. At least not for the last few minutes. I was thinking about my mother. I've been doing so on and off ever since I got the bridesmaids' letter."

"You've never talked about her much." Mrs. Malloy eyed me with unwonted sympathy as the waitress removed our plates. "Terribly sad it must have been losing her when you was so young. What were you, eighteen?"

"Seventeen. The same age she was when she married my father. She was eighteen when she had me. It seems strange now, but I didn't realize at the time how terribly young she was to die. Thirty-six." I poured myself more tea and sat not drinking it. "But I suppose children never see their parents as anything but middle-aged, if not actually old. Yet at the same time they believe their parents will live forever. I still half-believe she would have done if she hadn't fallen down that flight of railway steps at Kings Cross. It was ironic really . . ."

"Why do you say that, Mrs. H.?"

"She was a dancer. Ballet. Oh, she was never a prima ballerina. What jobs she got were few and far between and only ever in the corps de ballet. But she gloried in it. It was why she ran away from home and made her way to London, where my father—he was some sort of distant cousin—found her and married her before she could starve to death in a garret."

"Well, life isn't known for making sense." Mrs. Malloy laid a heavily ringed hand on mine. "You just have to hold on to your memories, is all I can say."

"And I do have wonderful ones." My eyes misted.

"That's the ticket, Mrs. H.!"

I reached behind me for my raincoat and slipped my arms through the sleeves, not because I was in any mad rush to get up and leave, but because I was cold inside and out.

"She was so special, a sort of magical person really, and everything she did, from taking pleasure in the violets she grew on the windowsills to reading me a story, seemed to be brushed with a kind of wonder. Yet I have this feeling that I never really knew her. It was as though some part of her was secreted away. I used to think it was because so much of her was wrapped up in my father. I believed that theirs was one of the great loves of all time, and that everyone else, even I, existed for them in a different sphere."

"But now you see it different?" Mrs. Malloy picked up the bill that the waitress had laid down in the no-man's-land between us. She checked it over, with the confident look of one who had shown Gwen how to get her sums right when they were kiddies. But at the same time I could feel her concern that I wouldn't snatch it away from her.

"Not about their love for each other. It's just that from having talked with my father recently—really talked for the first time ever, I wonder if my mother's upbringing impacted on her in ways I never understood. It took Daddy years to get over her death. I am so glad he has another chance of happiness with Ursel Grundman, his German lady friend. I phoned him last night but there was no answer."

"Out cavorting on the Rhine, I expect."

"I had so many questions for him," I went on, speaking

more to myself than to Mrs. Malloy. Once I got to thinking that I knew nothing about my grandmother Sophia, other than that she died when Mummy was a baby, I realized how very little information I have about my mother's life before I was born. Just the part about Daddy finding her in London and sweeping her off to the registry office.

"You said he was a distant cousin of hers, Mrs. H.?"

"Yes, he was introduced to her at some funeral. Afterwards he couldn't put her out of his mind. I don't know how he heard that she'd gone to London."

"Word gets around in families."

"I suppose." I finished buttoning my raincoat.

"Who was to know that she'd go walking out that door one day and never come back." Now Mrs. Malloy was misty-eyed.

"It was a Thursday." I was still talking to myself.

"A woman her age, she'd have thought as how she had a whole lifetime ahead, Mrs. H., to fill you in on things."

"I came in from school expecting her to be there. Mother was vague about some things, but never about being home for me."

In my mind I was back at the flat in St. John's Wood. I could see myself opening the door, it was rarely locked, and tossing my satchel down on a bench in the narrow hall. I could hear the click of my shoes on the parquet floor. I could see myself stepping into the sitting room. It was cluttered and haphazardly furnished, fantastical with its red-and-white toadstool curtains and invitingly livable with its worn comfy sofa and row of bookcases. A door to the right by the windows gave entry into my parents' bedroom. As usual that door stood open but my mother wasn't at the bar which ran the length of one wall, where she did her ballet exercises. No silhouette of her elevated arm and fluttering fingers creating a tree branch on the wall. The only person I saw was myself in the long mirror facing me. No sign of my father. But that wasn't surprising. He was often out in the afternoons looking for work in a hit-or-hopefully-miss sort of way to augment his trust fund. My feet dragged into the tiny kitchen that held a table and three chairs. On the one wall that wasn't turned into a miniature skyline by an uneven configuration of cupboards, my mother had hung my drawings and watercolors from art class. When putting up the last she had said without turning round: "You're going to win that art competition you entered. These are really good, Ellie. It's probably an inherited talent, even though your father and I can't draw a straight line between us." My eyes went from my still life of a violin, a loaf of bread, and a paisley scarf . . . to the note under the jam pot on the table:

"Dear Giselle, I have to go out for a few hours. If I'm not home by teatime, could you please fix a meal for yourself and Daddy? Something like baked beans, because I think he's being a vegetarian this week. Love, Mother."

Looking back, it was at that moment that my world turned into a series of still lifes . . . The phone rang, it was Daddy hysterical on the other end.

"So what took her to Kings Cross?" Mrs. Malloy's voice dragged me back into the present.

"Daddy thought she might have gone on a job interview. She'd seen an advertisement for a part-time ballet teacher in the evening paper the night before. And she had said she might inquire into it. But why she went really doesn't matter, does it? She tripped, she fell, she died." I got to my feet and tied my raincoat belt while looking straight ahead. "Sadly that's the end of the story."

"Rubbish!" Mrs. Malloy handed me the bill. "If you didn't want to reopen the book you wouldn't be going to see the bridesmaids, now would you?"

She had a point, and as we walked back out into the parking lot under a sprinkling of rain I very much wished she were coming with me to the Old Rectory rather than going to stay with her school chum Gwen.

# CHAPTER THREE

"It's a big house." The time was a little after noon. It was still raining in soft, petulant drops as Mrs. Malloy stood on the pavement of the country road with fields across the way. Her suitcases sat at her feet like three well-trained dogs, while she gave the Fiddler residence the once-over. "Nothing like the size of Merlin's Court, of course, but enough to keep Gwen hopping from morning till night from the looks of it."

"Perhaps," I suggested tentatively, surveying the red-brick Victorian dwelling with its plethora of chimney pots, "she has help in the house."

"Oh, I wouldn't think so." Mrs. M. pursed her purple lips, which she no doubt considered a perfect foil for the wild-cherry raincoat. "What with Mr. Fiddler being good enough to marry her, he was entitled to get a housekeeper out of it, is my way of looking at things. Course, if there's one thing to say for Gwen it's that she's the grateful sort. In a nice humble sort of way. I do hope she did something about them spots on her face. At thirty-five she still had them as bad as any teenager. And never could find a hair-style that did nothing for her. Sad, isn't it? Ah, well, we can't all be blessed with good looks, Mrs. H.!"

Having taken her sweet time batting her magenta lids, Mrs. Malloy proceeded up the broad drive with its neat borders of shrubs and flowers to the front door, where she rang the bell. Her cases did not trot dutifully after her on padded paws. By the time I had made two trips to lug them onto the step, she was already inside the hall. It was rather a grand space with a lot of carved wood and pictures in heavy gold frames. The wallpaper was florid in texture and pattern and it was all a little too rococo for my taste. But as an interior designer I acknowledged the importance of a home being representative of its owners' personalities.

Looking in on the woman standing with Mrs. Malloy's hands clasped in hers, I couldn't deny that the house suited her, from her bleached-blond hair to her high-heeled shocking-pink shoes. "Vulgar" was the word that nipped into my mind. Could this be one of Gwen's stepdaughters? She had now spotted me over Mrs. M.'s shoulder and with a well-executed expression of delight hurried to welcome me over the threshold.

"Come in, come in! Mrs. Haskell, isn't it? Don't worry about the carpet, dear," seeing me glance down at my shoes that had staggered into one or two puddles on route. "What's a little rainwater? And it's a very old carpet. Been in the family for years. Handmade in Algiers. Practically an antique. Oh, you're taking them off! No need on my account, but I expect you'll be more comfortable. Nothing nastier than damp soggy shoes, is what I often say to Fiddler."

"Fiddler?"

"My husband."

This was Gwen? Poor spotty-faced Gwen, who hadn't left the shelter of Mum and Dad's roof until she was thirty-five?

"Such a dear, lovely man. His Christian name is Barney, but I always call him Fiddler. It's one of our little love jokes, you might say, going back to when I was the r nny to his children and his first wife was still alive. Only of course then I called him Mr. Fiddler." She batted her eyelashes, which were at least two inches longer than Mrs. Malloy's, and gave an insouciant giggle. "Now I only call him Mr. Fiddler when in bed of an evening . . . or every once in a while of an afternoon."

I could only smile raptly as she took my raincoat and hung it next to Mrs. M.'s on the oak stand that looked as if it might also have come from Algiers. This Gwen was thin as a rail, in skintight black pants, a cowl-neck sweater, and didn't look a day over forty—if that. She had a topknot of platinum curls tied with a shocking-pink velvet ribbon to match her shoes, and jangled with jewelry every step of the way. Understandably, Mrs. Malloy looked none too pleased by this turn of events.

"Well, it's plain to see Gwen's landed on her feet." Her voice had more than a bit of a snort to it. "I was just telling her when you come up to the door, Mrs. H., that I wouldn't have known her if we'd met in the street. And of course I couldn't be happier for her."

"I knew you'd feel that way, dear." Gwen studied the writing on Mrs. M.'s blue sweatshirt with only a slight lift of her winged brows. "Always such a love was Roxie, so kind at helping me with my sums when we were at school. Now it's payback time. That's how I put it to Fiddler and as usual he quite saw it my way." She was now speaking to me in the lowered voice a grown-up might use while a little one was underfoot. "'You help out your old friend,' is what Fiddler said. 'Have her here as long as you like.' And of course I explained to him about that dreadful Leonard trying to worm his way back into her life after all these years. The cheek of it!"

"Mrs. Malloy's talked a lot about you," was all I could say with a certain person breathing down my neck.

"There's no need to go feeling sorry for me, Gwen."

"Now that's where I disagree with you," came the sparkling response. "All your life, Roxie Malloy, you've done for others. Putting your own needs and feelings aside, trying to bring a little sunshine and light into other people's misery. Giving and giving with never a thought of return. 'Where would I be,' I asked Fiddler, 'if the prettiest girl in the whole of Pankhurst Elementary School hadn't been my own guardian angel when the other kids went around calling me Spotty Face?'"

"Oh, well, if you're going to put it like that." Mrs. Malloy was clearly mollified. "Horrible how children can be! It makes you ashamed to admit having been one. But you mustn't put me on a pedestal, Gwen, just because I don't have an unkind bone in me body." She gave one of her pious sighs. "Mrs. H. is always harping on about me being too soft."

"Every day," I agreed.

"We're as God makes us and that's that." Mrs. Malloy didn't add: "With a little help for some of us from the plastic surgeons." If Gwen was aware of the eyes feeling their way up into her hairline and behind her ears she gave no sign. She was looking at a portrait on the wall. The shadowed figure of an old woman in a rocking chair.

"That's Fiddler's mother," she said. "It was done after she died."

"Well, I guess that's one way the artist could get her to sit still," Mrs. Malloy mused.

"It was painted from a photograph."

"Very nice," I said.

"And this is Fiddler's first wife, Mildred." Gwen had moved down the hall to point out an even larger portrait. It was of a middle-aged female who looked as though she had sat for years on a bad case of piles waiting for the Grim Reaper to beckon from the shadows. "A wonderful likeness, as you could tell from the resemblance, if you were to see her son and two daughters."

"The way her eyes pop . . ." Mrs. Malloy was clearly beginning to see herself as a serious art critic. "Would that be a symptom of the illness that took her?"

"No, it's just that she wasn't wearing her glasses." Gwen's smile slipped the merest fraction. "Poor Mildred. She was constantly losing them. Fiddler was always after her, in the kindest possible way, for being absentminded."

"She looks as though she could be sitting on them and getting a poke up the bum."

"Probably she was having one of her twinges. Agonizing they could be. The doctor was of the opinion"—this said with a certain emphasis—"that it was amazing how she didn't die sooner given the terrible state of her heart. There was never a question of her living more than a few years after I came to take care of the kiddies. And I like to think I helped make Mildred's last days as comfortable as possible."

"While taking ever such nice care of Mr. Fiddler." Mrs. Malloy nodded approvingly. "And the kiddies, too, of course."

This was all very pleasant, I thought, but I really should leave the two women to enjoy catching up on the years since they had last seen each other. I offered to take the suitcases upstairs. The exercise would have done me good after sitting for hours in the car just pushing the occasional pedal, but Gwen wouldn't hear of it. She said Fiddler would take care of the luggage when he came home for lunch shortly. There was a nice steak-and-kidney pudding in the steamer and an egg custard baking in the oven, but if I wouldn't stay to eat I must at least have a cup of tea to warm me on my way. Before I could decline she had skimmed ahead of us on her black scissor legs, the shocking-pink ribbon fluttering above her platinum topknot, into what she modestly called the front room. And after seeing Mrs. Malloy and me settled on a pair of extremely uncomfortable chairs that looked as though they might have come out of a monastery, she left us with the promise of returning in two ticks.

"Done all right for herself, has Gwen." Mrs. M.'s gaze rested on a towering china cabinet displaying a mammoth collection of ruby-red cut glass. I, on the other hand, was more taken with the draperies. They were of a particularly strong shade of mustard, fringed with purple, and graced not only the windows, but innumerable alcoves along with the entrance into an equally overfurnished dining room. "Nice fireplace," continued the home-furnishings expert from *House Beautiful,* shifting in her seat to eye the mantelpiece, above which hung a portrait of Gwen decked out in sequins and pearls.

"You must be happy for her," I said.

"Pleased as Punch."

"Those must be the stepchildren." I pointed to several eight-by-ten photos on the velvet-draped piano. "They look a pleasant bunch. A credit to their upbringing. It can't have been easy for them getting over the death of their mother and accepting Gwen in her place, however fond they are of her."

"You're back to thinking about your own mum." Mrs. Malloy lifted her feet onto a footstool hung around with tassels.

"It's impossible not to identify, especially with this visit to the bridesmaids looming."

"Life can't all be bingo and nights out at the pub, Mrs. H., is what I say. That's why in the thick of me own worries about Leonard I'm glad to be here. It's clear as one of them plate-glass windows that for all this big house and her new looks, Gwen needs me something desperate."

"Why's that?"

"You mean you didn't notice?"

"Notice what?"

"That haunted look of hers."

"I can't say I did."

"Perhaps that's because you didn't know her when she was a kiddie," Mrs. Malloy grudgingly conceded. "But I remember as if it was yesterday how she'd look when it was time to go to class and hand in the homework I'd done for her. It was like she was waiting for a policeman's hand to come down with a wallop on her shoulder and a voice to boom in her ear: 'You'd better come along with me, young Missy.'"

"So she's the sort to make mountains out of molehills," I observed. "Perhaps she forgot to put clean sheets on your bed. Or is afraid you'll realize she made the egg custard that's supposedly baking in the oven from a packet."

"Trust you to go minimizing things, Mrs. H. I tell you there's something serious troubling Gwen. And it's me duty to find out what it is and put her life back to rights before she works herself into needing another face-lift and loses a stone and a half she can't afford to lose."

"Being already a pitiful size six," I was saying when the door opened. A man of medium height with iron-gray hair brushed straight back off his forehead and a pair of very blue eyes came into the room. Having been taught by my parents to rise when a grown-up of either sex walked into the room, and tending to forget that I might now be classified as a grown-up myself, I stood up. Mrs. Malloy remained seated, but I could see her eyelashes flicker and her butterfly lips shimmer a deeper purple as she moistened them into a smile.

"Tell me you're Gwen's husband?" She was now crossing her legs at the ankles. They were good ankles, crisscrossed with the narrow straps of her high-heeled black patent-leather shoes. The man ceased shaking my hand to take appreciative note of them. Or perhaps he just had a kindly smile and a slight squint.

"You've hit it on the nose, I'm Barney Fiddler." He proceeded to take her hand and hold it even longer than he had mine.

"Isn't that nice!" His wife's lifelong friend was practically purring. "I was afraid you was a plainclothes policeman come to give Mrs. H. a ticket for parking on the wrong side of the street."

"Mrs. . . . ?" He turned, without releasing her hand, in my direction.

"Haskell," I supplied. "I'm on my way to visit some family friends in Knells."

"And you kindly brought our Roxie here on your way." He was back to gazing down at her.

"I do hope I won't be in the way," the wretched woman simpered.

"Such a very great pleasure to have you here, my dear. As you may imagine I have wanted to meet you for years. Gwen is forever talking about the best friend she ever had. And now we have this reunion of two delightfully grown-up little girls. Ah, and here is my darling now!" He turned at the clickety-click sound of footsteps, and hastened to remove a heavily laden tray from his wife's hands and lower it onto the marble coffee table. "Good girl," he said, patting her shoulder benevolently. "I see you used the silver teapot. Have to make this an occasion, don't we? I'll be mother and pour, darling, while you sit next to Mrs. Haskell on the sofa."

Thus freeing himself to take the chair next to Mrs. Malloy's when he was done passing the cups and saucers and little plates of ginger biscuits. There was no doubt that he kept glancing in her direction. The perfect host intent on making sure that her every need was anticipated.

"I didn't hear you come in, Fiddler, but I'm sure you remembered to wipe your feet before crossing the hall. You're as fond of that antique rug as I am." Gwen was all black angles and platinum-blond hair as she sat down. "And it looks as though you've already started getting to know Roxie and have met kind Mrs. Haskell."

"Yes, darling." His voice was soothing. "She told me she's going on to Knells to stay with friends."

"Three women who were friends of her grandmother's," Mrs. Malloy informed him as she picked up her teacup and elevated her pinky. "Mrs. H. hasn't seen them in years. Rather strange birds, if you ask me."

I wanted to say I hadn't, but settled for disclosing that they lived at the Old Rectory.

"What a coincidence!" Having finished being mother, Barney Fiddler sat down on one of the monastery chairs and looked from me to his wife, then back again. "Or perhaps it isn't really. Knells is a very small village. Just the pub and a church or two, a small row of shops, and a few streets of houses. But even so . . ." He paused to bite into a ginger biscuit. "Gwen must have mentioned her cousin Edna to you." He was now addressing Mrs. Malloy, who pursed her lips and furrowed her brow.

"I can't say as I remember."

"There's no reason I'd put Edna in letters. And anyway Roxie and I haven't been in touch for quite a while." Gwen sounded a bit snappish.

"But, darling," responded her husband, "Edna was the reason you came to Upper Thaxstead. It was her that sent you the clipping of my newspaper advertisement for a nanny. Surely you spoke of her to Roxie at the time, darling? I thought you two girls shared everything."

"I think it's coming back to me, Gwen." Mrs. Malloy looked eager to cooperate. "You said your parents wouldn't have agreed to your leaving home before your fortieth birthday if you hadn't been going to live near a cousin. A nice sensible older woman, that didn't believe in going to the pictures on Sundays or wearing gobs of makeup."

"Not a very accurate description of Edna." Barney chuckled as he again handed round the plate of biscuits. "From what I've heard she was a bit of a lass in her day. One good-for-nothing bloke after another before she married. But that's how these things go, isn't it? She wouldn't be the first or the last to take a turn or two around the paddock before getting on the straight and narrow." He had now fixed me with an intent blue stare. "You're going to the Old Rectory, you said. Lots of stories told about that house over the years. There was the vicar who dropped dead over his Sunday lunch. And his curate that went out with his new bride to work as a missionary in the Belgian Congo and came back a widower with a child. We've heard a good number of the stories from Edna, haven't we, Gwen?"

"I've never encouraged her to gossip. And, anyway, she's not the sort. She's a decent hardworking woman, past or no past."

"I'm still not sure," I said, trying to keep the frustration out of my voice, "about the coincidence. What connection does this cousin have to the people I am going to visit in Knells?"

"Edna works for them." Gwen could not have made the admission more reluctantly. "Has done for years. Long before I came to Upper Thaxstead."

"Does light cleaning." Barney appeared blithely oblivious to his wife's glum expression. "And she cooks the odd meal. At least that's how it works now with the three ladies. She says she was on the go from morning till night working for the vicar."

"The one that fell dead in his Yorkshire pudding?" Mrs. Malloy displayed a flattering interest.

"No, his son-in-law. The widower with the daughter. He took over the parish when he got back from being a missionary and stayed on till his death—some years after his daughter ran off to London to be a ballet dancer. I think Edna said she later married a cousin, one of the several-times-removed sort."

"She did," I said.

"Oh, you know about her?" Gwen had perked up.

"She was my mother." I sat there taking in the realization that she must have grown up in the Old Rectory, unless her father had sent her to live with relatives. I'd had no idea; not when she had taken me to visit the bridesmaids, or afterwards.

"A truly lovely person from the sound of her." Mrs. Malloy's pinky finger flagged as she sipped her tea, but the rest of her remained every bit the lady ensconced at the Ritz. "Mrs. H. and I were talking about her earlier, as we quite often do. Me being so much a part of the family—not at all like household help in the usual sense of the word. Now, as to whether the same can be said of your cousin Edna in her situation, I couldn't say." She smiled kindly at Gwen. "But I'm sure those three ladies Mrs. H. calls the bridesmaids are grateful for all she does for them."

"Why call them the bridesmaids?" Barney asked the obvious.

"It's how my mother referred to them. I've no idea why."

"And it would be her mother who died in the Belgian Congo?"

"I never heard where or how my grandmother died. All I know is that her name was Sophia." My voice was stiff. The same was becoming true of the rest of me from sitting on the hard chair. I put down my cup and glanced at the clock on the mantelpiece. Nearly one in the afternoon. It was more than time I got out to the car and on my way.

"It's so sad when people are snuffed out in their youth," Gwen said, sounding quite emotional. "Am I right in thinking, Mrs. Haskell, that your own dear mother, the ballet dancer, has also passed on?"

"Yes. She died in an accident. She fell down some steps on her way into the underground at Kings Cross . . ."

"Tragic." Barney leaned forward in sympathy. "What happened? Some sort of dizzy spell?"

"Darling, I'm not so sure Mrs. Haskell wants us to go on talking about this. It must bring back all sorts of sad memories." Gwen got to her feet, where she teetered for a few seconds on her high heels before clicking over to the piano. From the array of photographs in fancy frames she selected the largest and returned to my side. "Perhaps you'd like to see what the children look like, Mrs. Haskell. Fiddler and I are very proud of all three, as I am sure you can well imagine. Of course, they aren't children anymore, as you can see."

"A nice-looking group."

"They all went on to Cambridge, just like their teachers said they would from their very first days of starting kindergarten. No one ever had to help them with their sums. John got three degrees and Nancy and Patricia both got two each and all the best kind."

"Wonderful." I did not let my eyes wander from the photographed faces of the sober-minded-looking Fiddlers to where Mrs. Malloy sat in her pale blue sweatshirt with its embarrassing proclamation that she too had been to Cambridge. No wonder Gwen had eyed her with an enigmatical expression on first spotting it.

"I just wore this for laughs." Mrs. M.'s voice bounced across the room in a series of thuds. "My son George never went to no university, no more than I did. But he's made a huge success of himself has that boy, as Mrs. H. could tell you. Got his own factory, he has, for making exercise equipment. Still, I'm not saying there isn't a need for places like Oxford and Cambridge, so long as there's them that can't make it on their own after being at regular school all them years and getting extra tutoring to help them get jobs. Late bloomers is what I think they're called. Not meaning your brood, of course." She beamed at her hosts.

Silence flooded the room. Even Barney looked a trifle disenchanted with Mrs. Malloy. For a moment, I thought I might be taking her on to Knells with me after all, but husband and wife rallied commendably.

"Dear Roxie! Didn't I say, Fiddler, that the Queen couldn't impress her? That's because she's studied at the school of hard knocks."

"One of the toughest learning institutions going, darling. Only the strongest survive and not many make it through in such wonderful shape."

"All those nasty husbands." Gwen managed to look truly pained. "And now there's this Leonard Skinner, the worst of the lot from the sound of him, trying to weasel his way back into her life. We won't have it, will we, Fiddler? Roxie can stay here where we can spoil her to bits, until she's sure of being well rid of him. She'll have breakfast in bed every morning and lovely afternoon naps until she feels like her old self again."

"How about a cushion for her back?" Barney plucked one off the sofa and settled it behind Mrs. Malloy while continuing to address his wife. "She's had a long drive. So why don't you bring her lunch in here, darling? I'll pull up that little table for her, and after she's eaten every tasty morsel you can fetch a nice soft blanket and settle her down for the afternoon. Perhaps it might even be an idea to light the fire, as it looks as though it may rain on and off all afternoon."

"A good idea, Fiddler."

"Yes, it sounds just the ticket." The person being talked about in cosseting tones swung her legs off the footstool and heaved herself upright. "But first I need to go and say goodbye to Mrs. H."

"You're sure you won't stay for lunch?" Barney pumped my hand.

"I expect they'll have a meal waiting for her at the Old Rectory." Gwen eased him aside to make her own farewells and on her way out the door returned the photo to the piano. Her eyes lingered on it fondly before she picked up another and held it out for my inspection.

"This here's my cousin Edna and the man's her husband. It was taken when she and Ted got engaged."

"She looks in love." This time I wasn't being polite. The girl in the black-and-white photo radiated a dreamy-eyed passion. She was also pretty in a dairymaid sort of way. The man, on the other hand, wasn't good-looking and seemed as though he had been ordered to smile.

"Well, what romance there was didn't last. Ted made her life hell all their married life." With this Gwen offered me directions to my destination and asked me to say hello to

Edna for her, then gave Mrs. Malloy a hug before shushing us gaily from the room into the hall. I stood at the front door, eyeing Mrs. M. sternly.

"You were awful in there about that Cambridge stuff."

"I spoke me mind."

"After just telling me that you thought Gwen was troubled and needed your support?"

"That's not the same thing as sitting there listening to her brag." Mrs. Malloy drew herself up on her high heels. "If I hadn't nipped that in the bud it would have gone on as long as I'm here. And where would that lead to but a blazing row? That's what happens to a lot of friendships. Little things escalate into big things until there's no turning back. Hatred is unleashed, murder stirs in the heart, and . . ."

"Mrs. Malloy, you are being overly dramatic." I glowered at her.

"Just talking sense." She opened the front door for me. "It might be nice if you was to say something about how glad you are that you brought me to Gwen and Barney's because you've found out things about your mother and her family you didn't know. Now you drive carefully, Mrs. H.! And remember, you've got enough to think about with your dead grandmother wanting you there, without going and stirring up any wasp nests at the Old Rectory. Don't worry about me"—loftily spoken—"I'll have Gwen and Barney eating out of my hand in no time. Oh, and one more thing," she called after me as I headed off into the drizzle, "talk to Edna. I'll bet she's a fount of information on your mum and perhaps your gran, too."

Of all the irritating people, I thought as I got into the car. But all the same, now that the meeting with the bridesmaids was close at hand, I wished she were going with me, which was silly. Rosemary Maywood had sounded perfectly sane on the phone and no doubt the other two—Thora Dobson and Jane Pettinger—were also nice, respectable women who just happened to have an interest in the occult.

The rain was making me nervous about driving and I was wishing it would stop long before I turned off the road from Lower Thaxstead at the signpost to Knells. Fields now lay on both sides of me—spreading out to the occasional distant house like green counterpanes fringed with hedges. Several miles farther on I saw the beginnings of the village. I passed the post office and turned onto Vicarage Lane. Almost there, I was thinking, seconds before swerving to avoid the long, gray form of a dog that materialized without a shadow's warning in front of me. With sickening dread I felt the car do a short slither and a long slide through a hedge and into a ditch that I knew, with ominous certainty, had been waiting all day to swallow me up.

# CHAPTER FOUR

THE GREAT THING about not being a size six, as I could sourly have reminded Gwen Fiddler, is that you have that nice bit of extra cushioning when being bounced around like a frog in a coffee can. But I didn't sit dwelling on my good fortune. I undid my seat belt with shaky fingers and reached for the bag of peppermint humbugs Mrs. Malloy had left on her seat. Now on life support, I was able to plot my next move, which was to step out into the ditch and climb through its long, hairy grass back onto the lane. If Ben had been with me he would have just shot the car into reverse and with a soft bump or two had us facing in the right direction. But I like to take things in stages, weigh up all the possibilities, one of which was that a helpful man from the local garage might suddenly pop up beside me and insist on helping a matron in distress by getting behind the wheel and setting my world to rights.

I spotted a man—youngish, with a square face, closely cropped brown hair, and a boxer's broken nose. He was leaning over the garden wall of the first of a row of four attached cottages. Roses climbed the trellis that framed his front door. Lace curtains hung at the windows. It was all very charming, except that the man looked far from helpful.

His expression was pugnacious and he was yelling at the long, shaggy gray dog that was slinking in circles around a tree by his gate.

I had no reason to feel kindly towards the beast that had caused me to lose control of the car. But I couldn't see that at the moment it was doing any particular harm, other than cocking its leg every third step in a desultory fashion. I'm not one of those animal people who want to adopt every stray that comes along and am perhaps more of a cat than a dog person. Even so, when the man lifted a weighty hand and shouted: "Bugger off! We don't need your sort creeping around here!" I felt compelled to take a moral stand.

"Why can't you just say, shoo." I stood straightening my hair, which had unleashed itself from its neat coil during my excursion into the ditch.

"Give me a frigging break, lady! Your type don't get the point when spoken to in a civilized way." The fellow had now come out from his garden gate and was glowering at me through pinpricks of eyes in a scrunched-up face.

"Me?" My chin dropped in a series of thuds, or maybe it was my heart that was doing the thumping. I had rarely been so confused in my life. "Why should you be angry with me?"

"Barging in here, all set to destroy an entire way of life." He was now shaking his fist, balled up to the size of a boxer's glove, within inches of my face. "I went and left a good job in London 'cos me and the wife wanted the peace and quiet of country living. Think I'm going to let the likes of you force us to pack up and move?"

"How does it harm you that my car is in a ditch on the other side of the road? I can't see that your property values are likely to plummet all that much in the time it takes me to get it out." I'll admit to raising my voice. An upstairs window of the cottage next door flew open and a female voice screeched down at us.

"What's going on out there, Tom?"

The man unfurled his boxer's mitt and jabbed a finger at me. "It's the buggering woman."

"You mean her that's expected at the Old Rectory?" Revulsion throbbed through every syllable. The woman at the window was young and rather pretty but I decided, perhaps impetuously, that I had no wish to meet her alone on a dark night. Her hands presently gripped the sill but it did not take much imagination to picture them inching their way around my throat.

"You've got it, Irene," the man shouted up. "Miss Maywood said they was expecting her this afternoon."

"Just like I pictured she'd be. Looks the sort, doesn't she?" The woman was warming up nicely, even though it was beginning to rain again. "Nasty hard-faced bitch. I bet she'd turn her own mother in for cash."

"Look." I was floundering amid the injustice of the situation. "I don't have a mother and . . ."

"What, pushed her down the stairs, did you?"

This, given the way my mother had died, hit too close to home.

"How dare you!" I charged over to the wall bordering all four cottages and kicked it. Unfortunately it didn't collapse in a shower of bricks and I was tempted to administer another blow. But common sense, the eternal spoilsport, prevailed. So instead I just said, "Those three women at the Old Rectory know next to nothing about me. I've seen them once in my entire life."

"And, let me tell you, they were far from impressed." Tom came alongside me. "Miss Sneaky Pants is their name for you!"

I went rigid with wrath. What a way to talk about a young child, which is all I had been when my mother took me to visit Rosemary Maywood, Thora Dobson, and Jane Pettinger!

"Barging in on them uninvited!" Irene's words came

slamming down like hailstones, making the scattering of raindrops seem positively benign.

"It wasn't like that." I choked out the denial. But, truth be told, I wasn't sure what had occurred to initiate that first visit to the Old Rectory. My mother could have taken me there unannounced. Had the day ended in a row? Was that why it had been, in the years that followed, a closed subject? But then again Mother had been reticent about everything connected with her past. Now, before I could say anything further, the door of the third cottage opened and a stooped elderly man came feeling his way down his garden path with a walking stick.

"Trouble, Tom?" He inquired in a surprisingly vigorous voice. "Is she the one? Has the devil's handmaiden arrived in Knells?"

"On her way to see the old ladies, Frank."

"Viper!" The walking stick wagged in my direction. "Get back to the swamp where you belong and leave those three good women alone. They're all that stands between us and the folly of human nature, now that everyone in the village sees what should have stood out a mile."

He had lost me completely.

"You're right, Frank." Irene waved at him from her window. "But there's no good in raking over what's been done. We've all got to come together. I'm surprised that Number Four isn't out having her say."

"Here she comes," Tom informed her. And out the door of the last of the cottages appeared a large woman in a floral apron with her head in pink plastic rollers big enough for a child to roll in down a hill. She moved at a fast pace, with her cheeks blowing in and out like a pair of bellows, and the glint in her eyes would have been enough to make a pit bull whimper.

"This is her?" The latest arrival corralled her neighbors with a voice flung out like a whip and, amidst their shouts of agreement, she came storming out her gate. For one awful moment, I was sure she was going to pick me up with a giant hand (she made Tom's look as though they belonged on a baby) and hurl me into the ditch. On second thought, perhaps that wouldn't have been such a bad thing. I might have been able to crawl into the car, thus affording myself the luxury of being able to huddle behind locked doors and wonder what I had done to deserve finding myself in this awkward, not to say baffling, situation.

I suddenly felt extremely cross with Ben that he was off at Memory Lanes, a place with nothing more awful to bear than having to play a few hands of whist to an accompaniment of songs from *The Merry Widow* performed by a group of women with hairstyles dating back to the days of all-frizz no-curl perms.

Rousing myself back to the moment at hand, I decided to mention the salient fact that I was not thrusting my obnoxious self upon the three occupants of the Old Rectory.

"Miss Maywood wrote to me . . ."

"We've all written," Tom interrupted.

"And never so much as a one-line reply." Frank was back to brandishing his walking stick.

"Not a phone call," stormed Irene from her window. "Isn't that right, Susan?"

I was hopelessly befuddled. However topsy-turvy the world, Number Four could not in a million years, by any stretch of the imagination, be named Susan. A woman who looked as though she ate three blood-red steaks for breakfast needed a name with more meat on its bones. Something like Bertha or Hildegarde. Anything but—Susan! Even the pink hair rollers and floral pinny couldn't make her Susan-ish. The mind recoiled. As did the rest of me when she positioned herself in my path and ordered me in a voice that rumbled into a growl to come with her.

"I'll do nothing of the sort."

"Yes, you will, Miss Smarty Pants."

"I thought it was Sneaky Pants."

"You don't get to think." She had me in a vise-like grip now and was dragging me across the road under the appreciative glances of her hateful cohorts. "You're going to stand where I put you while I get that car out of the ditch. Then you're going to get the hell out of here and not come back. Anything you have to say needs to be directed to the Village Hall. There'll be no picking on three defenseless old women. Not while I have breath left in this body. Do I make myself clear, you sorry excuse for a secretary or whatever fancy title you like to give yourself?"

"I'm an interior designer," I retorted, sounding ever more idiotic. We were now down in the ditch and Susan had the passenger-side door of the car open. Rain was settling under my raincoat collar. Stupidly I had left the keys in the little pocket of leather surrounding the stick shift and she grabbed them up before giving me a shove onto the seat. At which moment my head cleared. Again I reminded myself that there are advantages in not being a size six. I might not be all muscle like Susan but I was damned if I was going to be booted out of Knells without putting up some resistance. When she went to slam the door I kicked it open, gave her a shove with both hands, causing her to shift just enough for me to duck under her arm. Lumbering out of the ditch I ran smack bang into a human wall made up of Tom, Frank, and Irene—who had either shinnied down a drainpipe or exited her cottage by the more prosaic means of the stairs and the front door.

"Get out of my way!" I shouted.

"Try making us!" Tom's square face was set. His short hair bristled.

I stood still, sensing rather than hearing Susan come up behind me. There was no dream-like quality to the moment, no rosy-hued hope that someone would appear out of the drizzle to rescue me. But that is exactly what happened. A woman was coming down the lane. A tall woman with wild black and orange hair billowing out around her shoulders. She moved with long strides, unencumbered by the rain cape that reached almost to her ankles.

"Shadow, where are you, Shadow?" she called, looking to the left and right and on reaching our gathering asked if we had seen a dog. "He's a lanky beast, rather like a greyhound with long hair. I left him in the garden at the Old Rectory when I arrived there about half an hour ago. He must have jumped the wall."

"He was over at my gate a short time back." Tom jerked a thumb over his shoulder. "Haven't seen him since."

"Could have cut over into the fields." Susan came up from behind me to stand with her fellows.

"I'd get after him quick." Frank sucked in his cheeks and tapped the ground with his stick. "Traffic's busy on the main road this time of day and the man that farms over the way doesn't take kindly to dogs in his fields."

"Yes, I wouldn't waste time." Irene was barely polite.

The woman's eyes met mine. They were a startling grass-green, the sort one only reads about in romance novels, and they were made even more remarkable by being set under straight black brows. Could this be the village witch? Given my situation I didn't really care if she was the Archduke of Transylvania. She spelled safety. And beyond that I felt an inexplicable feeling of familiarity that came not with an electrical jolt but as in a warm whisper from somewhere in my everyday world.

"Are you all right?" she asked me.

"No, I'm not," I shot glances right, left, and center. "These people seem to be in a muddle about who I am and what I'm doing in Knells."

"But surely"—her voice made me think of hot chocolate—"you'll be the one they're expecting at the Old Rectory."

"They told you they were expecting me?"

"You don't sound as though you're looking forward to the visit." She pushed her black and orange hair off her brow with long purple fingernails and I found myself thinking that it wasn't so surprising, perhaps—that feeling of recognition. She was younger than Mrs. Malloy by a decade or more, in her early fifties was my guess, and didn't appear to lay on the makeup with such a heavy trowel, but they were both undeniably theatrical in appearance.

"It's hard to look forward to meeting people who have told their neighbors up and down the street a whole bunch of nasty things about me."

"Really?" She looked from Irene and Tom to Frank and Susan.

"And with good reason," growled Mrs. Muscle Woman in a floral pinny. "Those dear good ladies at the Old Rectory have every reason for hating the idea of having Miss Amelia Chambers invade their home."

"Who?" I had the feeling that light might be about to dawn, although not, perhaps, without a struggle.

"Don't go talking daft." Tom wiped away the sheen of rain from his face and hunched his shoulders so that his neck disappeared into the collar of his plaid shirt.

"It's no good pretending you're not that horrible woman." Irene sounded as belligerent as ever; but her blue eyes looked a little uncertain.

"She's not, you know." The woman with the black and orange hair spoke out ahead of me. "Her name's Giselle Haskell and she's an old family connection of those three women you're so hell-bent on protecting. Her grandmother was their very dear friend and they have asked her to come for a visit."

Silence emanated from the cottagers. Trees stopped rustling, and the rain slowed to the occasional drip . . . drop, before stopping entirely. The question as to the nature of Miss Chambers's role in the scheme of things hung on my lips, but I couldn't get the words out. But while I wilted, Susan rallied.

"It's easy to see how you figured out who she was. You

with your psychic powers!" The words were punctuated by a sniff. A dainty sound so unsuited to her that I wondered for a wildly ridiculous moment if it might have been dubbed. Were we all in fact actors trapped in some horribly intellectual foreign film that would keep replaying itself until someone figured out what it was about?

"I didn't have to resort to mind reading," the woman with the black and orange hair replied to Susan. "Rosemary Maywood not only told me she was expecting Mrs. Haskell in the early afternoon, she showed me a photograph. That made recognizing her easy. Especially"—the green eyes sparkled—"as Miss Maywood also painted me a very clear picture of Amelia Chambers, who is due at their house at about four o'clock."

"Miss Sneaky Pants," I supplied.

"That was Miss Maywood's name for her. Apparently she has brown hair, might be described as good-looking by some, but is painfully thin. Barely a size six at best."

"Can't be you, then," Irene mumbled, looking at me out the corner of one eye.

"Never could abide a skinny minny, that's what I used to tell the wife when she'd talk about going on one of those diets." Frank also avoided looking directly at me. Instead he poked at a pothole in the road with his stick. "Haven't been the same since my Jessie passed on last Christmastime. Can't live with a woman close on fifty years and not feel it. Doctor said I'd like as not crack up. Isn't that right, Tom?"

"Said it in my hearing, he did," came the quick response of a man who knew how to grab an excuse and run with it. "And me and Susan and Irene are worn down to the emotional nub, keeping on the lookout to make sure you don't do something stupid, Frank, like sticking your head in the gas oven on a Sunday and ruining a perfectly good rump roast and Yorkshire. Very nice it is of Mrs. Pettinger to see to your weekend meals and it wouldn't do to go upsetting her, now would it?" Tom actually inched his head around to look me in the eye. "Her and the other two—Miss May-wood and Miss Dobson—have enough to contend with without any further distractions."

"What Frank and Tom are trying to get across, Mrs. Haskell," Susan chimed in with the force of a grandfather clock, "is that we've all been horribly distracted of late, what with one thing and that Chambers woman. We're sorry for the gaff—mistaking you for her and being so narky about it, but I'm sure when you sit down and talk with them at the Old Rectory you'll understand why feelings are running high."

"Edna Wilks is worried about those three ladies. Not a bad old stick, she isn't," proffered Tom. "Got a bugger of a husband, which means he'll live to be ninety. That sort always does unless someone pushes them off the twig."

"He means Edna that works at the Old Rectory." Susan showed me a conciliatory row of National Health teeth. "There four days a week, she is. It's her Ted that does the heavy digging in the garden and cleans out the gutters when needed—that sort of thing. Thora Dobson does most of the outdoor work herself. Put most men to shame, she would."

"Miss Chambers?" I prompted.

"Works for an evil property giant, Mrs. Haskell. One of the richest men in Britain, he is. Though why he had to fix his nasty sights on Knells is the question that's kept me awake more nights than I care to think about."

"Crafty bugger!" Frank growled down at his walking stick. "He's had this ticking over in his head from way back, he has. Started buying up houses round here some twenty years gone. And like a ruddy fool when the wife took sick I says to myself, why not sell and take her for a holiday on the continent, like she always wanted?"

"Don't go blaming yourself, Frank, just because you were the last holdout next to them at the Old Rectory." Irene pat-ted his shoulder and fixed her blue eyes on me. "One of the first to sell was the couple that owned the corner shop just off High Street on Hawthorn Lane. Apparently a rumor went buzzing round that a supermarket was going up not half a mile down by Gallows Cross and they panicked. It was before I moved here. But surprise, surprise, it didn't happen, not then and not later! If you ask me, it was Amelia Chambers's wicked employer that spun the story."

"I was taken in." Susan wiped her massive hands down the front of her damp pinny and shifted her gooseberry gaze between me and the woman with black and orange hair. "So was them that used to own Irene and Tom's cottages. That awful man always paid more—almost double sometimes what the properties would have brought from any other buyer. And to sweeten the pot we all got to stay on if we wished at a twopenny rent." Her face worked itself into a series of doughy shapes, like a ball of day-old pastry being thumped about by a furious pair of hands. "It seemed too good to be true. And of course it was."

"You never suspected that there was a scheme afoot to buy up the village for some commercial project?" I asked.

"We're a trusting lot," said Frank heavily. "But that don't mean we're complete fools. We had the town council get an assurance in writing that nothing like that was in the works. But turns out it isn't worth the paper it's written on; not when you get out your magnifying glass to read every word of the fine print."

"Couched in very clever terms," put in Irene. "With his millions that man could hire the very best lawyers, couldn't he? While all we've got down here is a nice old bumpkin of a solicitor to check things over. Eighty if he's a day and asleep at his desk, you might say."

"Me and the wife wanted to buy," Tom assured me. "We've always owned our own house, never thought of doing otherwise. But, like Susan says, the rent was so cheap, it was almost a joke. At first we thought we'd just stay for a year or two, save the lolly and when we found the right place move out to Upper or Lower Thaxstead." He looked up and down the lane glistening with rain and spangled with a sudden burst of sunshine, then over to where the fields spread gently out to be bordered at their furthest edge by a satin ribbon of road. "Trouble is, there's something about Knells that wraps itself around your heart."

"This village has been here since the fourteenth century." Frank now drew a handkerchief that looked as though it hadn't been washed since before his Jessie died, and blew his nose hard. "I was born in that cottage, same as my pa was. I played as a lad in the old churchyard and of occasion, when the devil took us, me and the Bradley lads that used to live at Number Four would shin up the drainpipe to peek inside the window of the rector's study."

"The famous rector who took off for the Belgian Congo?" I asked, hoping to get more information.

"No. His father-in-law. The old rector—Reverend Mc-Nair. Not William Fitzsimons. He's the one that was curate and went out as a missionary to force religion down people's throats, before coming back here to drum the pulpit for thirty years."

Fitzsimons, I thought. Here was additional information to what Gwen and Barney had told me. My cousin Vanessa was a Fitzsimons. Her father, Wyndom, had been my mother's brother, but his visits to the flat in St. John's Wood had been few and far between.

"Anyhow"—Frank had the look of a man talking into the distant past—"that was our Sunday-afternoon entertainment back then. Reggie and John and me, we'd flatten our noses against the windowpane hoping to catch the Reverend doing something he oughtn't, picking his nose or the like, that we could have laughed about with the other boys in Sunday school. But all we ever caught him doing was sucking on those cherry cough drops of his. Except for that time we saw him emptying his teacup into the aspidistra pot."

Susan responded with a gloomy laugh. "Gladys Bradley, Edna Wilks's mother, as was the daily help in those days, couldn't make a decent cup of tea to save her life. Gnat's pee is what my mother called it. Too weak to come out of the pot. But then tea wasn't Gladys's drink. My father wouldn't allow her in the house. Been a Methodist, he had, before coming over to the Church of England on marrying my mother. Same as your dad, Frank. Thought old McNair didn't talk enough about the evils of the bottle in his sermons."

Frank was back to reminiscing about his boyhood pranks. "Could have frightened the old geezer to death if he'd caught the lads and me. Or ourselves if we'd been at the window the afternoon he was found dead at his desk. Heart attack it was. Sixty-five years old. Same as I am now."

"Just days before his poor little daughter's wedding." Susan completed the sorry picture. "Sophia was her name. Only seventeen. And a nice girl. Far too young to be married off to anyone, let alone a dry old stick like William Fitzsimons. The whole village was heartsick when they heard what had happened to her. Dying out there in the wilds of Borneo."

"I thought it was the Belgian Congo," inserted Tom.

"All much of a muchness." Susan waved a hand the size of a ham. "All jungles and swamps from the sound of them. And hot enough to fry you like a pan of chips. No wonder Sophia didn't last a year."

"She was my grandmother," I said.

"Is that right?" Irene got back into the conversation.

"So you're Mina's daughter," Frank said. "Not more than two or three she wasn't when her father brought her back to the Old Rectory."

"A sad-eyed little sprite was Mina, you couldn't call hers a happy childhood, not with that old sour face for a father." Susan was now looking at me, her features somewhat softened. "Those that thought Reverend McNair didn't do enough thundering from the pulpit on the evils of drink got enough of it when William Fitzsimons took over. Foam at the mouth, he would. It was his favorite topic next to the evils of wanton women."

"Some men shouldn't have children." Tom's hair bristled.

How strange, I thought, to be learning more about my mother from strangers standing in a street than I had ever gleaned from her while I was growing up. I could feel the woman with the black and orange hair studying me intently from several feet away, but she didn't move and I couldn't.

"No one was surprised when Mina ran off to London and never came back after marrying that third or fourth cousin of hers," Susan went on. "Good riddance to Knells, is what she must have thought. It wasn't like she even had friends of her own age here. Kept shut away like one of those Victorian children, she was. Schooled her at home himself did her father. The only times she got to go out was to her ballet classes over in Rilling."

I could see why my mother had kept her father's memory under wraps. Mrs. Malloy, who could never quite remember if she had been married four times or five and was partial to a glass of gin, would not have enthused. Certainly not to the point of bursting the seams of her black taffeta frock to accompany me in laying a bunch of flowers on my grandfather's grave. Come to think of it, where was he buried? Was there a churchyard within a stone's throw of the Old Rectory? Had my mother, like the Brontës, grown up looking out upon a time-stricken cluster of tombstones? If so, small wonder that she had never seemed entirely connected to the everyday world of shopping lists and comedy programs on the television.

I looked down the lane, suddenly eager and at the same time afraid of all that I would find out from the bridesmaids. Strangely enough, I had forgotten that it was my grandmother who was my reason for being here. All I could see was my mother's shadowed face as she sat on a horsehair sofa in a room where there was a parrot in a cage by the fireplace, a dark red cloth with a balled fringe on the table, and a jug of lemon barley water on the sideboard.

# CHAPTER FIVE

SOMETHING FURTIVE AND furry moved out of a clump of shrubs to the right of cottage number four. Given the fact that I was half in the past and half in the present, which would have been disorientating even had I been comfortably settled in an armchair, I vaulted several feet in the air. My old gym teacher would have been astounded by this feat, considering that I had never been able to manage more than a bunny hop to make it over the wooden horse. Happily, Frank corralled me with the hooked end of his walking stick and Susan steadied me with an iron grip.

"I had forgotten all about your dog," I said to the woman with black and orange hair and impossibly green eyes.

"Been round back rummaging in the dustbins from the looks of him." Tom eyed the longhaired gray beast without much enthusiasm.

"He always looks as though he's in need of a brush and set." His owner patted her leg and made cooing noises to which he responded by turning tail and peeing up a tree. After which activity he sat down and stared mournfully off into the distance.

"Had him long?" asked Irene.

"He's not really mine." The green eyes went from the dog to me. "I'm looking after him for my mother, who's in hospital with back problems."

"Arthritis?" Frank inquired with the extreme interest that only the elderly seem to show in other people's ailments. "My wife was stricken with it something cruel for years before Thora Dobson came up with one of her herb remedies."

"No . . . a growth on her spine."

"Sorry to hear it, but I didn't mean your mother. I was talking about the dog."

"Sorry." The woman laughed. "I don't know what's wrong with Shadow."

"And you with your psychic powers?" Susan gave a foghorn grunt of laughter.

Frank wagged his stick in the animal's direction. "From the way he's sitting he looks stiff in the joints to me. But of course I'm no vet. Would have liked to be one, mind you. But didn't have the education. Started work at fourteen, like most of us that went to the village school. Of course there's always some," he mused, "that you just know is going to make it in this world without none of its advantages. There was this lad—some years older than me, he was, and thought by most hereabouts to be a thorough bad lot, but I always had the feeling he'd end up king of the heap one way or t'other. Not that the girls would have cared if he'd gone around emptying dustbins. Had the looks and the damn-you-all-to-hell attitude that had them all over him. Even my Jessie admitted to me after we'd been married some thirty years that she'd thought she was in love with him until she found out she was just one of a string wrapped around his little finger."

"Don't go looking at me!" Susan's stertorous denial carried conviction but she was fussing with her floral pinny. "My parents would have knocked me into the middle of next week if they caught me within inches of a gypsy

foundling without a proper name to call his own. 'Good riddance to bad rubbish,' is what they said when Hawthorn
Lane took himself out of Knells, right about the time"—she
looked at me thoughtfully—"that your grandmother Sophia
was married off all in a hurry to William Fitzsimons."

What was she implying?

"Poor lass! Didn't get the white wedding that was
planned," said Frank.

"Meaning?" Irene radiated a blue-eyed interest.

"On account of her father dying so sudden."

"Couldn't have been any other reason." Tom gave me a
smile that bordered on the benign. "Not with her being a
vicar's daughter. Bound to have been too busy doing the al-
tar flowers and helping her mum entertain the ladies of the
Women's Institute to get up to tricks. Besides, she was your
very own grandmother, wasn't she, love?" he added as if this
put the seal on it.

"It's very interesting getting a sense of Knells's past and
present," I said, "but I really should be doing something
about getting my car out of that ditch."

"Allow me." Tom sounded like Sir Walter Raleigh preparing to spread his cloak at my feet, where there happened to
be a puddle remaining in one of several potholes in the
lane. The sky showed patches of blue. There were only a
few clouds to be seen and even they were drifting away over
the fields like threadbare underwear blown off a clothes-
line. I wondered what the weather was like in Norfolk, and
if Ben and the children had managed to get out on one of
the nature walks so prominently featured in the Memory
Lanes brochure. When I refocused, it was to see that Irene,
Susan, and Frank had gathered alongside the ditch, heads
nodding, arms waving, as they issued a stream of instructions to Tom on how to back up without running one of
them over.

Shadow, the dog, pawed at my raincoat, and being the
rangy mutt he was, he managed to leave muddy prints from

hem to collar. I was tempted to turn around and let him do the back as well. That way, the bridesmaids might think I was wearing a smart, up-to-date leopard print, which I could later give to Mrs. Malloy, who was partial to the safari look. But the woman with black and orange hair was at my elbow, talking to me.

"This must be a real trip down memory lane for you, Mrs. Haskell."

I felt a chill, which had nothing to do with the breeze blowing strands of hair across my cheeks. "Susan said something about . . ." I watched the cottagers scatter as the car jerked out of the ditch. My voice was doing the same thing—coming out a lurch at a time. "Do you really have them . . . psychic powers, I mean?"

"Why?" She was looking at me intently and there was something about her perfume, softly floral—like violets on a windowsill—that set me further off balance.

"It was only that I was thinking just seconds ago about my husband and children." Shadow sat at my feet, one ear cocked as if eager not to miss a single word of what he clearly expected to be a fascinating disclosure. "They're staying at a holiday camp place called Memory Lanes. You've probably heard about them. They've been springing up all over England over the last few years. The way Butlins' did years ago. My parents thought they were awful. All that raucous 'let's have fun' and the beauty pageants, the worst thing since sliced bread. Or were they around before that?" Now I was talking too fast, one word toppling over the other. "Of course it was the logical thing for you to say, about my taking a trip down memory lane, I mean. After all, you do know I'm here to visit people I haven't seen in years, who live in the house where my grandmother and mother grew up. But, well . . . are you psychic?"

"Do you believe people can be?"

"I'm not sure."

She smiled and it was as though she drew me inside her-

self, back to a place I knew and loved. This stranger with
the weird, wild hair. And the eyes that had me feeling as
though I were looking into a kaleidoscope of fractured memories. Part of me wanted to climb into the car that Tom now
had back on the road. The rest of me needed to stay right
where I was, rooted not only to the past and present but
also to the future that was about to claim me.

"The ladies at the Old Rectory believe that I see things
hidden to most." I sensed she was about to say more. But
the cottagers suddenly surrounded us and for a moment I
panicked, remembering their earlier mob mentality. They
were instead almost falling over themselves to convey that
it wouldn't take my moving in and living amongst them for
thirty years to gain their acceptance and goodwill. Frank
took my arm and tottered me over to the car, Tom nipped
smartly ahead of him to open the driver-side door, and the
moment I was seated Irene reached in and buckled the
safety belt for me. When that was done Susan bundled in
the trailing end of my raincoat. After which one or all of
them shut the door and I rolled down the window to catch
what they were mouthing at me through the glass.

"Drive carefully." Irene beamed and waved her hand.
"The Old Rectory is just around the second bend, you can't
miss it. It's the very last house on the left where the lane
turns onto Church Road. Beyond that it's just more fields.
There's a sign on the gate."

"Ted could be working in the garden," supplied Tom,
"him that's Edna Wilks's husband, in case you've forgot.
Unpleasant old codger. Might snarl at you for so much as
telling him 'good afternoon,' but don't mind him."

"Always been that way since he was a lad. Can't think
why Edna married him. A pretty girl she was once upon a
time. Took her out a time or two myself till I met my Jessie."
Frank's craggy features softened into something between
happiness and sorrow.

"Now don't go keeping the girl twiddling her steering

wheel." Susan gave him a poke with a giant finger. "You'll just have to come round to my house one morning and we'll all have a good natter over coffee and one of my Dundee cakes."

"I'd love that," I said, and with a resolute wave put the car in gear and drove off down the middle of the road, where I hoped the ditch couldn't get me. Through the rearview mirror I could see the solitary figure of the woman with the black and orange hair framed by an overhanging branch from one of the cottages. A second glance showed Shadow, the dog, chasing after me—paws barely skimming the ground and ears streaming out behind him. This was all I needed. The next thing I'd know he would have circled in front of me. Either he would end up under the wheels or I'd end up having a serious accident this time.

Slowing to a crawl I breathed a little easier. He was now jogging, happily from the looks of him, alongside me, almost as if I had him on a lead and we were practicing for an upcoming appearance at Crufts. Although what breed he would have shown under I hadn't the foggiest. I was now at the second bend in the lane and could see what had to be the Old Rectory. Yes, there was the gate in the garden wall and I could read the lettering on the tarnished brass plate. I couldn't see a garage, although there might be one around the back. I parked at the curb and stepped gingerly out so as not to step on Shadow's tail, which was thumping happily, as though he had accomplished something wonderful in getting me safely to my destination. His owner's voice floated our way urging his return and with a last thump and a final soulful gaze he crept back up the lane.

"That's right, get off with you, nasty old mutt!" A small, wizened man wielding a pair of pruning shears several sizes too big for him crossed the sloping lawn as I was getting my case out of the car.

"He wasn't doing any harm," I felt compelled to say.

"Fouling pavements, that's all any dog's good for. Don't

know why Miss Maywood let that witch woman bring him along when she came here spinning her yarns." He was now gumming his words with a vengeance. The absence of teeth and the salt-and-pepper stubble on his cheeks and chin might have been endearing in a kindly old geezer. But I decided I had rarely seen anyone more repulsive. "And there was Edna telling me to keep an eye on him out here in case he jumped the wall while they was inside talking, like I got nothing better to do."

"You let him out, that's why he was running loose."

"And I say that's for me to know and you to prove." He was pointing the shears at me. Perhaps in his worked-up state he had forgotten he was holding them but I took a couple steps backwards, glad that I was still behind the gate. "Want to go running to the old girls, do you, letting them know Ted's not been respectful?" He stood cackling away to himself. Then a sly watchfulness slid into his lizard eyes and I stared back at him, telling myself that he was a poor mad soul. Perhaps if I stood very still and thought nice kind thoughts he would realize that I wasn't holding a hypodermic in one hand and a straitjacket in the other.

"I know who you are." Saliva foamed around his lips like the tide coming up on the beach.

Here we go again!

"You're Mina's daughter." Ted grudgingly opened the gate for me. "Even if the old ladies hadn't said you was coming, I'd have known you anywheres." His leer would have cracked a china cup.

"I don't look like my mother."

"No. A reed of a girl she was, with yards of red-gold hair. Never liked me, she didn't. Not from when she was a tiny child. Didn't give Edna any trouble." He released one of his foam-spattered chuckles. "That's my wife, or the old bat, as I calls her. She'll make a fuss of you, but don't you go being taken in. Her and her wicked deceiving ways! Led me a proper dance, she has, from before we was wed. Never good enough for her, I wasn't. Always dreaming of Mr. Wonderful."

I couldn't bring myself to thank him for confiding in me.

"The cemetery's just around the corner, not halfway up Church Road, next to St. John's. Could be you'll fancy a walk up there after you've had your tea and crumpets with Miss Maywood and the other two. Always nice to visit relatives, is what I'm getting at."

"Meaning?"

"That's where your grandfather and great-grandparents are buried. Say hello from me to the miserable lot of them. Religious nuts! Who needs them?"

Why ever would the bridesmaids employ such a man? Mercifully, he exited my life for the time being, disappearing through an ivy-covered archway set in the tall privet that separated the front garden from the back. Taking a deep breath, I studied the house, trying to merge the reality with my childhood memory of a place steeped in gloom. What I now saw was a gray stone dwelling with narrow sashed windows and a prim roof on which perched a row of chimney pots that looked as though they had been set there by a child's hand and dared to fall off. Not the grim-looking place I remembered. I had been an imaginative child and easily spooked, I reminded myself as I pried open the gate and headed up the cobbled drive. For years I had believed that a firm of goblins had set up their headquarters under my bed. The noises I heard at night were the whirl and grind of their machinery churning out bottles of spell bombs guaranteed to turn a child's homework into gobbledygook by morning, when it would be too late to do it all over.

The woman who opened the black-painted door certainly looked as though she had all her marbles, and in the right jar, too. She was neatly dressed in a plaid skirt, cream blouse, and cardigan, and wore octagonal rimless glasses. Her permed hair was only lightly threaded with gray and framed a face that was remarkably free of lines. If I hadn't known that she had to be at least in her early seventies, I would have thought her no more than sixty-five.

My smile probably came across as a little uncertain, as if I were trying it on for size. Her welcome was reserved, but not unwelcoming; even so, I found myself remembering that phone call in the middle of the night and wishing I hadn't come.

"Welcome, Giselle. I'm Rosemary Maywood. It's been a long time since you were here." She extended her hand.

"You know it's me."

"Of course, we've been expecting you." She didn't add that I was late.

"I know, but I wondered if you might think I was that other woman—Amelia Chambers." I was back to babbling. "My car went into the ditch. It wasn't hurt and neither was I, but some of the neighbors came out and they were telling me . . ." My voice trailed off as Rosemary stepped back from the door and I followed her inside.

"No, I didn't think for a moment you were she." She closed the door, took my case, and set it in a corner. And I added my handbag. The hall was narrow, darkened along one side by the staircase banisters. But there were two archways to the right and left of us, supplying elbowroom. They gave a view of the Victorian dining room papered with exuberant red and pink roses. And of a comfortable sitting room, where nothing matched but all the pieces, from the big, rather mannish sofa to the dainty crystal lamps, looked as though they had lived together long enough to settle in as a family of the sort where being nice to each other is more important than being singled out for a word of praise.

"We are expecting Miss, or I am sure she would say Ms., Chambers this afternoon." Rosemary hung my raincoat on the banister knob and guided me a few inches down the hall. "She is a very persistent woman, although I suppose, to be fair, she is only doing her job working for that ruthless man."

"The one who has systematically bought up all of Knells apart from this house?"

"You have been talking to the neighbors." Rosemary smiled thinly. "We'll get to all that in due time. Meanwhile let's hope this trusted assistant doesn't show up until after lunch, which we have been keeping warm in the oven. Our daily help, Edna Wilks, has made one of her fish pies and there will be plenty of vegetables from Thora's garden, as well as stewed fruit and custard to follow. Why don't we go and join them in the conservatory? We can take your case up later. You're to have the room across from Thora's on the second landing." Rosemary attempted to keep me moving but I had stalled in my tracks.

It wasn't the hall tree, with its arrangement of umbrella, pith helmet, and black witch's hat, that held my attention. It was the photograph, one making up a gallery of faces lining the staircase wall. A black-and-white photo of me. At about sixteen or seventeen years of age, looking plump and wistful with my hair plaited over my shoulder. My mother had assured me that one day I would look back and realize that I had been a pretty girl in my own special way. I could hear her voice, as if she had spoken to me yesterday—or even today. Then, creeping up on the heels of nostalgia, came a shivery feeling, of the sort that I had expected to feel on coming here, but hadn't, not on looking at the exterior of the house or upon crossing the threshold. Now it came to me that all the time I had been living my life elsewhere—learning to be a decorator, moving to Merlin's Court, falling in love and marrying Ben, giving birth to the twins, and welcoming Rose into our family—part of me had been here all the time. Stolen away without my knowledge, to be put in a frame and placed on a staircase wall with a group of strangers, some of whom were probably long in the grave.

"Jane's second husband was an archaeologist," said Rosemary.

"Oh!"

"And Thora dresses up as a witch for Halloween to amuse the village children." Rosemary was looking at the hall tree, obviously thinking that the pith helmet and pointed black hat were the cause of my distraction. "You can see why there wasn't room for your raincoat."

"I was looking at the photo." My voice sounded as though it were being relayed through a cardboard tube from a finished roll of toilet paper. "The one of me." I tried to lift my hand to point, but my arm was glued to my side.

"That's not you." Her octagonal glasses caught a flash of light from the wall sconce at the top of the stairs. "It's your grandmother Sophia. It was taken the summer she was seventeen, when Thora and Jane came for a month's visit. I was already at the house, had been for a year, while I worked at a chemist's shop in Rilling, training in the dispensary. Reverend McNair, your great-grandfather, was my uncle—my mother's brother."

"So you and Sophia were cousins?" I hadn't been sure of the connection. "What about Thora and Jane?"

"Friends from boarding school. Your parents didn't tell you much, did they?"

"Only that they themselves were distantly related. Mother was from the Fitzsimons branch. Daddy was from the side that had shortened the name to Simons. I sensed from when I was little that Mother hadn't had a happy childhood."

"Yes, Mina always hated this house." Rosemary fingered the collar of her ladylike cream blouse. "Couldn't wait to make her escape. She told us so when she brought you here that day. Her father, William Fitzsimons, had recently died and left the place to me. It was an awkward situation, at least I thought so, and I invited her down to ask if there was anything, among the furniture or china and glass, that she might like to take. She said there was nothing she ever wanted to see again. I think she only came because she thought it was the right thing to do."

An image came sharply to mind of my mother looking out the window as we sat on the train going home and then turning to me and saying: "Have you ever wondered why I've never wanted you to call me Mum or Mummy? It's because I never got to say the word Mother—that most beautiful name in the world." How could I have forgotten until this moment?

"The furnishings weren't to my taste either," Rosemary was saying. "So I got rid of the lot and moved in what I had accumulated over the years. Thora and Jane brought their own bits and pieces with them. The plan, right from when I got the news of the house being mine, was for the three of us to live together. Jane had recently been widowed for the second time. Her first marriage ended in divorce. And Thora was also on her own and had always loved the garden here."

"Nice for all three of you." I was back to looking at the photo on the staircase wall and Rosemary followed my gaze.

"It was taken in September of the year that Sophia became engaged to William Fitzsimons."

"Now I understand how you knew." The creepy feeling was ebbing away, leaving . . . I wasn't sure what . . . in its place. "That I wasn't Amelia Chambers, I mean."

"As you can see, Giselle, you're the very image of your grandmother."

"It's almost uncanny."

"I have to assume that is why . . . but we'll get to that later, if you don't mind. After we've had lunch and are all sitting having a nice cup of coffee, or tea, if you prefer." Rosemary was walking me briskly down the hall. "I have, by the way, met Mrs. Chambers. Thora, Jane, and I met her in London about a month ago."

"I remember one of the neighbors saying you had described her as having brown hair and being very good-looking."

"Stylish in a restrained sort of way. Classic features, that'd be my definition. Thora put it a different way. Just the sort to be a young man's fancy or an old man's darling is what she said. Her employer, who for the present will be nameless, is in his seventies: but still devilishly handsome, to quote Jane."

I had been doing a quick step to every word of this disclosure, with the result that I suddenly found myself in the conservatory. Here the pine planks of the hall gave onto a slate floor covered at random with hooked rugs that appeared no bigger than place mats because of the size of the room. It was glassed in on two sides, with an opening in the stone wall of what was once the exterior of the house. This gave entry to a kitchen of the good old-fashioned sort. Cheerfully painted an apple green and displaying some rather nice Devonshire pottery on the shelves of a large pine dresser.

"Do sit down and make yourself comfortable, Giselle." Rosemary indicated the faded chintz sofa overhung with foliage from just a few of the potted plants that crowded the conservatory at every turn. They came up from the floor and down from the ceiling. They sat in slightly smaller versions on the grand piano, they festooned tabletops and the wall-hung sink by the side door. I was tempted to say "Excuse me" several times while brushing up against the ones most determined to block my path. But I finally managed to seat myself on the sofa, only to leap up again when the cushion behind me moved. It turned out to be a cat. A big fluffy apricot one, with eyes almost as green as those of the woman with the black and orange hair.

"So sorry. I'll take her." Rosemary held out her hands, but I assured her that I had a cat of my own, named Tobias, at home.

"This one's named Joan, after one of Jane's friends."

"That's sweet." I resettled myself and didn't jump this time when another cushion, a tortoiseshell one this time, sprang to life and took a leap onto the coffee table, scattering magazines, mostly gardening ones, right and left.

"That one's named Charlotte."

"How many more are there?"

"Just Penny. A Siamese."

"Any dogs?"

"A lumbering old Labrador. He belongs to Thora. The only male in the group, but Thora named him Dog anyway to cut down on the confusion."

I leaned back against a cushion that was the real thing this time and felt something touch my hair. It was a long ferny-fingered hand. Not being inclined to get on stroking terms with any plant to which I hadn't been properly introduced, besides being afraid of knocking it over, I leaned forward, perhaps causing Rosemary to mistake my demeanor for impatience.

"I was sure Thora and Jane would be in here." She peered around as if expecting one or the other to pry their way through the jungle. "Perhaps they are out in the garden. Or they could have gone out through the back gate into the lane. But they knew you were due any minute." She sounded thoroughly exasperated and I had no doubt at that moment that she not only owned the house but also made it clear from the start who was boss.

"Here's our guest at long last!" A stocky woman of medium height with a shock of white hair trimmed short except where it fell over her forehead, dark brown eyes, and a ruddy complexion had entered from the hall. Two steps behind her came another woman. This one was thin and pale. Her hair was also white, but with a yellowish tinge and worn tied back from her face. Like Rosemary she wore glasses, but hers had black frames. The winged sort, that were in style once upon a time.

"She's not all that late," the thin one said.

"I meant, Jane," responded the stocky one, "we've been wanting to meet Giselle for a long time."

"Please call me Ellie." I got up from the sofa.

"Does suit you better." The brown eyes probed my face. "More friendly. I'm Thora Dobson." She had a gruff voice. "My shadow here is Jane Pettinger."

"Such a pleasure to meet you at last," joined in Jane. "So very like your grandmother Sophia, but of course we knew that already from the photo."

"The one on the stairs?"

"No, the one in the newspaper. From when you won that big art contest, shortly before your mother died. We just happened to see it and cut it out. Such a thrill! It's in one of our photograph albums in the sitting room. You must look through them while you are here. Do you still draw and paint, my dear?"

"I lost interest after Mother died." I wondered why Rosemary, in talking about the other photograph, hadn't mentioned that she had one—or at least a newspaper clipping of me at much the same age, and if this were the one she had shown to the woman with black and orange hair this very afternoon. Thora and Jane had come over to hug and kiss me, and when they moved back, Rosemary merely said that we should all sit down to lunch before it was completely ruined. At which point I apologized for being late, explaining again about the ditch.

"And then the neighbors got you talking! We quite understand. The important thing is that you weren't hurt. Such a relief." Jane drew a deep breath. "I had the most frightful dream last night that someone, I couldn't see who, met with a nasty end. Only they weren't dead, as it turned out. You know how those dreams go. But it's not just dreams with me these days. I've been the recipient of certain emanations. On several occasions I have seen a ghostly form stepping across the upper landing, and there have been other signs that Sophia may be trying to reach out to me from the other side." She picked up one of the smaller potted ferns and fanned herself with it.

"You and your emanations!" Thora turned to me. "Your husband phoned about half an hour ago to see if you had arrived. Had trouble hearing him because there was a lot of noise that sounded like opera going on in the background. Rather bad opera. Not that I am much of a judge."

"He's on holiday with our children."

"So Rosemary said."

"At a holiday camp called Memory Lanes."

"Oh, merciful heavens," exclaimed Jane. And I saw Rosemary cut her off with a nod.

"It was our vicar's idea. But it's probably not everyone's kind of place." I refrained from adding that being invited here, to commune with a long-dead grandmother, probably wasn't everyone's ideal invitation either. Presumably, we would get onto that topic after lunch, while sipping our coffee, or tea, in the sitting room. Such matters, I could imagine the bridesmaids thinking, were not to be charged at like a bull getting started in a china shop. Perhaps they would even produce a bottle of sherry, to add a touch of genteel elegance to the occasion of requesting my grandmother Sophia to waft forth. I was now pretty much sure of what lay in store for me. A séance, what else? The medium to be none other than the woman with black and orange hair.

"I met someone else in the lane." I didn't need to say more.

"That would be Hope," responded Rosemary. "A very interesting woman, although I wish she wouldn't encourage Jane's fantasies."

"Visions, dear, not fantasies."

Hope! Unlike Susan, the name was, I thought, exactly right.

"Cod's wallop! I forgot something," Thora said.

"To explain what kept you and Jane?" Rosemary put a Siamese cat out the side door.

"I was giving Dog a bath upstairs. He had got muddy out

in the garden. Always decides to help me dig when it rains. I'd just finished toweling him off when the phone rang for a second time. It was a Mrs. Malloy."

"For me?" I could have won a prize for asking the obvious.

"Said she was your personal assistant."

"In a manner of speaking."

"And why not? Sir . . . whatever he calls himself . . . has his Miss Chambers, doesn't he?" Thora scowled. "But back to Mrs. Malloy's message. I'm to tell you that if . . . now, let me see that I have this right—if that scurvy Leonard should show up here begging to know where she is, you're not to drop a word about how she's at Gwen's and having the time of her life."

"That's my Mrs. Malloy."

"Said you're to be sure and lock your door when you go to bed. Don't sleepwalk, do you?"

The side door into the conservatory opened and a short, prettily plump woman, of similar age to the bridesmaids, entered. She wore a print dress and half apron and she limped a little as she came, but that could have been because she had been hurrying. A fact made obvious by her flushed face and panting breath.

"Trouble," she said, leaning up against the door that had clanked shut behind her. "Ted's had an accident with the pruning shears!"

# CHAPTER SIX

"Wicked woman!" A snicker followed this screech. "I know what you did! And I'm telling! I'm telling!"

Peering through the foliage I spotted a birdcage. Inside was a green-and-yellow parrot of portly proportions, with a furrowed-feathered brow and that barrow-boy voice.

"That's what Ted is forever saying to Edna," growled Thora. "Old Polly there must have heard Ted rant those words a hundred times. He's always threatening to tell on that woman about something. She didn't rinse out the sink, she swept the toast crumbs under the carpet, she broke a cup. Poor Edna. She does her best. But she's seventy. Only a couple of years younger than Rosemary, Jane, and I. But we don't go out cleaning four days a week. And sometimes she even comes in to work on a Thursday, which is supposed to be her day off. God only knows how she gets through the weekends with Ted." Thora preceded me into the kitchen and sat down at the table that was already laid for lunch. "If I'd a kindly bone in my body, I wouldn't be talking about him like this. And I'd have gone along with Rosemary and Jane when Tom up the lane offered us a ride to the hospital. Nothing happens around here without one of the neighbors finding out in a flash. Would you like to eat now? It could be a while before Rosemary and Jane get back from the hospital. And you must already be starving."

"No, I'm fine. Let's wait a bit. They may ring to let us know how things are going. Ted's injury sounded pretty bad," I said.

"Could be, but then again you know how men carry on if they knick themselves shaving. Only have to bruise a knee to think their leg needs amputating." Thora gave a grunt. "Don't listen to me! Shock myself sometimes. But it gets my goat the way Ted treats Edna. Always accusing her of having some man on the side, because she used to enjoy the lads when she was young. Still, have to hope he pulls through. The man shouldn't have been climbing up that stepladder to prune that tree. Not that there was ever any talking to him. Odd, though, as Edna kept saying, that he fell with the blades of those shears pointing towards him." Thora got up from the table and put the kettle on. "Might as well have a cup of tea while we're waiting for news."

So the bridesmaids were in their early seventies. My mother had been eighteen when I was born, and if Sophia had had her when she was nineteen and I was now thirty-four . . . the numbers added up. My grandmother Sophia would now have been seventy-one. Not old by today's standards. What didn't fit the equation was my mother's older brother, Wyndom, and her sister, Louisa. I brought up this point to Thora, sensing that she didn't want to go on talking about Ted, when she returned to the table with our cups and saucers.

"Peculiar no one ever told you. They were her half-siblings. Your grandfather, William Fitzsimons, was a widower of thirty-five when he married Sophia. Believe the boy was about ten at the time and the girl seven or eight."

"I did know that they were several years older than Mother." I felt as though she needed defending. "We didn't see a lot of them when I was growing up and it doesn't surprise me now that she was reticent about anything to do with her past, given her unhappy childhood."

"Seems strange that your aunt and uncle didn't mention at one time or another that their mother and Mina's were not one and the same." Thora shook a lock of white hair off her forehead and continued to fix me with her brightly inquisitive gaze.

"Perhaps you never met Uncle Wyndom?" I asked.

"Only once or twice, when he was a little boy. Wasn't at the wedding. Neither of the children came. A hurried affair."

She might have said more, but I interrupted her.

"He grew into a man only interested in talking about his financial investments, until he lost most of his money. After that he went even more into his shell. He died a few years ago. I don't remember his ever saying more than a few words to me. And they were probably to point out that I needed to lose weight. His wife, Astrid, lived and breathed, she still does, for their daughter, Vanessa. She has no other topic of conversation."

"What about Louisa?" Thora asked.

"I call her Aunt Lulu. She's rather dear, in a naughty sort of way. Almost as though she never grew up. She's married to a man named Maurice who's the last word in pomposity. They have a son—my favorite cousin, Freddy. He lives in the cottage at the gates of our house. Aunt Lulu is a chatterer, but not about the past.

"Maybe," I added soberly, "she and my mother had more in common than they both realized."

"Same father, for starters."

"What was my grandfather like?"

Thora shifted Dog's head off her lap. She got up and checked a couple of saucepans on the gas cooker, adjusted the burners as low as they could go without sputtering out, and came back to the table. "William Fitzsimons wouldn't have been my choice of a husband. Wasn't Sophia's, either. Her father pushed the match. I never could make out why. He and William had rubbed each other the wrong way from day one. I heard them having a heated argument one afternoon, when Jane and I had come down for the weekend to see Rosemary, who was staying here while taking a dispensing course. The two men must have thought the house was empty. Mrs. McNair was out on parish work and we girls had gone to a tennis party, but I had to come back to get another racquet. We'd barely started the first set when I broke a string on mine."

"What was the row about?" I leaned my elbows on the table.

"Couldn't make out more than the odd disjointed sentence or two." Thora squeezed her eyes shut as if trying to bring the memory into focus. "The study door was shut and I didn't want to be caught eavesdropping. Although"—dimples appeared in her cheeks—"if I'd been caught standing on the staircase it would have looked as though I were either going up or coming down. The door was where the coat tree now is. Rosemary had it blocked up and the study taken out to enlarge the kitchen when we first moved in. But she decided on keeping the fireplace. Cheers the place up in winter."

"It does add charm." My eyes followed hers to the far wall. I was lying. In my opinion, the fireplace didn't do a thing for the room. It was too small, with a tile surround that looked as though it had come out of a public lavatory, and a mean, cramped grate that wouldn't have held more than two lumps of coal. I had a hazy memory of it from my childhood visit. Perhaps even then I hadn't liked it. Could it be that the parrot had been brought in to amuse me and had made some terrifying remark or that there had been a scary ornament on the mantelpiece? Would that explain why I had experienced a chilly sensation on entering the kitchen a few moments ago? In every other way it was a cheerfully functional room with its apple-green paint, pine cupboards, and neatly fitted appliances. On the windowsill was a jug of the same Devonshire pottery displayed on the dresser. And several hooked rugs warmed up the slate floor. Everything was spotlessly clean. Edna must work like a dog, perhaps goaded on by Ted's taunts. I wondered how he was doing, before bringing my thoughts back to Thora.

"What did you overhear of the argument between Reverend McNair and William Fitzsimons when you came back for the tennis racquet?"

"Something about the abomination of drink. Edna's mother was mentioned. Her name was Gladys. Used to be the daily help in those days. Everyone knew she tippled." Thora shrugged. "And it's true that it had begun to affect her work. Mrs. McNair caught her passed out on the sofa a few times. That was when Edna was brought in to help out. Don't ask me why William Fitzsimons sounded as though he'd just made a shocking discovery! He had already been curate at St. John's for two years."

"Didn't Reverend McNair"—I kept forgetting I was talking about my great-grandfather—"have a problem with Edna's mother's drinking?"

"Must have." Thora leaned down to stroke Dog, who was now lying by her chair. "He was a crusty old man, given to violent outbursts of temper. Probably never should have married, let alone had a child. He and his wife had Sophia late in life. She always had to tiptoe around them both. Mrs. McNair was one of those interested in everyone's business. Always out and about on her parish duties, but never making much time to see what was going on in her own family. Luckily for Sophia, they bundled her off to boarding school almost as soon as she was out of her pram. That's where Jane and I met her—Rosemary, too. They were cousins. Sophia was in the form below ours, but was always grown-up for her age. I'm sure the reason her parents allowed her to have friends come and stay was to keep her out from underfoot. Rosemary they rather liked, because she was a niece and they thought her a good influence."

This was interesting but we had become sidetracked. "Why do you think Reverend McNair—my great-grandfather—didn't give Edna's mother the sack? I was talking to some of the neighbors when my car went into the ditch. And one of them, I think it was Frank or Susan, mentioned her drinking, all this time later, so there must have been quite a bit of gossip at the time about a woman with her tendencies working for the rector and his family."

"Probably why he kept her on." Thora got up, opened the oven door, took a peek inside and then plugged in the old-fashioned coffee percolator. "Reverend McNair probably thought he could 'save' her." She lifted a saucepan lid and gave the contents a stir. "Also, wouldn't surprise me if thrift came into it. Gladys undoubtedly worked on the cheap. Would have had trouble finding another job." Thora set down her wooden spoon. "Don't think I'm saying that, Ellie, because Reverend McNair was of Scottish descent. My own mother was from Glasgow and a more openhanded woman you couldn't meet. Always inviting Sophia to stay with us during the school holidays. Damn it!" Thora turned to face me, her brown eyes somber. "If only she'd come that last year. Perhaps then there wouldn't have been a wedding and William Fitzsimons wouldn't have taken her with him when he went out to minister, as he was fond of saying, to the poor benighted savages in the Belgian Congo. You can't know how many times I've wished one of them had eaten him!" Thora sat back down at the table with a thump.

I suddenly remembered Ben. "Did my husband say when he would ring back?" I said. "I meant to ask but then Edna came in and everything became a scramble."

"Promised to phone again this evening."

"Did he say anything else?"

"They're all having a wonderful time. Sent his love."

"Good."

"Sounds as though you're missing him."

Thora's dimples appeared. I found myself wondering if she had ever been in love. Perhaps the look I gave her posed the question.

"I may be a Miss, but I haven't missed out entirely. For more than ten years I lived with a man named Michael. We couldn't marry because he was already married. His wife suffered from a mental illness and had been in an institution from before we met. Michael wouldn't divorce her."

I looked at her.

"And I'll show you my etchings, I told him. But it happened to be true."

"Your story sounds the sort of thing that happens in books."

Thora's expression gave no clue to what she was thinking. "Yes, in one of those gothic novels."

"I've read a lot of them," I told her.

"They all work out rather predictably. Sad little wife dies."

"Either by drowning in the ornamental pool in the Elizabethan garden, or from exposure to the elements after wandering out onto the moors in a thick fog." I didn't mean to sound flippant or callous, but I sensed Thora wanted to maintain an element of distance in telling her story.

"Leaving the hero and heroine making plans to head down the aisle." She smoothed out the linen tablecloth. "In our case, Michael's wife was put on a new miracle drug. She got better."

"And he went back to her?"

"Couldn't do anything else. None of it was her fault. If he hadn't she might have relapsed and neither of us was prepared to let that happen." Thora went to stand looking out of the window. "She deserved some happiness after all those years of living in the twilight zone. I hear from Michael on my birthday, just a card; but it lets me know he's all right."

"And his wife?"

"Took up gardening. For some reason that did get my jealousy juices going. It's the one thing I've always had to hold on to, the part of me that I didn't have to share. But that's life. Rosemary and Jane weren't lucky in love either. Jane's first marriage ended in divorce. Husband went off with another woman. Then she was widowed twice. Both times after being married only a few years. And Rosemary never got over Richard Barttle, not enough to ever want anyone else."

"Who was he?"

"Grew up in Knells, still lives here, in fact. Owns the photography place on Hawthorn Lane with his partner Arthur Henshaw. Richard and Sophia were great friends. You did know she was quite a talented painter herself? It must be where you get your gift."

"But I never did anything after winning that one art competition when I was still a schoolgirl." I was about to ask if there had been anything of a romantic nature between my grandmother and this Richard Barttle but at that moment Rosemary and Jane came into the kitchen and the conversation naturally turned to Ted and Edna.

"She's still with him at the hospital," Rosemary said briskly.

"And being very brave, of course." Jane seemed completely spent as she sat down in the chair Thora had vacated at their entrance. "He looked horrible. All covered in blood from the gash in his neck. Probably caught himself in the jugular, I doubt that'll he'll make it."

"It's Edna I feel sorry for." Rosemary removed a large casserole dish from the oven and set it down on a trivet. "She insisted we come back here, saying we could be sitting in the waiting room for hours without news. She seemed to really want to be alone. So we got a taxi home. But Tom stayed."

"If she could remain married to Ted all these years, she

can get through this, whatever turn it takes." After opening several cupboard doors, Thora found the jug she was looking for. "Can't imagine any other woman putting up with him, it's as much as I can do to deal with him puttering around the garden a couple of days a week."

"Thora," gasped Jane, "you do say the most dreadful things. You should be consumed with remorse. I heard you shouting at him this morning, something about him digging up your tulip bulbs." She tucked a strand of yellowish-white hair into the coil pinned at her neck with a large black bow. It looked like a butterfly in mourning, but its wearer seemed to be perking up a little.

"I wasn't shouting," Thora corrected. "Ted was the one doing the yelling. Perhaps I roared once or twice. It was raining and Dog was leaping about in mud when I was trying to put the bulbs back more or less where they had been."

"A mercy he didn't uproot your comfrey or lemon balm." Jane managed a wan smile.

"I'll say!"

"Thora's devoted to her herbs," Rosemary informed me. "Thinks they're the answer to every ill known to man."

"The lotion I made up for Frank-up-the-lane's late wife, Jessie, helped her arthritis," countered Thora.

"I doubt anything you would make up could do much to help Ted. But it won't do any good to dwell on the situation." Jane set down her glass. "We must try to stay strong for Edna. And for Ellie. This has hardly been the best of starts for her visit." I was about to reply that it wasn't as though Ted's injury had been planned, but that didn't sound right, and anyway Jane was still talking. "I've been so looking forward to meeting you, my dear. Unfortunately I wasn't able to be here when your mother brought you down for the day all those years ago."

"You weren't." I was vaguely aware of Rosemary setting the casserole in the middle of the table and Thora coming up behind her with a couple of steaming serving dishes.

"I had appointments that day with my solicitor in Cambridge and with my bank manager. If I could have postponed things, Ellie, I would have done it in a heartbeat. I was so looking forward to seeing Mina. None of us had really got to know her when she was growing up. Sadly, her father didn't welcome us to the house."

"Making it such a surprise that he left it to me," said Rosemary.

"Did that for spite." Thora now sat back down at the table. "William Fitzsimons didn't like his two older children any more than he liked Mina."

"Even so, it always struck me as peculiar that he left the house outside the family. And that's what he did, because your mother"—Jane looked at Rosemary—"was Reverend McNair's sister, making you no relation of William's. But perhaps he hoped it would rankle more with his disinherited offspring if he willed the place to someone they knew, as opposed to a stranger."

"I was sure you were here that day." I had been sitting and puzzling over the matter. "But perhaps I remembered it that way because Mother said there were three of you. And afterwards, when that day got fuzzier in my mind, I filled in the missing bridesmaid." The word popped out and I felt my face flame. But there was no point in leaving it dangling like a man on the end of a rope. "Mother always spoke of you as the bridesmaids. I never understood why."

There followed a pause in which all three women looked at each other.

"I don't imagine Mina talked about us often." Rosemary, who was seated next to me, placed a substantial serving of fish pie on my plate and urged me to help myself to vegetables.

"No, she didn't, but I hope you won't take that personally. She never mentioned her father. I hadn't heard his name until today. And all I ever knew about her mother was that her name was Sophia and she had died young. Now I have to fit a great-grandfather and a great-grandmother into the picture. But so far I can only think of them as Reverend and Mrs. McNair."

"Hugo and Agatha," supplied Jane.

I took a spoonful each of parsnips and brussels sprouts and added a larger helping of carrots; they smelled delicious, being sprinkled with finely chopped mint and chives, presumably from Thora's herb garden. "It wasn't until I talked to the people with whom Mrs. Malloy is staying that I found out Mother grew up in this house. Somehow I thought you three had always lived here."

"Growing dustier and more cobwebby with every passing year?" Thora passed me a jug of parsley sauce.

It was pretty much what I had thought. "I found the house scary when I was here as a child." I speared a carrot with my fork. Jane nodded. "Children are very susceptible to atmosphere. It's something we tend to outgrow, although lately I have begun to wonder if it's because we stop keeping an open mind."

"The house did look much the way you described it, Ellie, at the time of William Fitzsimons's death." Rosemary pushed her rimless glasses further up her nose. They had slipped down when she bent to unfold her serviette.

"I wonder if what I sensed," I found myself saying, "was Mother's dislike of this house."

"Loathing," said Thora, "would have been my reaction if I'd had to live here with such a father. In many ways Mina had it worse than Sophia did. At least Sophia only got stuck with William for a year. I've sometimes wondered if she wasn't glad to die in that car crash."

I stared at her, hearing Dog crunching in his bowl of food.

"What did you think happened?" Jane asked me.

"Somehow I got it in my head that she had died giving birth to Mother."

"Understandable." Thora was pouring parsley sauce over

her fish pie. "That would explain your mother's unwilling-
ness to talk about Sophia, wouldn't it? Feelings of mis-
placed guilt, you know. And I wouldn't put it past her father
to have made it seem the accident was Mina's fault."

"Sophia was leaving William," Jane said, "ending their
marriage of less than a year. And of course she had her precious baby with her. In her desperation to get away from
him, she was driving too fast. Her car hit a tree out on some
road in the middle of nowhere. It was hours before they
were found. Mercifully, Mina only suffered a few bruises. It
was too late for our dear friend Sophia." Jane's angular face
puckered. "That vile man wrote to her friend Richard Barttle, giving him all the details. I'm sure William persuaded
himself he was only doing his painful duty in relaying the
precise details of her death. But it was obvious—Richard
showed us the letter—the grieving widower relished letting
it be known that in  forsaking the holy estate of their marriage, Sophia had brought about her own destruction and
nearly killed her child."

I looked around the table at the three women. Now was
the time to pose the question that Rosemary had declined
to answer on the phone last night.

"What did you mean in your letter about my grandmother? Why would she wish to make contact with me
from beyond the grave?" There was no immediate answer
and I pushed on. "I've met Hope, the woman with the psychic powers, as one of the neighbors described her, and it
isn't hard to make the leap that she's somehow involved as
a go-between."

"We first met her a few weeks ago," Jane said, toying with
her food. "She'd just moved into a house between here and
Lower Thaxstead and was in the lane walking her dog.
Thora made a fuss of him, he's such a sad-eyed beast, and
after a few minutes' chitchat, invited Hope inside. It really
was uncanny some of the questions she asked about the
house, almost as though she'd been here before, in the old

days before Rosemary did it up. Then she said she sensed a presence and it was clear she was talking about Sophia."

"No one else? Her vibes didn't extend to my mother?"

"She spoke of a baby girl swaddled in shadows being brought here from a foreign country."

Jane laid down her knife and fork, at which point Rosemary remembered she hadn't led us in saying grace. She apologized for the oversight, said it was all the more important today in light of Ted's calamity, laid down her knife and fork, folded her hands, and bowed her head. The rest of us followed suit. Rosemary was as direct with God as I imagined she was with everyone else. She thanked Him for the food left on our plates as well as for that of which we had already partaken without first asking His divine leave. She requested that His will be done concerning Ted Wilks, that Edna be granted strength and comfort, and that He provide guidance in the matter which had brought me to the Old Rectory.

"Why is it called that?" I asked after a moment of silence. "Is there a new rectory?"

"Not for St. John's, dear." Jane dabbed at her lips with her serviette. "The parish offered William Fitzsimons the opportunity to buy the house. That's how it was his to leave to Rosemary. Since that time it's been the policy to provide the rector with a housing allowance and have him live in the home of his choosing. It's proved to be more economical and certainly our present rector's wife prefers it that way. She's the Danish-modern sort."

"To answer your question, Ellie," Rosemary cut in, "this house became known as the Old Rectory when the Methodists built a new one alongside the church they erected at the turn of the century. William grew up a Methodist; it's where he acquired his strong views on the evils of drink. I've often wondered what brought him over to the Anglican side. And now if no one wants a second helping of fish pie"—she stood up—"I will clear away. Perhaps, Jane, you will fetch the pudding."

While these tasks were being performed, Thora asked after my father and whether he had ever remarried.

"Not yet. But I think he's on the verge. He's quite smitten with a very nice German woman named Ursel Grundman. He did a lot of traveling after Mother died, just couldn't seem to settle down."

"Such a tragedy, her dying from that fall." Jane was carrying a Pyrex bowl of custard and another of stewed fruit.

"Who would think a person could be killed going down a flight of railway steps?" Thora shook her snowy-white head as she returned to the table.

"Mother's injuries weren't all that serious. She broke her leg, but there were complications. An embolism that went to her heart."

"So young." Jane sounded on the verge of tears.

"Only in her mid-thirties."

"We should have come to the funeral." Thora placed a hand on my shoulder. "We wanted to, but Rosemary was ill at the time and we didn't feel we could leave her."

"It's a long time ago," I said as I spooned stewed fruit into my pudding bowl.

"Such a lovely girl, Mina." Jane had joined the other two at the table. "I will always be sorry we saw so little of her and that I wasn't here when she brought you down that day. But she and your father—they were blissfully happy, I hope?"

"Devoted."

"And now he can take comfort in his precious grandchildren."

"He hasn't seen much of them, as I said, he's been abroad a lot. But I think he intends to make up for that, now that he is more settled."

"The acquaintance who helped us get in touch with you

said she had heard you have twins," Rosemary said, and then added casually, "Sophia's mother was a fraternal twin."

"They do say, Ellie, that twins run in families." Thora passed me the custard that had developed a skin from having been left sitting, and I spooned it aside before adding a helping to my fruit. I didn't like skin at the best of times and now felt I couldn't face it even to be a gracious guest.

Talking about my mother, thinking of her growing up a little lost soul in this house, had completely unsettled me. I wanted to get away, not just from the table, but from the bridesmaids and whatever melodramatic nonsense they had afoot. I wanted to be safely back at Merlin's Court, working myself to exhaustion wallpapering Rose's bedroom.

The conversation seemed to have dried up. The bridesmaids had to be wondering what was happening at the hospital.

"You must be anxious for word from Edna," I said.

"It would be a relief to hear something." Rosemary busied herself setting cups and saucers on a tray. "Perhaps you would like to freshen up. There's a downstairs loo, just through there." She nodded towards the opening into the conservatory. And glad to be moving, I went out into the jungle of potted plants in search of a door. Thora had told me after Rosemary and Jane had gone outside with Edna that the parrot was the same one that had been here on my previous visit. And that it threatened to outlive them all. It now squawked at me from behind a veil of greenery. "Cat will get your tongue! Cat will get your tongue!"

"Oh, shut up!" I muttered. There was a door behind the piano, but when I opened it there was nothing inside but the Hoover and a couple of spare lightbulbs on a shelf. After peering around some more and coming up short, I decided that Rosemary must have meant that the loo was out in the hall. Sure enough, when I stepped from the slate floor onto the pine planks, I saw a door under the sloping rear of the staircase. Unfortunately it didn't yield the desired view of a toilet and a sink. It opened onto a flight of rough-hewn stone steps leading steeply down to the murky depths of a cellar. Not a place I wanted to visit on the spur of the moment. Retracing my steps into the conservatory, I stumbled over one of the cats, either Charlotte or Joan, and in reaching out to save myself from a spill, grasped hold of a doorknob. Here at long last was the loo, just outside the kitchen, where I would have been able to spot it but for a rubber plant that, from the size of it, had to be as old as the parrot.

When I came out again I heard all three women in conversation in the kitchen. It struck me that this would be a good time to take my suitcase, handbag, and raincoat up to the second landing, where Rosemary had said my room was, so that they wouldn't be left taking up space in the narrow hall. Moments later I was heading up the stairs and reached the first landing and the second without looking to the right or left, only to be assailed by the scent of orange blossom. Air freshener, I thought. Probably it was a little musty up here. I set the case down on the floor and noticed a trail of confetti leading towards the door on my left. And it was then that I heard a voice begin to sing softly: "Here comes the bride . . . Dum-dum-dee-dum-dum . . . Oh, how she cried . . . A pity she died!" Feeling faint, I had to brace myself before looking around. There was no one there. It had to be a joke, I told myself. One being played against Jane. I would repeat the story and she would be thrilled to bits that I also had experienced what she called her "emanations."

Saved by the doorbell. Dropping my handbag and raincoat on top of my case, I sprinted downstairs.

# CHAPTER SEVEN

WHEN I REACHED the hall Thora was standing outside the sitting room.

"Ellie, come and meet the devil's emissary, Miss Chambers. Rosemary says you knew we were expecting her sometime this afternoon. But we hoped it would be later, around four o'clock." She glanced at her watch. "Cod's wallop! It's almost that now. When we heard the doorbell we thought it would be Edna."

Thora took my arm and guided me into the sitting room. It would have been churlish to shake her off; she had been nice to me even to the point of confiding about Michael, who had gone back to his wife. So I dredged up a smile and tried to forget what had happened upstairs as I followed her through the wide doorway. A woman was seated on the bulky but comfortable-looking sofa. She had a clipboard-style notepad on the lap of her tailored ivory linen suit. But for her expression, which was decidedly businesslike, she might have been a fashion model, like my cousin Vanessa. She had the face and features for the job. Dark eyes under perfectly arched black brows and a sweep of smooth golden-brown hair that curved just above her suit collar. Jane was seated across from her in a striped velvet chair whose fringed trim might have been the cats' handiwork. Rosemary was standing in the middle of the room with a coffee cup in each hand.

"Ellie," she said, glancing my way, "Amelia Chambers has graciously paid us a visit. I don't think she will be staying long but we might as well make ourselves comfortable."

"Good afternoon," I said dutifully, to which the visitor responded by crossing her long legs and murmuring something inaudible. At which point I felt justified in having disliked her on sight. No woman should get the face *and* the legs. And the legs meant she had the perfect figure, because legs like those were never found anchored to a tub of lard. It was the law of the jungle, as Mrs. Malloy would have said. A little late, but I could now empathize with Mrs. M. on meeting the new Gwen. Trim as a whistle and with a faultless complexion. Miss Chambers did not even have the age factor against her. She was about my age. In her early to mid-thirties. I hoped she would snag her stockings with the heel of one of her shoes that matched the ivory suit to perfection and probably cost the price of a small car.

Whatever had come over me? Such hostility towards a woman I didn't know from Eve. And then I realized. Apparently, I hadn't got over my childish susceptibility to atmosphere. Amelia Chambers had taken one look at me and loathed me on sight. She couldn't have made it clearer if she had got up and slapped me across the face. The antipathy was there not only in those crossed legs but also in every line of her body.

"Ellie's grandmother was my first cousin," Rosemary was saying, "which I suppose makes us second cousins or first cousins once removed, I'm never sure which it is."

"I'm more knowledgeable on the intricacies of business." Ms. Chambers tapped her notebook with the pen attached to it by a cord. "It's understandable, of course, Miss Maywood, that you would wish to have a younger member of the family present during this conversation. I understand

that anything requiring a signature can be emotionally tax-
ing for older people."

"I'm here for other reasons," I told her.

"I don't believe I caught your last name?" Her smile
looked expensive. No over-the-counter lipsticks for her.

"I didn't provide it." Rosemary finished handing around
the coffee cups, did not offer milk or sugar, and took her
seat.

"It's Haskell," I said.

"I'll make a note of it." The pen was applied to the
notepad.

"Mrs. Haskell. And you?"

"Ms. Chambers."

"Just for my files." My smile came from a cheap lipstick
I'd had for years, but I liked the color.

"Ellie, come and sit here." Thora patted a chintz-covered
footstool comfortably big enough for two between her chair
and Jane's.

I did as I was told, being careful not to slop my coffee in
Ms. Chambers's direction. Heaven forbid that she should
get stains on the ivory linen suit or, worse yet, get splashed
full in the face. Focusing on our mutual antagonism helped
keep that awful wedding song out of my head. For some
reason it had reminded me of the poem I had told Mrs.
Malloy about, "Rosemary, Thora, and Jane. Lived at the
end of the lane . . ."

"May I ask, Miss Maywood, why the other two ladies are
present at this meeting?" Amelia Chambers sat with her
pen poised.

"They're my friends," said Rosemary.

"With a vested interest in your financial affairs, grounded
in the expectation of an inheritance upon your death?"

"What a nasty thing to say." Jane's winged glasses looked
ready to take flight along with the black bow at her neck.

"Why didn't your boss come himself, instead of sending
you to do his dirty work?" Thora's growl now verged on a roar.

"He's a very busy man."

"That we understand." Rosemary set down her coffee cup and raised a hand to calm her friends. "Even so, it might have helped smooth matters along had he been prepared to grant us more than five minutes of his invaluable time when we paid him a visit at his office in London. Particularly"—she undid a button and then redid it on her cardigan—"considering that we are old acquaintances."

"Who is this man?" I was on the edge of my footstool. The wedding song had faded for the moment to a distant hum.

"Ms. Chambers's employer is Sir Clifford Heath."

"But"—I looked at a landscape painting on the wall and noticed that it needed straightening—"that's the man who owns the Memory Lanes holiday camps. My husband and children are at the one in Norfolk, as we speak."

"So you said." Rosemary was working another cardigan button. "Presently, Sir Clifford Heath, as he now calls himself, is intent on turning Knells into one of his family-type fortnight-away-from-home places."

"What do you mean, calls himself? Did he give himself the title?"

"Unfortunately not, Ellie. Her Majesty the Queen knighted him. Poor overworked woman. I expect someone put the sword in her hand when she wasn't looking and she found herself tapping him on the shoulder without having a clue if he was the undergardener or the Pope. It's the rest, the Clifford Heath part, he's invented. That wasn't his name when he lived in Knells."

"Not that people aren't entitled to change their names if they don't like them," conceded Jane before I could speak. "And none of us begrudge Sir Clifford his success. He was always clever and must have worked exceedingly hard."

"We can also see, whilst not admiring his tactics, why he would put Knells on his hit list." Thora's voice had softened to its usual deep tones. "Wasn't always treated well here.

And there were other factors, sufficient to make any proud man bitter. But to take revenge upon an entire village, the majority of whose inhabitants weren't around in his day, that's beyond the pale."

"Sir Clifford's motivations are none of my concern." For some inexplicable reason, Miss Chambers was looking at me and her smile would have been enough to frighten children under the nearest table, the more so because it was as exquisitely tailored as the rest of her.

"Oh, I think you are being too modest." Rosemary could smile with the best of them. "You are his *personal*," emphasis on the word, "assistant."

"And what is that supposed to mean, Miss Maywood?"

"One assumes you are more than a well-paid secretary."

"My duties are extensive."

"I'm sure they are." Rosemary actually chuckled. Quite nastily, too. "You are, as you must be fully aware, a very attractive young woman."

"If you are implying . . ." Ms. Chambers forgot herself sufficiently to grind her perfect teeth.

"Merely that you are a visible asset to your employer." Rosemary adjusted her glasses on her nose. "What did you think I meant?"

"That Sir Clifford and I have a romantic relationship." Ms. Chambers had lost some of her poise. I thought I could see a wrinkle in her linen skirt and the hand that gripped her pen was not one hundred percent steady. "It's none of your business, but to set the record straight, Sir Clifford is my stepfather. He married my mother when I was a teenager. They divorced a few years later, but he provided for me while I was attending university. Afterwards he hired me for a relatively junior position and I worked my way up. That's it in a nutshell."

"Very kind of him." Rosemary got up to refill her own coffee cup and sat back down without bringing the pot around to the rest of us. Something, I was sure, she would normally not have done.

"I'm very good at what I do." Ms. Chambers made a couple of strokes with her pen across the notebook.

"Commendable!" Thora said.

"I'm sure your dear mother will be proud," Jane twittered.

My empty coffee cup sat adrift on my knees like a raft from the *Titanic* waiting for would-be survivors to jump into it. The air throbbed with tension.

"It's time"—Amelia Chambers drew up her jacket sleeve and looked at her watch—"more than time that we get to the purpose of this meeting. I'm to inform you that Sir Clifford regrets your refusal to accept his more than generous purchasing offer for this house, Miss Maywood. The result is unnecessary aggravation to yourself. Surely something a woman of your age does not need, given the futility of the situation. Sir Clifford will ultimately have his way. All other properties in Knells belong to him. He has permission from the appropriate national and local authorities to proceed with the conversion of Knells into the next Memory Lanes. In other words, Miss Maywood, you remain thc one minor stumbling block. But I am to tell you that you will be removed."

"By legal means?"

"Of course." Ms. Chambers tucked away her pen in the top of her notebook. "Sir Clifford is a law-abiding citizen."

"But not a kind one," I said.

"Ellie"—Rosemary held up a hand—"we really don't want to keep Ms. Chambers here longer than necessary. The message to be delivered to her employer is that I am prepared to reconsider my position. And that I hope, in light of his former connection to Knells, he will grant me a week in which to do so. Now"—she rose to her feet—"given my rapidly advancing years I feel in need of a nap. Thora and Jane," she said, turning to them after setting her coffee cup down on a table, "ᵢ am sure you could both benefit from one also."

"Dropping on my feet." Thora, who exuded the vigor of a woman eager to get back to the garden and chop down a couple of trees, stifled a yawn with her hand. Jane did likewise. And before Ms. Chambers had half-completed her protest that Sir Clifford had expected the papers signed this afternoon, she was somehow marshaled out to the hall, handed her umbrella and coat, and nudged out the front door.

"One has to be firm with that sort of person." Rosemary returned to the sitting room with the rest of us crowding in behind her. "And fortunately we had her sufficiently unsettled under that flawless persona that she wasn't dying to be invited to stay for tea." Rosemary returned to the chair she had vacated moments before.

"Aren't you going to lie down?" I asked her.

"Certainly not."

"What about your nap?" I didn't like to add that she looked in dire need of a rest.

"Surely, Ellie, you realized I only said that to speed Ms. Chambers on her way." Rosemary smoothed out the arm cover on her chair while Thora and Jane watched her from where they were now seated on the sofa. "We have to explain to you about Sir Clifford Heath and why he is the reason we asked you to come."

"But I thought you said it had to do with my grandmother?" I sat down feeling betrayed.

"And so it does," said Jane. "It's about them both—Sophia and Hawthorn Lane."

"Who?"

"That's who Sir Clifford began life as, so far as we know. It's possible, I suppose, that his mother took the time to call him something before she abandoned him when he was no more than a few days old on the doorstep of a house in Hawthorn Lane. A sad beginning." Jane dabbed at her eyes.

"I think it would be best if one of us took over telling the story. It will speed things up and make it easier for Ellie to follow." Rosemary addressed the sofa. "You do it, Thora. Jane will flutter about and I am a little tired."

"Very well," said Thora. "The foster agency that took him on decided, for want of any other ideas, to name him Hawthorn Lane. A rotten thing to do." She grimaced. "Never allowed him to escape his beginnings. He was a dark-haired, dark-eyed baby and people got the rubbishy idea he'd been dropped off by gypsies. Hawthorn went from one foster home to another, some here in Knells and some in the other villages around here. No one ever wanted him for long. Every time a penny went missing he was out the door. Gypsies are thieves, people believe, so it was bound to be him. Wasn't surprising he grew more troublesome and rebellious, until he was packed off to a reformatory school. Sophia told us all about him when she and Rosemary, Jane, and I were at boarding school together. She was in love with him even then. Most people would say that a fourteen-year-old girl couldn't be in touch with the real meaning of the word, but it was one of those Cathy–Heathcliff relationships. Two souls connecting from the very first moment of meeting. That's what Sophia called him—Heathcliff. It was her secret name for him. Only told us because we were her closest friends. Said he deserved his own name. One given to him by someone who loved him till death and beyond."

"So that's why he changed his name to Clifford Heath," I said slowly, "but he also elected to keep at least part of his original name in coming up with one for his Memory Lanes holiday camps."

"Could be he was sending a message that he's got a long memory indeed." Thora shrugged. "But on with the story, Ellie.

"Sophia told us that she met Hawthorn when she caught him scrumping for apples in the back garden. Said she saw his face looking down at her from the tree and she thought he was one of Pan's people. She was seven and he was ten. I'm sure her parents had no idea that there was this *Wuthering Heights* business under their noses, until Hawthorn went to that reform place.

"She used to write him letters when we were at boarding school. Had one of the older girls who had permission to go into town post them for her. Rosemary, Jane, and I took over when we entered the fifth form a year ahead of Sophia. When she turned sixteen she was able to post the letters herself. All through those years Hawthorn wrote back, signing his letters 'Your loving Aunt Betty.' Because, as Sophia used to say earnestly: 'almost everyone has an Aunt Betty.' She was in many ways a very serious girl. The teachers called her 'sensible.' It was only in her painting that she revealed a wilder, more passionate side. Said Hawthorn was the only one who really understood the ideas she was trying to project. Our art teacher certainly didn't. Called what Sophia did a lot of sploshing about with the paintbrush. Never gave her high marks. But somehow we three—Rosemary, Jane, and I—knew she was good even if we couldn't put into words why."

Thora paused. It was clear that she had got sidetracked somewhere down memory lane and Rosemary, who appeared to have nodded off, urged her to continue, which she did after taking a sip from the coffee cup she had set down on Amelia Chambers's departure.

"Hawthorn returned to Knells the year before Sophia left school. Got a job in the photographer's studio, the one now owned by Richard Barttle. He started out sweeping up and doing other odd jobs, but the plan, Sophia told us, was for him to establish himself in Knells as a young man who had outgrown his wild ways and was ready and eager to settle down. She naively hoped that this would encourage her parents to give their approval when she and Hawthorn broke the news that they wanted to become engaged."

"And did he settle down?" I asked.

"When it came to work." Thora settled back on the sofa. "Began taking photographs when there was a need on the owner's half day off. Seemed to have a flair for it. There was quite a bit of talk about how good he was amongst the young people we played tennis with, when Jane and I came down to spend time with Rosemary while she was learning to be a dispenser at the chemist's in Rilling. But it was hard to tell with the girls whether it was his talent they admired or his stunning good looks. He'd turned into quite a dish, as we used to say. What made him even more appealing to some girls was that wild untamed quality of his. 'Like a fallen angel,' I remember one of them saying. Not that any of our set would have gone out with him. They were all inclined to be snobby when it came right down to it and they knew their parents wouldn't have had Hawthorn in the house. He had quickly gained a reputation, deserved or otherwise, as a seducer of sweet little virgins, to add to the one he already had as a ne'er-do-well. It got so that the local young men were afraid to take their sweethearts to him for the engagement photos. Because word was out that they fell in love with him while he was clicking the camera. Don't doubt he took every opportunity offered him for a tryst in the hayloft of one of the abandoned barns."

"Did you tell that to Sophia?" I asked.

"Wouldn't have come as news to her," replied Thora. "Said she didn't expect Hawthorn to live like a monk while they were apart. He was young, only nineteen, this was the time for him to sow some wild oats. She was a strange girl in some ways. Passionately romantic and at the same time realistic. Maybe a lot of sixteen-year-olds are that way. All she asked of Hawthorn was that he be discreet and not get anyone pregnant. A fairly tall order in those days. But I don't know that there was ever any talk about anyone having a baby by him."

"Even so, if he really hoped to gain Sophia's parents'

approval it might have been better if he'd chained himself up in the nearest abbey," I said. It was difficult in listening to Thora's recounting of events to fully accept the fact that she was talking about my grandmother.

"You're right, of course, Ellie, but I'm not so sure it would have made any difference. Sophia hadn't been home for a week after leaving boarding school when Reverend McNair called her into his study and told her William Fitzsimons had asked for her hand in marriage and there was to be no silly nonsense about refusing him."

"But that's archaic!" I protested.

Thora bit her lip as she nodded. "That was Sophia's reaction. There were some terrible rows between her and both parents—Mrs. McNair was all for the idea, she thought William was absolutely splendid, saw him making a big name for himself in the church. His plan to go out as a missionary to the Belgian Congo would be the first step in getting himself noticed. She believed he'd end up as Archbishop of Canterbury. And William was ambitious. Undoubtedly it was the main reason he wanted to marry Sophia, although she was a pretty girl. A little plump but it suited her. Her eyes were what one first noticed—a lovely shade of gray, very like yours, Ellie, and she had masses of long hair, usually worn the way you are wearing yours now." Thora paused before adding: "Rosemary was here all the while the rumpus was going on."

"It must have been difficult to see a friend so unhappy and feel helpless to do anything about it." I was leaning forward on my footstool, wondering if I should suggest another round of coffee, but decided that wasn't the drink required. They all looked as though they could have done with a good stiff brandy.

"The situation wore me down to the point where I was ready to throw up my training in Rilling and move away." Rosemary still sat with her eyes closed behind her octagonal glasses. "Sophia was kept shut up for weeks after being shouted at by Uncle Hugo for being a willful, unnatural daughter. Of course, when William was present she was made to come down and be pleasant. Then out of the blue she quietened down and said she would marry him. The engagement was announced in *The Telegraph* and Aunt Agatha immediately began plans for the wedding that was to take place a couple of weeks before William was due out in the Belgian Congo. Thora, Jane, and I were to be bridesmaids."

"So that's why Mother called you that."

"She must have got it from her father." Rosemary had clearly decided to take over from Thora in finishing the story. "Afterwards William always referred to us by that collective name. He did so with one of his sneers. In fact we never performed the role of bridesmaids for Sophia. But we were in the house trying on our frocks that Sunday afternoon, a week before the wedding, when Uncle Hugo was found dead of a heart attack in his study. And of course that altered everything. The ceremony was scaled down to a bare-bones affair and . . ."

"Yes?" I prompted.

"Sophia's plans for running off with Hawthorn at the final hour were scratched."

"She had that planned all along, from when she meekly agreed to marry William?"

"She was, as we have indicated, a girl with a strong practical streak," Jane broke in before Rosemary could speak. "They would need money and the more Hawthorn saved from his job the longer they could manage until they found other work somewhere else. We weren't in on the secret. Sophia kept Rosemary, Thora, and me in the dark until she broke down on the evening of Reverend McNair's death. She was really a very decent girl, who had been jostled around by forces too strong for her. She blamed herself for her father's heart attack."

"Saw it as retribution," Thora broke in just as Jane had done moments before.

"And she agreed to marry William." I felt a little sick. I couldn't imagine what it would be like to spend a wedding night with a man I loathed. And Sophia had loathed him. I was certain of it. As had my mother loathed and feared him in the years that followed. They had been there on that day when she brought me to this house, those shadows that unfurl out of the subconscious to blur the present with the past when misery is never properly laid to rest.

"The wedding went forward on the day planned in a simple ceremony in the vestry. No bridesmaids. No guests." Rosemary was tapping the arm of her chair. "Only Richard Barttle as the best man and Aunt Agatha in attendance. Uncle Hugo's funeral had taken place the previous day. There wasn't even a proper wedding breakfast, according to what Edna has told us, just tea and sandwiches before Sophia and William left to catch their train. We hoped Sophia would write but she never did, not even to tell us the baby had been born. And shortly after that she was dead, killed driving her car into a tree, something she surely had no business doing, because she had never had a license in England and had always said she was afraid of learning to drive."

"And how did Hawthorn react to Sophia's marriage?"

"He went around spewing talk of revenge."

"Against the entire village, or specifically against the woman who loved and left him?" I was looking at all three women. "Is Sir Clifford Heath intent on tearing down Knells and replacing it with a Memory Lanes holiday camp to get back at those who symbolize the rejection that made him an outcast as a boy? Or is he out to bury all memories of Sophia under the rubble?"

"That, Ellie," said Rosemary, "is what we think Sophia wants you to find out."

# CHAPTER EIGHT

"IT SOUNDS RATHER a tall order." I got out of my chair and paced around the room, a habit I had picked up from Ben, who had worn out two rooms of parquet flooring before he had been at Merlin's Court a month.

"I'm sure it does, dear," replied Jane soothingly. "And believe me, Rosemary, Thora, and I resisted the notion of involving you when Hope first suggested it. But she has been so insistent that Sophia is calling out to you from beyond the grave and that the message she wishes to impart concerns Sir Clifford and his plans to visit his vengeance upon Knells. So after much thought, and some disagreements amongst ourselves, it was agreed that Rosemary would write to you."

"Providing just enough of a tease to get me here."

"You're cross, Ellie," said Thora from the sofa. "Quite frankly, I don't blame you one bit. You haven't heard a word from us in years. We weren't there at your mother's funeral or afterwards to offer a helping hand to you or your father in your bereavement. And now here we are, caps in hand. There aren't any satisfactory excuses to be made, which is why Rosemary—even though she is the one who finally wrote to you—felt it was an impertinence to involve you."

While adjusting a brass candlestick on the mantelpiece—straightening things was my response to tension—I kept my back to all three women. "Had you simply written to let me know about Sir Clifford and his plans for Knells, I might not have cared too much one way or the other."

"Oh, dear!" Jane sounded like a schoolgirl caught putting a frog in the headmistress's bed. "I do see what you are getting at: You think we've brought Hope into this as a ruse to lure you into thinking it's Sophia who's asking for your help, not virtual strangers. But I assure you, Ellie, we didn't cook this up. From her first visit on, Hope convinced us she sensed our beloved Sophia's presence and her desperation to make contact with you."

"And it never occurred to you she might be a fraud?" I returned to my footstool.

"Of course it did." Rosemary sat scrutinizing the rearranged landscape painting and candlestick through half-closed eyes. "Or I should say I had very strong suspicions that the woman was playing some sort of game for her own dubious ends. Thora and Jane swallowed every word as if it were an elixir from the gods. Being the guileless women they are, they couldn't think of any possible motive for her popping up out of the blue at a time when I am making difficulties for Sir Clifford."

"You think Hope may be working for him?"

"The thought occurred." Rosemary stirred in her seat but did not get up. "All that wild black and orange hair—and those impossibly green eyes. No one has eyes that color unless they wear contact lenses. She could have made herself over so that we would more readily buy into the possibility that she was able to commune with the dead. But when it comes right down to it, Ellie, I don't believe Hawthorn . . . or I should I say, Sir Clifford, would stoop to playing silly games."

"He's been dipping into his nasty bag of tricks for years," I countered, "buying up the villagers' properties a cottage at a time, just as if it were a game of Monopoly, until he could sweep the board. Do the other residents know he is Hawthorn Lane?"

"No," said Rosemary. "We didn't know until that visit to London."

"And when you balked at selling he could have come up with this scheme of dragging me into the picture."

"It's possible." Jane looked from me to Rosemary and back again. "But somehow it seems more the sort of thing a woman might do. Most men don't have that kind of imagination, do they? And Hawthorn was always so intensely masculine. Besides I don't see how such a ruse would work to his advantage. Reflect upon it. If Hope were to fake a trance and claim Sophia was instructing her to urge Rosemary to sell Sir Clifford the Old Rectory as a means of righting old wrongs, we would immediately smell a rat."

"I know what you are thinking." Thora studied my face intently. "He could be picturing us as three silly old women, as gullible as God makes them. But somehow I don't think so, especially in Rosemary's case. She was always the brainy one out of all of us, including Sophia. And even though Hawthorn didn't give her more than five minutes of his time when she went to see him in London a few weeks ago, he must have realized she is still a woman to be reckoned with."

"That's neither here nor there." Rosemary crossed the room to stand in front of the landscape painting which she tapped with a finger until it was once more slightly crooked, before moving over to the mantelpiece to realign the candlestick. "Whatever the cause, Hope is now part of the equation. And it is as much your right, Ellie, as it is ours to determine whether to believe her or not."

"Sir Clifford could have provided her with all sorts of compelling details to make it seem that she had a psychic connection with the house and Sophia," I persisted, not quite sure why I was doing so. I had felt an instant rapport with Hope. And I wasn't one to dismiss the idea that there are those who can see beyond the veil into other realms of existence. Could it be that I was beginning to like the bridesmaids, despite my scare on the upper landing, and objected to the idea of them being hoodwinked? Or was I afraid of some other more formless danger with myself at its dark core?

"We must also bear in mind," Rosemary was saying, "that Ms. Chambers is undoubtedly correct in asserting that Sir Clifford, with all the pieces in place, has the power to force me to sell him this house. Making it foolish for him to take additional steps that could give the impression he is not one-hundred-percent confident he has me by the tail."

"Perhaps he's allowing his thirst for revenge to deflect his business judgment," I argued. "From what you've told me he's a man who allowed his emotions to lead him into behaving stupidly in the past. He returned to Knells after his stint at reform school supposedly intent on gaining Sophia's parents' approval. And what did he do? He squandered his time sowing his wild oats, until it's a wonder half the fathers within miles weren't out after him with their shotguns."

"But he's not a hot-blooded, foolhardy youth anymore," Jane pointed out.

"I suppose not, given the fact that he is now over seventy. Instead of nibbling on young girls' necks he may prefer these days to go straight for the jugular." It was an unfortunate thing for me to say. I had forgotten Ted and how he had stabbed himself in the throat with the pruning shears. But I saw Rosemary turn white and grab hold of the mantelpiece to stop herself from tripping over the hearthrug. And Thora hurried over to wrap a sturdy arm around her shoulders.

"Steady on, old friend," she crooned. "Such an eventful afternoon. I'm afraid we've all shuffled Ted into the background. Ellie, of course, doesn't know him and I didn't see him out there in the garden, looking, I'm sure, horrible and bloody. You and Jane had the worst of it, going outside to help Edna as best you could until the ambulance arrived."

"He wasn't a pretty sight." Rosemary squared her shoulders and straightened her back, but allowed Thora to help her as she returned to her seat.

"Ghastly. Eyes rolled back in his head and that dark trickle coming out of his mouth." Jane bustled over to a cabinet from which she withdrew a bottle. "Sadly, he was never a particularly appealing specimen of manhood at the best of times. My husbands—the two that died—looked heroic and noble right till the end. But there would be no way to make Ted look either even if you tied him to a flagpole and flew him over Buckingham Palace. But we mustn't think the worst. He may bounce right back from this accident. Here, dear"—she handed Rosemary a minute glass filled with a reddish-purple liquid—"sip this down. It's the last of the elderberry wine from last year's crop, and I'm sure just what the doctor would order."

"Ellie will think me an alcoholic!" Rosemary accepted the glass and held it gingerly under her nose before pursing her lips and taking a dubious swallow. "A person of backbone should not have to resort to artificial stimulants in order to deal with the ups and downs of everyday life. Tom from up the lane was a tower of strength. Very kind about it, too. And if I didn't crack up on seeing Ted in extremis I don't know why you and Thora think I'm about to do so now."

The two other women exchanged a look and one or both of them said something about delayed shock, coming on top of Amelia Chambers's visit . . . I wasn't able to catch everything being said. Dog had started barking at the top of his lungs and came skidding into the sitting room with a couple of very unladylike cats in pursuit just as the doorbell pealed.

"I expect that's Edna now," said Jane.

"Let's hope it's good news." Thora was pouring Rosemary another glass of wine.

"Would you like me to get the door so you can catch your breaths?" I asked.

"That would be kind," one of them said from where they

stood in a close-knit triangle, and I went out into the hall, bracing myself to say the right things to Edna, who had known my mother even if she and I were complete strangers.

But it wasn't Edna at the door. A middle-sized man, with black hair slicked back off his forehead into waves guaranteed to cause seasickness in the most seasoned sailor, greeted me. But what put me off most was his flashy imitation-silk tie.

"Yes?" I attempted a smile as falsely bright as the one he shone on me.

"Sorry to intrude." A bold-faced lie if ever there was one.

"I'm just staying here for a few days," I told him, "but if you let me know what it's about, I'll tell the ladies who live here."

"No need to bother them." He stood jiggling the loose change in the trouser pockets of his cheaply smart suit and bouncing on the balls of his feet. "Don't tell me, because I've already guessed—you're Ellie Haskell. And if I may say so, you're every bit the looker I was led to expect. But I won't keep you hanging about on the step. Just give a whistle inside will you and let my one and only know I'm here to take her back into my loving arms. Playing hard to get, the little minx!" His grin widened so that his resemblance to a stoat should have put him on the cover of *National Geographic*. "Thought she'd do a bunk and make me come chasing after her. So here I am! Always try and give the little woman what she wants, is my way of thinking."

What I was thinking at that moment wasn't fit for print. I came out onto the doorstep, which put me nose to nose with the man. Perhaps noting the menacing glint in my eyes, he shifted to my left. Very sensible, although it wasn't him I was itching to kick.

"I assume it's Mrs. Malloy you're looking for," I said coldly.

"That's her. My own darling Roxie!" He exuded delight and the pong of hair tonic. "Where is the little rascal hiding herself? Don't tell me she didn't recognize my footsteps coming down the street!" Seeing that he was ready to piffle on, I cut him short.

"So you're Leonard Skinner."

"The one and only." He was back to jiggling coins, otherwise I was sure he would have thumped his chest.

"Really? I should have thought there were dozens in the phone directory."

"Not like yours truly."

"You're probably right," I conceded. "I don't suppose the others all had the gall to walk out on their wives, then show up twenty-some years later expecting all to be forgiven."

He assumed a crestfallen expression that wouldn't have fooled a two-year-old. "I wrote and explained all that to Roxie. About how I'd had amnesia and . . ."

"You probably caught it staying out too late at night." I smiled at him in what I hoped passed for a kindly fashion. "And I'm sure you still need to take extra-special care of yourself, so I won't keep you hanging about on a nasty cold doorstep, Leonard." I turned to go inside. "Besides, Mrs. Malloy isn't here."

His good humor was gone, as if sucked down a drain. He looked ready to throw a punch, but vented his feelings by sucking in his lips and glowering at me in a pop-eyed fashion. "What do you mean, she's not here? Her neighbor—a Mrs. Mills—said Roxie was taking off with you for a few days of living it up. Fat chance, I'd say, in this mausoleum of a house." He swept out a hand and let out a very satisfactory ouch when he scraped his knuckles on the stonework.

How typical of Mrs. Malloy! I could picture her soulful expression when she passed along the information as to where she was going and with whom. Not a word of which must be breathed to the husband who had forsaken her but was now desperate for a glimpse, however fleeting, of her winsome face—thigh—big toe or whatever. I had no doubt that Mrs. M. had left her neighbor happily convinced that she was a conspirator in one the great romances of all time and that it was her bounden duty to facilitate a happy ending.

"Poor Mrs. Mills," I said, "she's going to hate herself in the morning. Now, if you will excuse me, I'm going back inside. Your Roxie is truly staying somewhere else. You will only be wasting your time and that of the local police department if you continue to hang around."

"Come on, lovey." He had put the smile back on so that it almost hid his anger. "Tell me where she is. The woman loves me, she always did, she always will. You can't say she been happy these last years, now can you?"

"You've got a point there," I said.

"You see! She's been pining, isn't that right?"

"Absolutely. For the pound and a half of stewing steak that you were supposed to bring back when you went out to do the shopping and forgot to come back. There's no way I'm going to tell you where she is, except to say that it is miles away from here. Sorry! Mrs. Mills didn't know as much as she thought she did. The old blabbermouth!"

Pushing the door open, I went inside, closing it behind me with a decisive click. Bother Mrs. Malloy, I fumed. Leonard was a complication I did not need, with Ted Wilks at death's door and a meeting still to be arranged with my grandmother Sophia. But there was no time to wallow in aggravation. The bridesmaids must be wondering what had been keeping me. Not sure how much to tell them about Leonard, I crossed the strip of hall and went through the wide archway into the sitting room, only to find it empty. The tray with the coffeepot along with the cups and saucers had been removed. A couple of cushions had been plumped up and the clock on the mantelpiece ticked away in the self-conscious manner of someone left talking to himself. Before leaving the room, I crossed to the window, whose curtains were open to the front garden and the lane beyond.

Yes, there was Leonard prowling around my car like a

prospective buyer. I was about to pound on the glass when I saw him touch the handle of the driver's-side door. But he turned his head, saw me looking out at him, and with a shrug he moved off. Not, however, without taking a good look at the license plate. Lovely! I seethed. From now on I wouldn't be able to drive down the lane and back without being afraid he was tailing me. True, he had said he had come here by train, but there was nothing to stop his hiring a car. Certainly not the cost, because if he didn't have some woman's credit card in his pocket or know just the right sap to spot him the cash, I was the Queen of Sheba. I watched until he disappeared around the bend in the lane. I hoped it would rain, causing his cheap suit to shrink until the trousers were up to his knees and the sleeves about the elbows. Somewhat cheered by this ridiculous picture and his resulting embarrassment, for if ever a man existed to cut a dash it was Leonard Skinner, I went in search of Rosemary, Thora, and Jane.

I expected to find them in the conservatory, but only the parrot was there to greet me with a few well-chosen words, which included a couple of profanities and the admonition to stick my head in a bucket.

"The same to you." I parted the screen of greenery to make a face at him.

"Oh, bugger off!" He puffed out his green-and-yellow chest and, nastiness coming before a fall, toppled off his perch to the bottom of his cage. "You'll pay for that!" he screeched in the voice that so uncannily mimicked Ted's, and then he added a word that made me back up in such a hurry that I kicked aside one of the smaller potted plants: "Murderess!"

"Is that you, Ellie?" Thora's voice came to me from the kitchen and I negotiated my way with all possible speed through the rest of the jungle into the cozier atmosphere of apple-green walls, Devonshire crockery, and the bunches of herbs hung from a rustic rack suspended from the ceiling.

All three bridesmaids were seated around the wooden table. With them was Edna, her head bent and a handkerchief pressed to her face.

"She came in through the back door," explained Rosemary, who was pouring tea while Jane handed around a plate of sandwiches. "She'd been here for about half an hour before the bell rang."

"Ted is dead," Thora said, as if she were giving me the time of day.

"Thora!" cried Rosemary.

"It's okay, Miss Maywood. I know Miss Dobson isn't one to mince words. He passed away a short while ago." Edna lowered the handkerchief, to reveal reddened eyes and tearstained cheeks. Her lips quivered and she sucked down a sob. "I'm sorry. I should be glad he never regained consciousness. I don't think I could have stood watching him suffer. It's bad enough picturing in my mind what happened with him falling like that off the ladder. I just don't understand it . . . those pruning shears all sticky with his blood." She drew a deep breath and tucked the hanky in her skirt pocket. She didn't have on the apron she had been wearing earlier. It had been horribly stained. "Tom said we should take the shears with us to the hospital, so's the doctors could look at them and try and figure out what happened. And then . . . well, if Ted didn't make it, there'd have to be an inquest and they'd be needed for that."

"Tom's wife says he watches too many of those police programs on television." Rosemary placed a trembling hand over Edna's clasped ones. "The inquest will be just a formality. There always has to be one in accident cases. And we will all be here to help you get through it. Even Ellie, if she can possibly stay for it, because you were always so kind to her mother when she was growing up here."

"Such a sweet girl, Mina." Tears gathered in Edna's eyes. "The only time she'd ever get cross was when I'd call her Wilhelmina."

I stared at the bridesmaids.

"You didn't know that was her full name?" Thora looked back at me from across the table.

"No."

"She was named for her father, William."

"Then I understand why she hated it."

"Would you like to lie down?" Rosemary asked, turning her attention back to Edna.

"That's more than kind." Edna summoned up a watery smile. "But I think I'll ask my cousin Gwen that lives in Upper Thaxstead if I can stay over at her house. She nursed her husband's first wife through her final illness, so she understands how hard these times can be."

It was as Edna blew her nose in her hanky that I remembered that she was Gwen's cousin and it was possible she had heard of Mrs. Malloy and her intended visit. Even if she hadn't it was likely to come out now because of Ted's death. However snobby Gwen had become, basking in her big house and her stepchildren's degrees from Cambridge, she could hardly fail to offer Edna some emotional support at a time like this.

"Gwen and I aren't what you could call close," Edna went on to say. "Even though it was me years back that told her about the job working as a nanny for the children of the man she's now married to. But family is still family when all's said and done. And there's no one else left. My brothers and sisters are gone. I keep thinking how it would have been if Ted and I'd had children. Such a comfort they can grow up to be, but we weren't blessed, so there's no use going on about it. I've got to think myself lucky for having my husband all these years. Some would say he put me through a lot, and so he did, but that's most marriages, isn't it? Take the rough with the smooth."

"Men do have their funny ways," was Thora's response and I wondered if she was thinking about her Michael, who for all his devotion to her had gone back to his wife.

"Even my last two husbands had their off moments," Jane agreed. "The one who was an archaeologist started digging through neighbors' dustbins after he retired. Looking for broken pieces of pottery and piecing them together so he could determine how much wear they'd had and whether they'd been dropped by accident or smashed in a fit of rage. And the one who was an accountant not only counted sheep out loud before going to sleep but separated them into groups according to age, sex, and sheared and unsheared, and gave the fastest ones a handicap of five hundred paces. Then there was my first husband, who bought me a ring and a fur coat the day before he went off with another woman."

Edna smiled mistily. "Luckily, I never had to worry about that sort of thing with Ted."

No, because he was too busy worrying about you having a man on the side, I thought. Looking at her now, even with her woebegone face, she was still a pretty woman. In her youth she must have been all peaches and cream. Her figure was pleasingly rounded. And her thickly curling hair, which had gentled into a shade between gray and brown, had probably been fair. She got up from the table and I noticed her slight limp, wondering as I had done on first seeing her come into the conservatory whether it was an old injury.

"Edna, what have you done to your foot?" asked Rosemary, rousing herself from staring into space.

"It's nothing, Miss Maywood. Just a slight sprain. I felt something twist when I skidded on a patch of wet grass running back into the house. One of the doctors at the hospital took a look at it. Tom insisted, and I was told to rest it as much as possible, but they always say that, don't they, just to try and keep you happy." Edna continued her halting way over to the cooker, where she set the kettle on to boil.

"I can see the bruise through your stocking." Thora came up behind her and turned off the burner.

"Nothing to fuss about, Miss Dobson." Edna belied this reassurance by leaning up against the sink and biting down on a wince. "I just won't be able to move as fast as usual for a few days and going up and down stairs may be a bit of a bind, but I'll manage pretty much the way I always do."

"Meantime, I'm going to make you up one of my poultices." Thora put an arm around her shoulders and led her inexorably into the conservatory. "You lie down on the sofa with a couple of cats for hot-water bottles, while I go out into the garden to pick some comfrey and cook it up to a nice green mess on the stove. Nothing like it for drawing out a bruise."

"Well, if you insist." Edna sounded more than ready to give in. "But what about your dinner? I left a nice macaroni and cheese in the refrigerator, but I'd planned to grill some rashers of bacon and tomatoes to go with it. Miss Maywood asked for something simple seeing that you ladies all have a lot to talk over with Mrs. Haskell; still, I do feel I'll be letting you down if I leave you to fend for yourselves."

Thora's soothing murmurings drifted into the kitchen and we could see her bent back as she tucked Edna up on the sofa with its canopy of greenery.

"Ellie, I completely forgot! Who *was* at the door?" Rosemary asked.

"It was someone for me." I sat down.

"Your husband?" Jane looked up. The black bow had slipped low on her neck and her winged glasses were askew as if she had shifted them to wipe her eyes.

"No, someone looking for Mrs. Malloy, whom I took to stay with friends in Upper Thaxstead."

"The man she spoke to me about on the phone?" Thora was back in the kitchen. "The one she didn't want to know where she was? What was his name now?"

"Leonard. I didn't tell him anything, except to get lost."

"Do you think he will?"

"I expect so," I lied. "I told him she was miles away from

here, which is, strictly speaking, the case. Upper Thaxstead isn't just round the corner."

"You don't think—" Thora fixed me with those brown eyes, made even darker in contrast to the fringe of snow-white hair that just cleared eyebrows. "You don't think, Ellie, that he thinks she is here?"

"I believe I convinced him that wasn't the case." I felt awful fibbing like this. But it didn't seem fair to make Leonard an ongoing issue. I almost wished he would figure out, by one sneaky means or the other, that Mrs. Malloy was at Gwen and Barney Fiddler's house and then she could make her own decision whether to fall into his arms or strangle him with his imitation-silk tie.

"Well, we should have realized it wouldn't be Edna at the front door." Rosemary finally spoke, while handing me a roast-beef sandwich. "We always leave the conservatory unlocked for her during the day, so she can come in round back."

"And of course Dog wouldn't have barked if it had been Edna. We just weren't thinking." Jane removed her glasses and gave them a polish with her serviette before dabbing at her eyes. "It breaks your heart, doesn't it? Edna's always been such a gem, and just look at her now, still thinking of us with all she's going through, Ellie." ·

"It would be nice if she could finally find some real happiness." I lowered my voice as I picked up the remains of my roast-beef sandwich. It was smothered in horseradish just as I liked and I polished it off feeling a little ashamed of enjoying every mouthful. But I reminded myself that I needed to keep my strength up. The macaroni and cheese might be a long while in coming. This thought was bolstered when Rosemary suggested that Jane and I accompany her back to the sitting room. That way we wouldn't be in the way while Thora made up the poultice, and our talking wouldn't disturb Edna, who might even now be dozing off.

"It may seem heartless but we do have to get back to the matter which has brought you here," Rosemary said when we again were seated—she in what I was now sure was officially her chair, and Jane and I on the sofa.

"I imagine Hope has suggested conducting a séance." I managed to sound quite matter-of-fact and both women looked relieved.

"It would seem the obvious course of action." Rosemary reached sideways for the footstool on which I had sat earlier and propped her sensibly shod feet on it. "At first I was against the idea. I've always thought such things a lot of twaddle. Dangerous twaddle at that, where susceptible minds are involved. But Jane has been all for it from the time the suggestion came up, and even Thora has agreed. I am not sure if it was Hope who first put the idea into words or exactly how it happened. But the long and the short of it is that I have decided to participate if you will, Ellie."

"I explained to Rosemary"—Jane turned around on the sofa to face me—"that we didn't have the right to deny you the opportunity of hearing what your grandmother wants to say to you."

"Added to which," I couldn't resist saying, "you're hoping that whatever it is, it will somehow help in this situation with Sir Clifford."

"There is that, dear. We've been wondering, at least Thora and I have, if Sophia will ask you to go and see him and try to talk him out of destroying Knells. An appeal from you, the granddaughter of the woman he loved, might just do the trick, don't you think?"

"Not really, if he loathes the very thought of her memory, which seems to me entirely likely, seeing that she threw him over to marry William, a man she claimed to detest."

"But only think of the circumstances!" Jane took my hands and pressed them between her own. "Her father dead, her mother distraught, and then Sophia's own tragic death less than a year later."

"That may be the part he can't forgive."

"But we can't be sure of that, dear. He may well have come to realize that she was a victim of life in Knells, perhaps more so than he was himself. It could be that he wants to take revenge on the village on her behalf. And if you were to explain to him that existing, as she surely must, in a place where all is love at its sublime forgiving best, he might realize she wants him to let all the old resentments go. Otherwise"—Jane was warming to her theme—"he could put his immortal soul in jeopardy, thus making it impossible for him to rejoin her in the next world."

"Jane is an incurable romantic," said Rosemary from her chair.

"Would I have been married three times otherwise?" A giggle followed these words, but Jane's face quickly sobered. "But there's more. I've been having these dreams. Some of them nightmares, where everything gets mixed up so that I only remember bits and pieces on waking. But always there's this sense of urgency, a need to get to some truth that I should know, if only I could step back far enough to look at the full picture. Ever since Hope came to this house I, too, have sensed Sophia's presence and I'm overwhelmed with the feeling that we—Rosemary, Thora, and I—have failed her in some vitally important way. Then there are those times"—Jane smiled ruefully—"when I'm not sure of anything."

I felt exactly the same way, except on one point. I was hungry despite the roast-beef sandwiches, and I had not a doubt in the world after eating Edna's fish pie for lunch that the macaroni and cheese would be delicious if not quite up to Ben's culinary standard. He always used white cheddar along with a smaller addition of Camembert. The secret ingredient was a crumbling of Stilton. And speaking of secrets, despite the bridesmaids' apparent openness, this house seemed full of them.

# CHAPTER NINE

IT WAS NOW NINE o'clock, if the clock on the sitting-room mantelpiece was telling the truth, and I saw no reason to think otherwise as it had an open honest face. Thora had brought our supper into the sitting room. As I had expected, the macaroni and cheese was extremely tasty. It didn't come accompanied by bacon and tomatoes, though. Thora explained that she wanted to get in and out of the kitchen as quickly as possible, seeing that Edna had dropped off into a deep sleep after having the poultice applied to her foot and secured with a bandage torn off an old sheet.

"Everything is old in this house," she said to me. "The people, the furniture, Dog and the cats. But we've been happy here. The Old Rectory has become a contented house again. For all that Reverend and Mrs. McNair weren't the sort of parents who understood young people, Rosemary, Jane, and I had some enjoyable times staying here, going to tennis parties and riding our bicycles into Rilling. Everybody cycled in those days, but now the traffic's so bad we worry when Edna takes the bike to go up to the fish shop in the High Street, even though she goes the back way up Church Road and along Hawthorn Lane."

The conversation at that point naturally turned back to Edna and what she was likely to do now that Ted was gone. Rosemary brought up the possibility that she would move in with Gwen. But Jane shot down this idea, saying that the two women only saw each other once a month on one of Edna's Thursdays off. And when she had on a couple of occasions happened to see them in a tea shop in Lower Thaxstead, Gwen had looked as though she were there only under duress. Jane added that it was of course possible that the woman always had a face like a jug of sour milk, which had somehow led the conversation round to our all having a cup of tea. Thora went out to make it and returned with a loaded tray, which contained a plate of rock buns and jam tarts. Edna, she reported, was now awake but had insisted she couldn't possibly eat or drink anything. Her stomach was all in knots.

After the teacups and plates had been handed out, Jane began talking about Ted's funeral, whether or not he would be cremated and when it was likely to take place, and if the inquest would cause much of a delay, and so on. Rosemary bore this for about five minutes before asking me about Ben and the children, but eventually this topic led to their being presently at Memory Lanes. And a silence settled on the room. Everyone sitting thinking her own thoughts, until Jane finally brought up the séance.

"Ellie has kindly agreed to our idea that it take place tomorrow evening," she now said as I swallowed my last mouthful of jam tart. "I told her that Hope, when she was here earlier today, had suggested seven o'clock. Unfortunately it won't be dark then, but that's the problem with having one of these things in summer."

"I'm not sure a dark windy night is necessary," responded Rosemary tartly, "but what do I, or any of us for that matter, know about the rules pertaining to summoning up spirits? And from what she told us Hope isn't entirely sure herself, not being a professional medium."

"Describes herself as a 'sensitive.'" Thora got up to remove the tea plates from our knees and placed them on the cabinet from which the bottle of elderberry wine had been produced earlier. "Said she offers no guarantee of getting Sophia to speak to us. I for one got the feeling she's not entirely comfortable with performing the procedure."

"You make it sound as though she's going to take out someone's appendix." Jane gave a rather shaky laugh.

"If she were, there'd be other doctors standing around in gowns and masks ready to take over if things went wrong," said Rosemary. "But I don't know what any of us could do if the séance got out of hand and the room was invaded by demons flapping about us in droves, sucking out our souls and leaving us to spend the rest of our lives glued to our chairs like zombies."

"Perhaps we should all wear garlic necklaces," suggested Jane.

"I think that only works with vampires," I said.

"Then what about a crucifix?"

"Why not hope that Sophia shows up on her own?" Thora was now gathering up our cups and saucers. "And not talk about it any more tonight, or we'll all have nightmares."

"Everyone's tired." Rosemary got to her feet. "Ellie, especially, has had a long day, so let's make it an early night. Thora, why don't you take her luggage upstairs and show her to her room?"

"I took my things up to the second landing just before Amelia Chambers arrived." I suppressed a shiver. "But would you like me to put my car in the garage? I noticed you have one beyond the side archway."

"Trouble is"—Thora grimaced—"it's chock-full with the lawn mower and a couple of wheelbarrows. It's a scramble to get our old bike in and out. Would you mind leaving your car in the lane overnight? Tomorrow I can move some of the stuff into the shed at the back of the garden."

"There's no need to do that," I assured her. "The car isn't in the way out there, is it?"

"If you're sure that's all right." Rosemary was moving to the door. "We don't tend to get vandals around here. It's too off the beaten path. Jane, why don't you go and check on Edna and see that the cats are all in for the night, while Thora and I take Ellie upstairs?"

"Go on ahead, Rosemary, and climb into bed, you look done to death." This suggestion of Thora's received no resistance and when the two other women went out into the hall she asked if I would like a book to take up with me.

"That would be lovely."

"Always helps, doesn't it, to make you feel settled when going to sleep in a strange house. A chapter or two and you're out like a light. Unless you're the sort who gets so caught up in the story you can't put the book down until the last page. By which time it's six in the morning and you feel like a rag. Better promise me you won't do that"—she chuckled—"or Rosemary will have me in the doghouse."

Dog, who had clambered onto the vacated sofa, cocked an ear on thinking he was being brought into the conversation. Thora patted him as she headed towards the bookcase. "Silly old boy," she said. "You've never occupied a doghouse in your life. Spoiled rotten, that's what you are! Sleeps on my bed," she added over her shoulder to me. "And always shares a nightcap with me. Ovaltine's his favorite. Jane doesn't give her cats milk. Says it gives them diarrhea. So whose door do they scratch on at night? Mine! They know better than to bother Rosemary. She's not an animal person, except perhaps for having a sneaking fondness for that blasted parrot! I wish the cats would eat it. Tried to show them how to open its cage and offered to grill it, sauté it with truffles, or pop it in a casserole but they're just not interested."

"And Polly hasn't been blackmailing you for thousands?" I said as Thora began pulling books off the shelves and studying the titles. After what I had experienced since being invited to this house, I was ready to believe a bird capable of human wickedness.

"Polly knows I don't have a bean to my name apart from my pension and that's gone the moment I draw it. There's my share of the household expenses and stuff to buy for the garden. Rosemary's jolly good, made it clear from the start she didn't expect me to contribute as much as herself or Jane—who is reasonably well placed, although none of her late husbands were rolling in money. Nor, for that matter, is Rosemary herself. William Fitzsimons didn't leave her any money to keep the house going and there's nothing from her job, because she didn't continue on to retirement age."

"Why was that?"

Thora put the books she had been holding back on the shelf. "Shouldn't have said anything about that, Ellie. Jane is always telling me I let my tongue wag too much. Think how I chewed your ear off about my love affair with Michael while Rosemary and Jane went with Edna to the hospital. It's not that there's any big secret, Rosemary just found the job stressful. And who wouldn't? My nerves would have cracked the first day if I'd worked in a chemist shop. All those bottles of medicine and pills, I would have been terrified of handing out the wrong thing and having the person drop dead before getting past the perfume counter, let alone out the door." She was talking a little too fast, just as I did when I was uncomfortable, and she dropped a couple of books on the floor. "Oh, there it is," she said, looking down, "the one I was looking for; it's a wonderful old gothic romance written at least sixty years ago by someone I'd never heard of. Found it in a used bookstore, last week. Probably paid more than I should have. But the proprietor said it was worth it because of the leather binding." Thora was still visibly flustered when she handed me the book, whose title I saw was *Secrets of the Crypt*.

"I'll start reading it as soon as I get into bed," I promised.

But, truth be told, I was more interested in knowing what she was afraid she had let slip, or come close to doing so, about Rosemary.

Could it be that Rosemary had been sacked from her job at the chemist's for handing out the wrong prescription? Or was it worse than that? Had she been helping herself to bottles of codeine, sleeping tablets, or whatever she fancied? These weren't nice thoughts to have about one of my hostesses and I jumped guiltily on hearing someone come into the sitting room. It was Edna who had entered. She was wearing her coat and hat—a black felt one, very suitable under the circumstances, and had her handbag strung over her arm.

"I just came in to say I'm leaving, Tom's going to take me over to my cousin Gwen's." She looked from me to Thora. "I gave her a ring on the telephone, I thought that would be all right, Miss Dobson. I told her about Ted and she said she was sure it would be all right with her husband if I was to come and spend the night. It won't be for more than that. Tomorrow I'll be feeling more myself. Have to, won't I? I'm not the first to go through this and I won't be the last, that's what I have to keep telling myself."

"It must be hard," I said, although given Ted's abominable nature, it was difficult not to think that in time she would realize she had been granted a "Get Out of Jail Free" card.

"Edna, wouldn't you rather stay here?" Thora appeared to be over her former discomfiture and fully focused on the sad-faced woman with the apron bib showing under the partially buttoned coat.

"Better not. You know I've not a thing against Mrs. Pettinger's cats. But I don't think on this night in particular I could get a proper sleep with the thought of them coming in to jump all over me. As I said earlier, Gwen can be snippy and her husband's too much of a ladies' man for my taste, but well—they are family when all's said and done. Only thing is, they've got another lady staying with them. An old school chum of Gwen's."

"That's Mrs. Malloy, who works for me at home," I told her. "When she found out I was coming here she decided it would be a good opportunity to renew the friendship. She needed to get away because her husband's been trying to get back in touch with her after a long separation."

"Mrs. Pettinger told me he showed up here this evening," she said.

"Yes. But there's no need to bother saying anything if Mrs. Malloy is up when you get there. I'll try and see her tomorrow and tell her about Leonard."

"Whatever you think best, Miss Ellie." She smiled. "I hope you don't mind me calling you that, on account of being so close to your mother when she was growing up?"

"I like it." I felt the prickle of tears and my heart warm to her. "Perhaps we can talk about her sometime, when you're feeling up to it."

"That'd be nice. And now I'd really better be off, unless you'd like me to pick up those books first."

Thora looked down at the floor. "Absolutely not, Edna. As if I'd let you! I dropped them when I was going through an armful looking for one to lend Ellie. We were talking earlier and I got the feeling from one or two things we were saying that she enjoys a gothic novel as much as I do. But I couldn't remember just where I had put it."

"But here it is." I tapped the leather-bound volume.

"Your mother wasn't much of a bookworm; all she lived for was her ballet dancing. Who'd have believed it—her taken so young." Edna shifted her handbag into the crook of her arm. "And here's me not stopping to think how lucky I was to have Ted for fifty years of married life."

"That's not what you need scolding for." Thora went over and gave her a hug. "It's that you've taken the poultice off your foot."

"I couldn't have got my shoe on with it, now could I?

Anyway I'm sure it did its job just like all of your concoctions, Miss Dobson, because I'm walking much better. Oh, I almost forgot," she said as we followed her out into the hall, "I left a saucepan of cocoa on the stove, just waiting to be warmed up again. There's enough for all of you. Bye for now. See you in the morning."

"You will not." Thora held the front door open for her.

"All right, then"—Edna turned and patted her shoulder—"I'll wait to come in till the afternoon. And don't go telling me otherwise. Keeping busy's pretty much all I've got left." She pointed. "Look, there's Tom waiting for me just a couple of steps up the lane. Mustn't keep him waiting any longer." With this she limped down the steps, firmly rejecting Thora's offer of assistance, saying it was bad enough being a widow, she didn't intend to become an invalid, and shooing both of us back inside.

"She's a dear, wonderful, stubborn woman." Thora led the way up the staircase with its gallery of photographs, including the one that looked like me, but was of Sophia as a young girl. I looked to see if there was one of my mother. But all I saw were unknown faces.

A wall lamp on the first landing lighted our way. I hadn't paid much attention on my previous trip upstairs. Now I noticed that the small rectangular space had the same timeworn pine floors as the hall and included an iron balcony swathed in greenery overlooking the conservatory. There were two doors across from each other and another angled into a corner. "That's the bathroom. The bedroom on the right is Rosemary's and the one on the left, Jane's." Thora turned a corner to our left and proceeded up a half-flight of steps to a similar-sized space, except that this one was L-shaped. I drew a deep breath. This time there was no confetti. No scent of orange blossom. I picked up my raincoat and handbag. Thora handled my case.

The door right at the top was to her bedroom, she told me, before leading me down a strip of faded carpeting and around a corner. We went up a couple of steps into a surprisingly large room furnished with a nineteen-forties dressing table with some of the silvering gone from the mirror. There were also a couple of tallboys, several chairs and tables that looked as though they had made their way up here to get out of people's way, and a wardrobe with one door standing open, probably because it wouldn't stay closed unless secured with a rubber band. An iron bed covered with a patchwork quilt stood under windows that were positioned high on the wall and looked as though they might have had bars on them at one time. This must have been the nursery once, I decided, as Thora put my case down on the trunk, the kind I had taken with me to boarding school, that was at the foot of the bed. Had it been Sophia's? I wondered. My eyes skimmed the couple of pictures and the embroidered sampler on the walls to fix on the spiral iron staircase a few feet from the boarded-in fireplace.

"Rosemary had that built shortly after we moved in." Thora stood with her hands on her hips, giving the room a once-over. "Provides access to the attics, although we hardly ever go up there. But when we do, it certainly beats swinging like Tarzan's Jane on a rope ladder. Actually, our Jane is the only one of us who wouldn't have minded. You wouldn't think it to look at her"—Thora's dimples appeared—"but she was a whiz at games when we were at school—hockey, netball, rounders, swimming, and she could run like the wind. She's still wonderfully fit. Only reason she doesn't ride the old bike in the garage is because it's really kept for Edna. And Jane won't encroach on what she sees as other people's turf. Besides, she loves to walk. Goes over to see friends in Upper and Lower Thaxstead on foot all the time."

"But it's miles." I thought of my drive from Gwen's to Knells.

"A bit of a stretch if you're not used to it, but not all that bad if you take the country road and cut across the fields by way of the footpaths. I've done it myself. But this isn't the best time to talk about stretching your legs, is it?" Thora took the book she had lent me and set it on the small chest of drawers that served as a bedside table. "Let me show you in here." I stepped after her into a rectangle containing a shower stall no bigger than a refrigerator, a tiny pedestal basin with a couple of towel hooks above it, and a built-in blanket chest, painted pink with transfers of butterflies, taking up more than its share of room. The toilet appeared to have been added as an afterthought. It was wedged into a corner and looked as though it required a sign above the tank reading Standing Room Only.

"I need to show you how to flush it. You have to hold the handle down and count to ten." Thora demonstrated as she spoke. "If you don't, the tank doesn't clear and it will gurgle away all night. Count to eleven and it will overflow and you'll have to put on a pair of Wellington boots before getting out of bed in the morning. Would you like to practice?" To oblige her I did so and was rewarded by a normal-sounding flush ending with a sort of burp. "You're a quick learner." Thora patted me on the shoulder and returned with me to the bedroom. "I'll leave you to settle in, unless there's anything else you think you might need."

"Nothing at all—you, and Rosemary and Jane, have done everything to make me comfortable." I sat down on the bed.

"But something's bothering you."

"I was just wondering if this was my mother's room."

"Don't think so." Thora bent and kissed my cheek. "I'm almost sure she had my room. But I can ask Rosemary in the morning. She'll remember because all the furnishings from William Fitzsimons's day were still here when we moved in. And she made careful lists of what was what before inviting Mina to come and see if there was anything she wanted, especially those things that were her own."

"I would have been pleased to sleep in her room if she

had been happy here." I sat with my hand cupped to my face. Thora's kiss had stirred some memory so that it floated halfway to the surface before drifting back down to the murky depths, to be washed over by the present moment.

"Have a little read and then get a good night's sleep." Thora moved to the door.

"There's one other thing," I said, getting up. "Ben said he would phone this evening and he's probably waited until the children are in bed. If he rings now it could wake the whole household."

"But you'd like to talk to him, Ellie. Don't worry, I'm not going to turn in for at least an hour and I don't suppose Jane will, either. We agreed to an early night because it was plain Rosemary was exhausted and we don't like her to overdo. She's such a good soul under that buttoned-up exterior. Letting Jane have her cats and putting up with Dog lumbering around the place." A couple of woofs were heard from outside the door and Thora laughed. "Sounds like I'm being summoned. Good night, Ellie." She went out but a second later popped her head back in. "If you'd prefer a bath to the shower by all means use the bathroom on the first landing, and if you're like Edna and don't want the cats sleeping on your face be sure and close this door securely. They have their ways of nudging it open."

With that she was gone, but I stood without moving for a few moments, prepared for her to make yet another return. She didn't. And I got down to the business of removing my nightdress and bathroom necessities from my case. The rest of my clothes could wait until morning or perhaps I wouldn't bother to unpack them at all, I thought, opening both doors of the wardrobe and inhaling the musty smell of old wood, mingled with a faint, but still unpleasant, whiff of mothballs. What it needed were bags of the lavender which Thora undoubtedly grew in her herb garden or among the flowers in the borders.

There was a black hat on the shelf above the clothes rod and I took it down, turning it around in my hands, fingering the spotted veil and the feather tucked in the grosgrain band. It looked like something a vicar's wife might wear on visits to the parishioners. After a moment's hesitation, I put it on and crossed to the dressing-table mirror. My face stared back at me, pale and inquiring. The black brim didn't suit me. It cut off my eyebrows and covered my ears. Had the hat belonged to my great-grandmother Agatha McNair? Could it have been the one she had worn when out and about on her good works? Was it the one she had worn to funerals, including her husband's? I took it off and returned it to the wardrobe shelf, realizing as I did so that I didn't know when she herself had died. Nothing I had heard about her had warmed the cockles of my heart, other than that she had allowed her daughter to have her friends come to stay at the house. And that, from what I remembered Thora's having said, was mainly so that Sophia wouldn't get too friendly with any of the village young people.

How, I wondered as I gathered up my nightie and went into the narrow bathroom, had Sophia managed to convince herself that she would ever be allowed to marry Hawthorn Lane, or her Heathcliff, as she had called him? Even had her parents been presented with a magic looking glass and seen that he would one day be called Sir Clifford Heath, I doubted they would have turned beaming one to the other, proclaiming that he was the perfect son-in-law. However rich or successful he might become, his early life could not be banished with a magic wand. I would have liked to think they were more concerned with his bad-boy image—especially with the girls—rather than his lack of the appropriate background. But even that didn't excuse forcing Sophie into marriage with William Fitzsimons. Why didn't they send her away to finishing school or on a shorthand–typing course, for that matter?

I sat down on the pink blanket chest and undressed slowly, hoping that the phone would ring. But there was the question of how much I could tell Ben without getting him worked up to the point where he donned his suit of shining armor. I could almost hear him clank-clanking as he paced in circles, at risk of throttling himself with the telephone cord. He wouldn't take enthusiastically to news of the proposed séance, of the gardener's coming to grief with the pruning shears, of neighbors who had tried to run me out of town, and of the wedding song. He would insist I had landed in a madhouse. And if I didn't crawl out the nearest window the moment I was off the phone, he would arrive to find that the bridesmaids had called in the local taxidermist and I had been stuffed and put in the hall for use as a second hat stand.

Unless—I elbowed my way into the shower to a rumbling in the pipes before I'd hardly begun turning the knob—I could get him all fired up to do his part in foiling Sir Clifford's vengeful scheme. That way I could assure the bridesmaids that life in Knells would return to normal. If there were such a thing. After all, I thought, as a miserly stream of lukewarm water sprinkled my chest, how hard could it be for a man of Ben's ingenuity to upset the apple cart at Memory Lanes? Get the nannies to riot, the musical ensembles to play heavy-metal rock music, the poetry readers to forsake Robert Louis Stevenson for the work of someone who didn't know the word "rhyme" and went on for pages about the meaning to be found in a head of cabbage. Families would flee back to their own homes. Word would spread to the other holiday camps scattered throughout England. People would demand the return of their deposits. The brochures would be used to line the bottom of canary cages and—hey, presto!—Sir Clifford would be out of business and Amelia Chambers out looking for a job.

With this pleasing picture in mind I got out of the shower and reached for the towel. It was extremely skimpy, but that was probably because it had thoughtfully shrunk itself in the wash, so as to take up less room on the peg, thus allowing room for the addition of a facecloth. My sponge bag filled up the diminutive basin like a life buoy. After putting on my nightie, I placed it on the blanket chest and while brushing my teeth I toyed with the notion that with the culinary skills he had at his disposal Ben should perhaps strike at the heart of what was often most important to people on holidays. The food! All he'd have to do was impress the chef with his credentials, offer to help out in the kitchen, and make sure every meal turned out inedible. A burner turned up full blast here. Another turned down to a flicker. Too much salt. Not enough—while he waxed forth about the new concepts in cooking coming down the pike. To the sort of chef hired for three meals a day of hearty family fare he could talk gibberish and it would come out sounding like genius, and the poor soul on the receiving end would imagine himself about to take the Parisian world of haute cuisine by storm. The idea reeked of possibilities. But as I slipped on my dressing gown I doubted that Ben would go for it. So what was I to say when he phoned?

Picking up my clothes from where I had dropped them on the floor, I returned to the bedroom and puttered around for several minutes. Sorting out what could be worn again, laying these over the back of a chair and stowing my shoes in front of the wardrobe, before crossing to the window to draw the curtains. It was still light enough to have a fairly good view of the garden and I was sure I saw something, or rather someone, hovering beside the garden shed at the back. Could it be Leonard Skinner? I wondered. But the next moment there was nothing. Except a low-hung branch swaying in the breeze.

Assuring myself that I was as easily spooked as when I was a child, I sat down at the dressing table, unpinned my hair, and combed it through my fingers, not feeling sufficiently bothered to go back to the bathroom and collect my brush. I looked better without the hat, but that wasn't saying much. It had been, I reminded myself, a long day. And my sleep had been broken the previous night by that phone call from the person warning me not to accept the bridesmaids' invitation. I had forgotten to add that gem to the list of reasons Ben might have for not wanting me to be here. Proving just how tired I must be underneath my nervous energy, I told myself, and resolutely climbed into bed. The mattress was comfortable, the sheets smelled as if they had just come in off the line, and there were two comfy pillows in beautifully embroidered cases. Still, I doubted I would have an easy time falling asleep and reached out a hand for Thora's *Secrets of the Crypt*.

By the middle of the first chapter I'd decided she had definitely paid for the leather binding. Every other line contained a cliché dear to the gothic-lover's heart. I had already encountered the stony-faced, bombazine-clad housekeeper on a dark bend of the staircase. Awakened in my turret room to glimpse a cloaked figure disappearing behind the false bookcase. Met an unpleasant child wearing the clothes of a century or so past who threatened to ram my candle up my nose. Taken a walk out on the moors in thick fog. Spent the night trapped in an abandoned quarry. And, most terrifying of all, I had been summoned to an interview by the master of Cragstone Castle. Or, I should say, I had accompanied the drab but spirited governess, Phoebe Phillpot, in all these activities. I sat with her, wide-eyed and palpitating of heart, in the shrouded drawing room as she listened to Lord Rothbourne inform her that he was no callow youth, but a hardened man well past his prime, being all of thirty-five. I listened with a reluctant welling of pity as he recounted the details of the hunting accident—which involved a riding crop and a golden-haired debutante riding pillion—that had resulted in his being reduced to living his life in a bath chair. Or shuffling around with a stick. I experienced a flicker of hope when he mentioned the German doctor who had suggested the possibility of an operation. And felt my heart plummet when Lord Rothbourne listed the risks involved, which included the possibility of total paralysis, loss of eyesight because of some conductor-nerve involvement, and a worsening of his irascible temper. Along with Phoebe, I jumped when, to emphasize how undesirable this would be, he pounded on the piano keys, breaking his cane into flying pieces. And again my heart knew compassion when he explained that he had once been a world-renowned concert pianist. But had been unable to play a note since the discovery that his wife came from a family riddled with insanity and he had been forced to place her in the care of his devoted old nanny.

Devoted old nanny my foot, I thought, turning a page. She'd probably poisoned poor Lady Rothbourn with a nice bowl of strengthening gruel and buried her under the begonias. "Mustn't have the master upset, now, must we?" It was all completely ridiculous. But I couldn't wait to find out if Phoebe would save Lord Rothbourne from being set alight in his bed by a disgruntled housemaid. Or reveal to him that she was herself a gifted pianist who would make it her life's work to get him to play again. I wondered how long it would take for him to realize that if she were to unloose her hair and put on the family jewels she would be breathtakingly beautiful and a more than fitting wife if he could just figure out what to do with the first one. Gentlemen of the old school are notoriously incapable of thinking nasty thoughts about dear old nannies. Or could it be that it was the greatcoated, dour-looking visitor from Australia with a twitching eye—always a bad sign—newly arrived on page twenty-seven, who would prove the villain of the piece?

I yawned, but I wasn't sufficiently sleepy to put the silly book down even though the clock on the bedside table showed it was twenty past ten. Just one more chapter, I was thinking when the door opened and Jane came in with a cup and saucer and a plate with two Rich Tea biscuits on it.

"Oh, good, you're awake! I saw the light under your door, otherwise I would have gone away again. I would have brought you this cocoa earlier, but I had to give Charlotte her injection. She has them twice a day for diabetes and the naughty puss didn't want to be found tonight." She handed me the cup and saucer and set the plate down on the bedside chest.

"This is kind of you." I sat forward and smiled at her.

"My pleasure, dear Ellie, I always bring the drinks up at night. It's one of the small things I try to do routinely as part of my share. I'm not good in the garden, like Thora, or much use at housework. I always seem to dust what's already been dusted and put things back in all the wrong places. That's probably why when I opened the cupboard door to get out the tin of cocoa, some things—a bottle of garlic powder, a box of rice, and one of those little packets with the tubes of food coloring fell out. The lid came off the garlic and it went all over the floor. That put me behind, too, sweeping it up."

"I'm always dropping things," I said.

"That's sweet of you to say." Jane sat down on the edge of the bed. "But I'm glad Rosemary wasn't there. It's the little things that are inclined to upset her. As a rule, she's always so good-natured. It's because she is caring that she considers it so important to put things properly back where they belong. She says that if the foodstuff is left all higgledy-piggledy on the shelves it makes extra work for Edna when she's doing the cooking. Rosemary is very fond of Edna. They always got on from the days when Edna used to come in to help out her mother with the cleaning. Rosemary may appear stiff at times but she was never a snob. And she thought Ted was wrong for Edna from the start. She tried to talk her out of marrying him." Jane looked down at the book that I had half-tucked under the pillow. "Is that the one Thora lent you, Ellie?"

I nodded because my mouth was full of biscuit.

"She mentioned that she'd had trouble finding it when I took in her cocoa—not that she was blaming me." Jane took off her glasses to polish them on her sleeve and her eyes looked paler than ever without them. "We were just chit-chatting about this and that. Thora and I often talk over the day at night and this one has certainly been eventful, sadly so for Edna."

"I hope her cousin Gwen is being supportive," I said, picking up my cup of cocoa. It was delicious, hot and chocolaty, possibly the best I'd ever had.

"I've never met the woman, but I've built up a dislike of her. Edna often comes back upset after seeing her. I can tell from the way she goes all quiet the next day. It's wrong, isn't it? How very sad, Ellie dear, that some people seem to live to make other people unhappy. And that, from the sound of him, could certainly be said of William Fitzsimons. Oh, I am sorry"—Jane got off the bed—"I keep forgetting he was your grandfather."

"So do I."

"Merciful heavens, there's something else I've been forgetting! You had a couple of phone calls."

"I didn't hear it ring once."

"Perhaps you were in the shower."

"That must have been when."

"And the pipes make that terrible rumbling." Jane shook her head sending the black bow at the nape of her neck even more off kilter. "The first call was from your husband. Of course I offered to fetch you, but he said in such a gentlemanly manner that if you had gone up to bed I wasn't to disturb you."

Disappointment flooded through me, to be followed almost immediately by relief. Perhaps it was better this way.

"I didn't feel I could insist, even though I knew you'd be

sorry to have missed his call. He sounded—ever so nicely—in a bit of a hurry."

Oh! Ho! Couldn't wait to get back to another poetry reading or musical recital! Could it be that the charms of Memory Lanes were beginning to grow on him? Of course, I reasoned with determined fairness, he might not be having a whale of a time without me. It could be that one or all of the children were clamoring for his attention.

"He said to tell you that everything was fine and that he will try and get back in touch tomorrow, but not to worry if he doesn't because every moment is jam-packed. If you should need him, there's an emergency number you can ring which I have written down on the pad by the phone downstairs. The other call was from Richard Barttle."

I looked at her.

"He was a very dear friend of Sophia's."

"I remember. Doesn't he have a photography studio in Knells?"

"That's right, with his partner, Arthur Henshaw. They are both such kind men."

"Why did he want to speak to me?" I had finished my cocoa and set the cup and saucer back on the chest.

"For old times' sake, I suppose—because you're Sophia's granddaughter and because he knew your mother—not well, her father wouldn't have allowed that, although Richard was the best man at the wedding. But I think that was a matter of necessity; William didn't have any friends of his own living nearby, at least none that I ever heard of or saw, and Richard was on the spot."

"I wondered before I found out about Sir Clifford," I said, reaching for another biscuit, "well, the thought crossed my mind that Sophia might have been in love with Richard."

Jane sat back down on the bed. "No, that was Rosemary."

"But he didn't feel the same way?"

"Not because he was in love with Sophia. They were only

very dear, one might even say best, friends. She was always aware that he was a friend of Dorothy's."

"Who's Dorothy?"

"Silly of me"—Jane smiled ruefully—"you're much too young to have heard of that old-fashioned expression. Being a friend of Dorothy's means that a man isn't interested in women in . . . that way, if you understand me."

"You're saying Richard is gay?"

Jane now looked thoughtful. "I believe Sophia knew from the time he first realized it, and with her feelings for Hawthorn entering the picture, it increased the bond between them. They were both part of the village but at the same time outsiders, going against the tide."

"Was it very difficult for Richard?"

"It had to have been, if taking a drop too much drink was enough in those days to send someone straight to hell; but he stuck it out here. Moving away, he once told me, would simply have meant moving his problems with unkind-minded people to a new location. He's a strong, stubborn man. And a decent one. That tends to shut down the snick-ering and nasty remarks. Besides, society is a bit more open-minded now. The sad thing is that it was his mother, to whom he's been the most devoted, caring son, who kicked up a stink when he and Arthur Henshaw moved in together."

"You'd have thought she would want him to be happy."

"Alas, not old Mrs. Barttle. She's that type, Ellie, the sort that thinks there isn't a man alive good enough for her son. Arthur hadn't been to the right schools or come from money. Worse"—Jane's smile reappeared—"he had a tattoo on his arm of another fellow's name, rode a motorbike, and wore his hair long—tied back in a ponytail. And that was years before it was common."

"He sounds a bit like my cousin Freddy, only he doesn't have a tattoo. But he does have an earring. I'd like to meet this Arthur."

"That's why Richard rang. He wants to see you while you're here and said to ask if you would go round, perhaps tomorrow morning, to his place. He and Arthur have a very nice flat above the photography studio. I'm sure they'll take you up there for a cup of coffee. They always grind their own beans, so it'll be a bit of a treat for you and make a break in your day. Now I really must let you get back to your book, dear, if you aren't ready to fall asleep."

"I think I am."

"Then I'm gone." She whisked out the door but didn't quite close it behind her. Remembering what Thora had said about the cats being likely to come in and pounce on me, I pushed back the covers. I was fond of cats. I had my own dear Tobias at home. But I wasn't up to them tonight in groups. So I staggered, for I had suddenly come over dreadfully sleepy, across the room. It stretched out before me like the fog-covered moor on which Phoebe the governess had managed to get lost. Had there been a passing carriage, with a masked driver at the reins, I would have hailed a lift back to bed. But I forced my legs onward. At last! I leaned against the wall and after considerable fumbling pushed the door shut and pressed down the old-fashioned iron latch. Only to see it pop up again in slow motion. After watching, in total befuddlement, my hand reach out to meet with the same response, I suddenly saw a key in the lock. It grew bigger and then it grew smaller. After a couple of failed attempts I managed to turn it before stumbling back to bed. My last thought as I spiraled into sleep was that Mrs. Malloy had told Thora on the phone that I was to be sure to lock my door.

I felt heavy and sluggish even in my dreams. Part of the time I wasn't sure if I was dreaming or awake. I was lying in bed and people kept coming in and out of the room but I couldn't lift my head to speak even when it was Ben standing over me. Only it wasn't Ben, but another dark-haired man with hawkish features and burning black eyes. My mouth tried to form the words that I was glad he was out of his wheelchair but that I wasn't Phoebe the governess, at which he threw back his head and uttered a fiendish laugh that turned into a gurgling in the shower pipes. Then he leaned forward and kissed me. It was a tender kiss, but one seared with passion, and he said of course I wasn't Phoebe the governess or Ellie the housewife, I was his beloved Sophia. I tried to tell him he was wrong. Wrong about everything. I hadn't agreed to marry William, not even with my father lying dead in his coffin; not until the bridesmaids had talked me into it, or perhaps they had wanted me to marry Ted, I was so tired I couldn't quite remember. Then he lay down beside me and stroked my hair and told me the other girls had meant nothing to him and he had never promised any of them the family jewels. I told him, without any sound coming out, that there had never been anyone else for me and that William had only wanted to make love using the method prescribed for missionaries and that the poor benighted savages out in the Belgian Congo had been very kind to me. And that a wonderful black midwife had delivered my beautiful baby girl, but I wished she hadn't named her after William and that it frustrated me that I didn't know my own child's middle name.

While he was kissing me again and I was struggling to say that he mustn't, because I did love my husband after all, a fog rolled in. And I was back at Merlin's Court, slogging up a stepladder with a tin of paint. Only, when I looked inside, it wasn't real paint. It was food coloring with the red and the green and the yellow and blue all swirling together, and I knew it would look terrible on Rose's bedroom wall. It would frighten her when she woke up at night, so I stepped off into the fog and knocked over the paint pot, which was now somehow filled with garlic powder. But it didn't smell like garlic powder, which was good, because it now covered the floor. Spreading and rising like desert sand as I fought my way out of bed. Because I knew now that I was in the bedroom at the Old Rectory and Rosemary would be upset if I didn't sweep it up. I went and opened the trunk, looking for a broom, but there was nothing inside but a couple of cats eating a fish pie, so I closed the lid and got back into bed, which was odd seeing that I was already there. After that there were no more dreams until I heard a voice mutter in my ear, "Go away. First thing tomorrow morning, otherwise I'll be forced to kill you, just like I did your dear mother."

## CHAPTER TEN

I LAY ABSOLUTELY RIGID. There was no doubt at all that this time I was awake. My mind was clear. Every part of me was prickling with fear, but when I opened my eyes I couldn't see or hear anything. Not so much as a whispering shadow, although when the voice had spoken I had felt evil breathing down my neck. I was having trouble breathing myself and suddenly realized why. The patchwork quilt, along with the sheet, was covering my face. Shoving them off, I scrambled out of bed. With the curtains closed it was pitch-dark in the room. It took me a while to find my way to the door and fumble for the light switch. There was no bedside lamp. And there was no one in the room but me. Unless, I thought, as I blinked several times to adjust to the brightness, whoever it had been was hiding in the wardrobe.

I looked, certain as I did so, that whoever it was would have gone out the door with all possible speed. But when I checked the key, it was still turned in the lock. I fleetingly considered the window. It turned out to be unlatched. But I would have heard it being opened and closed when the intruder made his or her escape, presumably by way of a ladder propped against the house wall. A ladder that would have needed to be removed—hardly a speedy task. And before that stage of the game, whoever it was would have had to take vital extra moments to redraw the curtains. What about the bathroom? I had to keep moving, I couldn't let myself dwell on what the monstrous voice had said about my mother. Not now. Not yet. If I did, I would start crying or go into a huddle. Time enough after I figured out how the entry and exit had been achieved.

The bathroom idea didn't pan out. The window was above the toilet, which would have made for easy access, but it was a round one, not much bigger than a dinner plate. A person might possibly be able to stick his head through it when it was open. Nothing more. He'd be left looking as though he'd been put in the stocks. I returned to the bedroom and sat down on the trunk at the foot of the bed for a moment before looking towards the spiral staircase. Could it provide the answer? Catching up my nightgown so as not to trip, I nipped up the pie-shaped steps. Two whirligig rounds and I was on a wooden platform, level with the attic floor. Dangling to my left was a string which when pulled provided light equal to that of the bedroom. The space was well organized as such places go. There were several shelves stacked with boxes mounted on one wall, an old sofa positioned against another, and several other pieces of furniture grouped together in a corner. Along with a rolled-up carpet, a couple of lamps, a galvanized iron washtub, an enormous mirror, and a trunk similar in size to the one in the bedroom below. Otherwise the floor was clear for me to cross to the row of narrow windows that overlooked the lane. I realized that none of them would lead out onto a fire escape, unless one had sprung up like Jack's beanstalk. It was the sort of thing I would have noticed from the front gate. But I hadn't paid much attention to whether there was a tree conveniently close to the house wall. There was one, in fact there were two, but they were spruces, and even had a person been able to climb down their twig-sized branches, their tips didn't come within six feet of the window ledges. I sat down on the trunk, not caring that it was coated in cobwebs and the back of my nightdress would be filthy as a result. The horror of that evil voice muttering over me as I lay in bed could not be held at bay any longer. My mother murdered? Why? It had always been dreadful enough accepting the unfairness of her dying from an accidental fall. So pointless! So unlikely! All she had done was break her leg—nasty, painful, but not the sort of thing people died from.

It was at that moment that I began to wonder if I had dreamed that voice, just as I had dreamed that Hawthorn Lane—for that's who it was, I'd decided—had kissed me and lain down next to me on the bed. Because it didn't make any sense. A push down a flight of railway steps wasn't any sort of way to try and murder someone. Even had Mother fractured her skull she would most likely have recovered. And what could possibly have been the motive? She hadn't been in touch with the bridesmaids or anyone connected with the Old Rectory for years. But, the stubborn part of my mind insisted, that voice had sounded so real; there had been nothing fuzzy or dreamlike about it. Through all the other parts I had felt that heavy inertia. Could the difference be, the rational segment of my brain suggested, that I'd dreamed the voice when I was on the very edge of sleeping and waking? Surely that was the sensible—the only—explanation. Hadn't I already thought that I had got out of bed and looked in the trunk and found it full of cats?

I imagined myself telling the story to Ben, the one person who was always prepared to bend over backwards to take me seriously, and it wasn't hard to picture the look on his face. No one else would hear me out without thinking I was at least somewhat disturbed to be taking such nightmares seriously. And that's of course what it had been. I was growing more convinced by the moment. I had already faced up to the fact that there appeared to be no way that anyone could have got in and out of my room, because of the locked door. I had fallen asleep after a stressful day, during which a man had died in a freak accident. My subconscious must have made a connection with my mother's death because she had been on my mind from the moment I received the bridesmaids' invitation. And to top everything off I had been reading that silly gothic novel, inventing my own characters as I went along. The wicked old nanny, for one! I'd even given her a croaky voice in my head. Yes, I was feeling better by the moment; it must have been the nanny I had conjured up in my half-waking state. Even the sheet and patchwork quilt covering my face had a logical explanation. I must have pulled them up myself when I thought I was getting back into bed after looking in the trunk.

It was a relief to realize I didn't have to march down to the bridesmaids' bedrooms and demand to know which one of them had pulled a Houdini stunt and insist on knowing the reason why. I banished the thought that I was willfully pulling the wool over my eyes. I told myself that the bridesmaids' invitation had stirred up a lot of issues for me, so that it wasn't stretching the bounds of probability to conclude that last night's phone call had also been a dream. As for the wedding-song business, that had to have been a joke on Jane and her emanations. It was when I pictured Mrs. Malloy's disbelieving face and could almost hear her exclamation of disgust that I remembered thinking I had seen Leonard Skinner lurking behind the garden shed. But that would have been a non-issue, regardless of whether I'd dreamed up my nocturnal visitor. Even had he managed to get into the house to search for Mrs. Malloy and had wanted to punish me for keeping her from him, he wouldn't have known my mother was dead. Unless Mrs. M.'s neighbor had mentioned the fact, which seemed highly unlikely, blabbermouth though she might be.

I got off the cobwebby trunk. I was now feeling wide awake, if still somewhat haunted, added to which I have always loved rooting around in attics, so I raised the trunk's lid and reclined it against the wall. The scent of lavender was suddenly all around me. Inside were a number of hats, in the style of the black one I'd found in the wardrobe. Underneath the hats, which I set on the floor, was a rather pretty, very long ivory lace mantilla. Without thinking, I draped it over my head. But before taking time to preen in the huge mirror of the sort that might have hung in the drawing room of a home like Cragstone Castle, I looked back into the trunk. It was still half-full. With what I couldn't tell. Dropping the mantilla I reached in and pulled out a heavy tissue-paper-wrapped bundle, and upon peeling off these flimsy layers I found myself holding a heavy linen bag.

Curiosity made my hands clumsy as I undid the string tie at the neck. I didn't think that I was expecting to find anything wonderful. Maybe I was still trying to take my mind off my mother. Certainly I wasn't prepared for what I found myself holding: a wedding dress. An ivory silk one, simply cut, with a scalloped neck and of tea length. No frills, no flounces, but the skirt looked as though it would float out into graceful folds with every step. The material had rusted in places, but it was still beautiful and in candlelight would have looked perfect. All it needed, I decided as I held it up against me and stepped in front of the mirror, was a beautiful lace veil. Whoops! I looked down at the mantilla and grabbed it up off the floor, laying it and the dress over the back of a chair that must have found its way up here from the dining room. I again reached into the trunk and pulled out what remained. It was another tissue-paper-wrapped bag, somewhat larger than the first. I think I knew what was inside before I undid it. And moments later I was holding three lavender silk frocks. Bridesmaid frocks. Identical in design to the wedding dress apart from color, having three-quarter-length sleeves instead of full-length ones, and rounded necklines. Again, there were rust marks, but no tearing away of the material. The realization squeezed my throat shut and set my heart hammering. These were Rosemary's, Thora's, and Jane's bridesmaid dresses and the wedding dress intended for Sophia's walk down the aisle on the day she was to recite her marriage vows to William Fitzsimons. But they had never been worn—her father had died and there had been a simple service in the vestry.

Not until this moment did I have a real sense that this man and this woman were my grandfather and grandmother. Had he been every bit as unpleasant as he sounded? What had she ended up wearing on her actual wedding day? A dress—perhaps navy, because she was in mourning? A gray suit? Something bought quickly for the occasion? Or something she already had in her wardrobe? Surely Mrs. McNair wouldn't have had her wear black? I folded up the wedding dress first and placed it back in the bag, rewrapped the bag in tissue paper and returned it to the trunk. Then did the same with the bridesmaid dresses. The veil I rolled up and put in a box that contained a circlet of silk orange blossom. Had it been the veil's original storage place? And if so, why had it been taken out? I returned the hats, lowered the trunk lid and slowly crossed the attic to the platform of the spiral staircase, turned off the light and went down to the bedroom. My eyes immediately went to the trunk at the foot of the bed. It was unlikely I would discover anything close in significance to my other finds, but even so I looked inside. A moment later I was sitting on the floor holding a little girl's pair of pink ballet slippers, the soft-toed kind—for someone not old enough to get up on pointe. My mother's. I held them against my heart and my tears fell over them. Then I got up and turned the key in the door, still holding the slippers. It was almost morning and I didn't want one of the bridesmaids to bring me a cup of tea, only to wonder why I had locked myself in. I could have given the real reason—that the latch didn't hold and I had wanted to keep the cats out—but I didn't want to

risk giving offense. There had already been too much un-
happiness in this house. After that I climbed into bed with
the shoes, pulled the quilt up to my chin, and fell instantly
asleep, as if some hand had been waiting there to drag me
down into formless, but ever-shifting, shadows.

It seemed like days later when I came groggily awake to
see the hands of the clock pointing to nine-thirty. Someone
was tapping on the door, and when I called out, "Come in!"
Jane appeared with a tray filled with a mug of tea, a plate
piled with buttered toast, a dish of marmalade, a brown egg
in a Bunnykins cup, and a small glass of orange juice.

"We thought you might enjoy breakfast in bed," she said,
lowering the tray onto the bedside chest. This morning she
was wearing a mustard-colored dress that brought out the
yellow in her white hair. Her hair was pinned back with the
same black bow, but instead of being coiled up at the nape
of her neck it hung down in a tired-looking ponytail. Her
eyes looked equally tired, and I felt guilty sitting propped
up against my comfortable pillows while she waited on me.
"It's not a bit of trouble," she said as if reading my mind.
"I'm always up before cockcrow. Rosemary and Thora like
to have more of a lie-in, although no one could call them
late risers. They're usually up by seven-thirty. Today's an exception. They only came down as I was making the tea. Did
you sleep well, dear?"

"Like a top," I lied.

"I was out like a light before I'd got one foot in bed"—she
handed me the mug—"but I can't say I got a good night's
sleep. I had the most awful dreams, worse than any I've had
lately. I kept wanting to wake up, but it was though
someone were pushing me down in a bog. But I don't suppose that's surprising, given the sort of day we had yesterday. I'm so sorry that you've been put through so much.
And now there's the séance looming ahead. But we won't
think about that, will we? Tonight is yet hours away."

"Are you sure it's a good idea?" I asked her.

"I did. In fact I was the one who pushed for it—more than Thora and Rosemary, who took a long while before being brought round to agreeing to it. So I'll never forgive myself if something goes wrong."

"What do you think could?"

"Supposing it's not Sophia who comes in response to Hope's summons?" Jane's pale eyes widened behind the black-winged glasses. "What if it's Reverend McNair on one of his rampages? Or William Fitzsimons damning us all to hell? After all, Hope isn't a professional medium, although I don't suppose anyone gets a degree in that sort of thing. But we musn't think along those lines, must we?" She made an obvious attempt to brace up. "Now you go ahead and enjoy your breakfast, and come downstairs whenever you're ready. No rush. Don't feel you can't go back to sleep if you want to."

"Thank you, Jane, but I think I will get up." I swung my legs out from under the covers.

"Whatever you like, dear." On these words she was gone from the room and I settled in to finish the mug of tea and devour my breakfast. I was amazingly hungry. Nervous energy again, I told myself, although I didn't feel particularly haunted by my nighttime experiences. Sunshine streamed in when I opened the curtains, making the very idea of ghoulish intruders seem even more ridiculous than I had come to realize while up in the attic. Finding Sophia's wedding dress and those of the bridesmaids had been poignant, as had, in a deeper sense, the discovery of my mother's ballet slippers. But perhaps they had been necessary in helping me lay the past to rest. I would take the slippers home with me, but for the remainder of my stay at the Old Rectory—which I hoped would be short—I would keep them under my pillow. I put them there now and suddenly had the uncomfortable feeling that something was missing. Thora's book! If it wasn't under the pillows it should be somewhere on the bed, among the covers. But it wasn't. I pulled off the quilt and shook it out into a large square. And then I saw *Secrets of the Crypt* poking out from under the bed. What a fuss about nothing, I thought, putting it on the trunk, because there wasn't room with the breakfast tray on the bedside chest.

With that, I went into the bathroom, where I brushed my teeth with gusto, washed my face, and coiled my hair into a loose knot low on my neck, the way Ben liked it, dabbed on some eye shadow, brushed on mascara, and replaced my sponge bag on the pink blanket chest. While I was dressing in a skirt and top in my favorite sage green, I thought lovingly about him and the children. I was eager to know what he thought of Memory Lanes. To tell him of the bridesmaids' connection to it. Meanwhile, I hoped my family was fully occupied and having a good time. I didn't allow the possibility that Ben might develop a taste for harp music disturb me. In fact, I positively glowed with goodwill, not only towards those I loved, but to complete strangers everywhere. It was as though I had emerged triumphant after spending a night in the dungeon at Cragstone Castle.

Carrying the tray downstairs, I did allow myself to make one exception to my bonhomie. And it wasn't Sir Clifford Heath. In my newfound spirit of optimism, I was sure that, whatever the result of the séance, Sir Clifford could be brought round to behave like a worthy knight of the realm in regard to Knells. It was Leonard Skinner that I could not bring myself to take unconditionally to my heart like a brother. Not when he presented such a threat to the happiness of my dear Mrs. Malloy. It would have been nice to imprison him in a dungeon until he developed a recurrence of his amnesia. But as such places no longer abound in England and I had no wish to find myself afoul of the law, I would have to settle for talking some sense into Mrs. Malloy. I would tell her she would be out of a job at Merlin's Court if she took him back.

By the time I entered the conservatory I'd decided this

might not be the best approach. For one thing I couldn't do without her and our daily chats; for another, given her perverse nature, I would only succeed in driving her into the wretched man's arms. I'd have to come up with another approach, perhaps threaten to report her to the Chitterton Fells Charwomen's Association, of which she was currently president.

"Nasty, rotten blackmailer," piped a voice in my ear. It was of course Polly, the horrid parrot; but I didn't respond in kind because I had just noticed something that I'd missed yesterday due to the amount of foliage. It was a spiral staircase, exactly like the one in my room, and it connected with the balcony on the first landing. While I was parting the leaves of a rubber plant on an old washstand to get a better look at it, Rosemary called out to me from the kitchen.

"Is that you, Ellie?"

"Coming," I replied and went through the archway to place my tray on the table, where Thora was sitting having a cup of tea. Jane was bending over a row of plastic bowls on the floor, spooning cat food into them, while furry forms climbed all over her feet, and Rosemary was at the sink washing up. Her ensuing conversation was mainly about whether I had slept well, whether I had got started reading the book Thora had lent me, whether I had enjoyed my breakfast, and culminated in a question as to what I wished to do with my day.

"Perhaps you would like to stay in and read," suggested Thora, who had expressed pleasure that I had been entranced by life at Cragstone Castle.

"Whatever you choose, Ellie." Jane gathered a couple of cats into her arms, leaving Dog free to lumber over to their bowls and polish off the remains. "But do remember, dear, that Richard Barttle would like to see you."

"Can't that wait for an evening?" Rosemary stood drying off her hands on a tea towel. Today she was wearing a pale blue twin set over a gray plaid skirt and the colors suited her. "Richard is a nice man and I understand why he wants to meet you, Ellie, but it's such a fine day, I would think you'd do better going out for a leisurely walk."

"But she could walk to his studio," Jane pointed out. "She wouldn't need to drive her car. She could go up Church Road and along Hawthorn Lane and have a look at the horses in the field by the old mill."

"And then I could go on and see Mrs. Malloy, who's staying with Edna's cousin, Gwen Fiddler," I said.

"If you're sure that's what you want to do." Rosemary hung the tea towel on one of the three wooden spokes beside the sink. "It's a long walk even if you go the back way and take the footpaths. And you don't want to come back exhausted with the séance set for seven this evening." Before she could say more we all heard someone tap on the conservatory door and Thora opened it. I expected her to return with Edna, but it was Susan of the mammoth proportions and pink hair rollers from cottage number four whom she brought into the kitchen.

"Here's Susan," she said unnecessarily, "come to ask how Edna's doing."

"I was never so shocked as when I heard the news about Ted." The woman planted herself on a chair at the kitchen table and placed her massive hands on the knees spread under her skirt, which was partially covered, as it had been yesterday, by a floral pinny. "Here in the morning, gone by afternoon! But still I suppose that's not all bad. Take me fast, is what I always pray to the Lord, none of this messing about with tubes up the nose and down below. Takes away all your dignity." She patted a lopsided roller back into place. "And how are you today?" she inquired, looking at me. "Got to meet that Chambers woman yesterday, I suppose. Needs a fist put through her face, if you ask me. Don't tell me if you don't want to, Miss Maywood"—she swiveled her gaze towards Rosemary—"but did you get anywhere with her? Did you put it to her fair and square that she could tell her boss we'll all be out with pitchforks if he forces you to sell up?"

It was abundantly apparent that it was this topic even more than her interest in Ted's demise that had brought her here. Not that I doubted she would want to hear all the ghoulish details pertaining to the pruning shears before she made her departure. Mercifully, Thora explained that I had been on the point of leaving to make a couple of stops and Susan graciously excused me, adding that she would like to have me over for a cup of coffee and a good long natter. But not tomorrow. Because tomorrow was Thursday and she always had her hair washed and set on Thursday morning and in the afternoon she had to come home and re-roll it to get it back the way she liked it. And then there was this program she had to watch on the telly.

"So, better make it Friday, love."

Love? This from the woman who yesterday had been on the verge of crushing me with her bare hands into something not fit for the junkyard?

"That's awfully kind," I said as I stepped over Dog in my haste to keep up with Thora, who was already heading out of the kitchen.

"I'll have Frank and Irene come and make a proper party of it. Tom will likely be at work. He drives a van, delivering fish to people that don't want to buy that dyed smoked haddock and piddling pieces of cod from the supermarket. And Friday's his busiest day."

"There's nothing like fresh fish," piped in Jane, and all three cats mewed agreement.

"Ellie will let you know, Susan. She could be busy. We've a lot of plans and she can't remain with us very long." Rosemary set the kettle on the cooker, looking none too pleased about it, and got down a cup and saucer from the cupboard.

"Off we go!" Thora herded me out into the hall, and I

picked up my handbag from the coat stand, where I'd put it on coming downstairs, and listened to detailed but cogent directions on how to find Richard Barttle's photography studio and how to get to Upper Thaxstead from there.

"Sure you won't take your raincoat?" she asked while opening the front door for me. I told her I didn't think I'd need it. She agreed that it didn't look like there was much chance of rain, although one never could tell, but if things changed while I was with Richard, she was sure he would lend me an umbrella. She added that I shouldn't worry about getting back for lunch, although if I showed up, there would be something for me. And I went down the steps to the sound of Susan's voice announcing that she liked two spoons of sugar in her tea and that she wouldn't object to a biscuit or a slice of cake and what exactly did Amelia Chambers, the nasty cow, have to say for herself?

I spared only a passing glance at my car as I went through the gate and out into the lane, just enough to see that it had all its hubcaps and that its antenna had not been snapped off by some passing youths intent on livening up their night. After which I turned cheerily left at the fork, beyond which the fields stretched out like a green sea. About a hundred yards along Church Road I paused to take a look at the sign listing the times of services at St. John's, which looked very much like St. Anselm's, whose vicar had arranged the holiday to Memory Lanes. Although I didn't think St. John's was Norman, but only posing as such, having instead been built in the mid-nineteenth century. I was tempted to stop and take a look around the churchyard, but I was afraid my ebullient mood would ebb if I stood looking at the family tombstones, particularly the one marking William Fitzsimons's final resting place, he not being precisely the grandfather I would have chosen. So I walked on and turned along Hawthorn Lane, which immediately brought Sir Clifford Heath to mind. I wondered, as I looked at the charming cottages lining both sides of the street, which doorstep he had been deposited on by the mother who for one reason or another had not felt equipped to rear him? It was impossible not to feel sympathy for him, whatever his later shortcomings. As I stood admiring the picturesque Old Mill, I remembered my dream, in which he had figured, I had to admit, so appealingly. I felt an urge to meet him and discover how hardened a villain he had really become. I was so fully occupied wondering how he now looked that I reached the High Street with its scattering of shops, passing cars, and ambling pedestrians before I realized I must have passed the studio and had to turn back. Yes, here it was—Barttle and Henshaw, Photographers. Its bay window contained only one portrait of two soberly dressed children standing sideways under a tree— the girl holding out a glossy red apple to the boy. What made it especially interesting, in addition to the expressions on those faces, was that the photo, apart from the apple, was in black and white. After a second look, I pushed open the iron-studded oak door and entered a space that gleamed with white paint trimmed with black. Its stark simplicity emphasized the warm gloss of the honey-colored wood floor. Elegance was provided by the graceful positioning of a Chippendale chair, seemingly casually draped with a paisley throw. Only five or six photographs were on display and not all were portraits. One in particular caught my eye. It was of the Old Mill, which I had passed on my way, and included the shadow of a tree—rather than the tree itself. Again, it was in black and white with a single introduction of color. This time of blue wildflowers peeking up alongside a brook that appeared to be gliding over boulders and stones.

"Do you like it?" a voice inquired, and I turned to see a man standing behind the crescent-shaped white counter, on which reposed nothing but an old-fashioned black telephone.

"I love it," I said.

"I'm not surprised." He smiled and his thin, aesthetic face warmed. "The Old Mill was one of your grandmother's favorite subjects to paint in Knells." He came around the counter, and even close up it was hard to believe he was in his seventies. His hair was still more brown than gray and apart from the crows'-feet around his eyes he had next to no wrinkles. Neither was he dressed like an old man. He wore corduroy trousers and a lightweight cotton sweater over a plaid shirt. It was an ensemble I might have chosen for Ben. "Don't look so spooked." He held out his hand. "There was no need for you to tell me who you are. You're the very image of Sophia. Far more so than your mother ever was. I was very sorry"—he now gripped my hand in both his own—"when I got word of Mina's death."

"Thank you."

"It shouldn't have happened." His voice took on an agitated edge and in that moment I knew who he was.

"It was you." I found myself sitting on the Chippendale chair that probably was there for art's sake and not to be sat upon by anyone. "It was you who phoned me in the middle of the night and warned me not to accept the brides— . . . Rosemary, Thora, and Jane's invitation to come to the Old Rectory."

He stood looking down at me, not denying it.

"Why?"

"Why," he echoed, "phone at all? Or why wait until three in the morning?"

"Both!" I watched the paisley throw slither onto the floor.

"To answer the first part, I didn't want to see you risk the same fate as your mother. As to the second, it took me until that unconscionable hour to convince myself I wasn't being a needless alarmist. Or I should say, it took that length of time for Arthur to get me to brace up." Without waiting for a response, he went to a door that opened onto a flight of stairs painted the same stark white as the studio walls and called out to someone above. I was feeling close to fainting. But I was brought to attention by the thunder of descending footsteps and I was looking sideways into the eyes of a brawny man with a tattoo showing below one of the short sleeves of his black T-shirt. The shirt featured a dragon spewing fire emblazoned on the front and he wore his gray hair in a bushy ponytail that went halfway down his back.

"Ellie," said Richard, "I'd like you to meet Arthur Henshaw, my partner in both the personal and business sense."

"Hello," I responded in a toneless voice. How could I be pleased to make anyone's acquaintance after being told for the second time in the space of a few hours that Mother had been murdered? For what other interpretation could I put on Richard's words? He could hardly have meant that the excitement of a visit to the Old Rectory would be sufficient to cause me to trip and fall down a flight of steps. And if he was correct in his belief that my mother had not met with an accident, but with someone intent on getting her out of the way, how could I go on believing that I dreamed up the person who had entered my bedroom last night? Hadn't that voice—had it been a woman's?—said the very same thing: that I was risking the same fate as my mother?

"Ellie knows it was I who made that phone call," I heard Richard tell Arthur but I couldn't bring either of their faces back into focus.

"Why don't we take her upstairs to the flat?" Arthur suggested to Richard.

It was like listening to people auditioning for parts in a play, except that I was also on stage and I had no idea what was going to happen next. Other than that I was going to be forced to play out the next scene, in which anything might happen. No one handed me a script that I could thumb through to find out how the last act ended. Nor did I have a clue as to whether these two men were to play the roles of heroes or villains.

# CHAPTER ELEVEN

"DRINK THIS DOWN, it will help you feel better—get over the shock." Richard handed me a brandy snifter.

"Thank you, but I'm not much of a drinker." I stared mindlessly down into the amber depths, then downed the brandy with quick gulps.

"That's what your great-grandfather, Reverend Hugo McNair, wished his parishioners to believe. You may have heard of poor Gladys Bradley and her problem. But it wasn't only Edna Wilks's mother who used to tipple at the Old Rectory. It was the man who preached teetotalism from the pulpit. That was why he was always sucking on those cherry cough drops of his—to cover his taste for cherry brandy. Gladys was the one who sneaked him the bottles, it was the reason he couldn't give her the sack. I'm sure Agatha McNair never guessed. She was the sort who saw only what she wanted to see, not what was right under her nose. It was William Fitzsimons who caught on and threatened to inform the bishop if McNair didn't pressure Sophia into marrying him."

"Richard, I don't think this is the time to go into all this," Arthur said, tapping him on the arm with a hand almost as big as one of Susan's. We were in the flat above the photography studio. I was aware of chrome-legged chairs and tables and a long, brown sofa, and some really beautiful ultra-modern glass sculptures in a rainbow of jewellike colors.

"It's all right, Arthur," I said as if this were my one line in the play and I'd been practicing it for weeks. "I'm interested." Untrue, but it was better than talking about who had murdered my mother, and why.

"If we're going to dig into the subject"—the man with the bushy ponytail sat down on the end of the sofa closest to my chair—"what I'd like to know is why it would have mattered a hill of beans to his lordship the bishop if McNair did enjoy a drink. Doesn't sound as though it kept him out of the pulpit, not if he was always ranting on against the stuff. Makes him a hypocrite. A guilty conscience will do that to you every time. And guilty for nothing, because I never heard that the Church of England makes its members take the pledge."

"True," said Richard from where he was leaning against an armoire, "but McNair's congregation was a mixed bag. A good number of them had come over to St. John's from having been Methodists until they married and got roped into going down the road to the other church. Once the wedded bliss wears off a bit, as it tends to do for most couples . . ."

"Speak for yourself," Arthur told him.

"Then it doesn't take much, such as finding out the rector is an imbiber, to send the not-so-converted chasing back to their old pews. In a village the size of Knells the defection of a dozen or so members of the congregation means a considerable difference in what goes into the collection plate. Besides which, Reverend McNair would have had to explain to the bishop why he was losing customers. And his lordship, not being of the nonconformist mentality, might have concluded that rather than enjoying the occasional, or possibly frequent, glass of oh-be-joyful, McNair was a staggering drunk. In other words, William Fitzsimons must have convinced him with a few well-chosen words that he had him over a barrel . . . of cherry brandy, at risk of being publicly shamed and out of a job."

"What a predicament," I said.

"Hugo McNair, like a lot of men who roar about their households like lions if anyone so much as treads on their toes, was something of a coward when anyone faced him down."

"Oh, I don't know." Arthur leaned forward in his chair so that the dragon on his T-shirt was reduced to pair of green nostrils spewing fire. "I can do my share of stomping and snarling and flinging saucepans around. And I don't shrivel up into a quaking huddle when anyone rallies to say 'Boo!' back to me."

"You're the charming exception that proves the rule." Richard smiled absently back at him before saying to me, "Here. Have another poison. I won't report you to the church elders if you do. And I promise you it's not drugged."

At that moment, the paralysis that had turned me into a zombie for the past ten minutes seeped out of my pores, leaving me limp but alive again. "The cocoa. The cup Jane brought to me in bed last night." I got up and paced the shining wooden floor of the flat's sitting room. "Of course! It was drugged! How could I have been so stupid as not to realize? The feeling even when I was asleep that I couldn't move, that my limbs were weighted down with concrete, that I was trapped in a bog. That's how Jane also described how she felt. But of course she could have been making it up, if she was the one who had put whatever it was in my cocoa. Or someone else could have drugged her, too—either Thora or Rosemary, because it had to be one of them who did it. Whoever came into my room in the middle of the night and whispered in my ear that she had killed my mother wouldn't have wanted to rouse either of the others when making her getaway. For all I know they could be light sleepers given to getting up in the wee hours and prowling around the house. It was horrible! She probably had to shake me half-awake so that I could hear what she was saying, but needed me to be thoroughly sluggish so that I couldn't nip out of bed after her. Or"—I whirled around, spilling half the contents of my brandy snifter— "do I have it all wrong? Maybe it wasn't Rosemary, Thora, or Jane."

"I haven't got the full gist of what you've been saying," Arthur said, getting up from the sofa to take the snifter away from me, "but explain the last bit first."

I turned towards Richard, who had moved away from the armoire to stand beside the glass-and-chrome amoeba-shaped coffee table. "When I ignored your request that I stay away from the Old Rectory, perhaps you decided that you needed to make your point clearer. How do I know that you aren't making up this business about my mother's being murdered to scare me away because you've got some evil plot afoot that I could ruin just by being here? Could it be that you're in league with Sir Clifford Heath, for instance? Maybe he's promised you some vast sum of money if you agree to help him get the bridesmaids—I mean, Rosemary and the other two—to let him have the Old Rectory? Maybe, for all Amelia Chambers's confident talk, there is some legal stumbling block to his forcing them out?"

"That does sound plausible," Richard responded without visible rancor. "It doesn't happen to be the case. I can't tell you with certainty that Mina was deliberately pushed down those steps at Kings Cross, but I feel—with every bone in my seventy-odd-year-old body—that such was indeed the case."

"There's more to it than your masculine intuition." Arthur went over and placed a hand on Richard's shoulder. "But before you lay out the reasons one by one, why don't we have Ellie explain exactly what happened last night from the time Jane brought her the cocoa?"

"I've told you. But all right." I sat back down in the rust-colored art deco chair. "I'll take it step by step. Not leaving anything out, including the book, *Secrets of the Crypt,* that Thora gave me to take up to bed. It was one of those gothic novels, with the usual beleaguered heroine trapped in a house of secrets and things that go bump in the night. That's what helped me convince myself that I had dreamed up the woman coming into my room."

"Are you sure it was a woman?" Arthur asked, handing me back the brandy snifter, which he had replenished.

"Of course I'm not a hundred percent sure." I finally took a swallow and felt the fumes ignite my mouth like a Christmas pudding. "I just accused Richard, didn't I? It was a muttering voice and it's hard to tell sometimes, even when someone is talking out loud. Some women have deep voices. Thora does, and Hope, the woman with the black and orange hair."

"We know who she is." Richard sat down on the sofa next to Arthur, who told him not to interrupt.

"She has a rich, full-bodied voice. I remember thinking that when she spoke to me it was like hot chocolate."

"Wonder if she drinks a lot of cocoa." Arthur raised a bushy eyebrow and it was Richard's turn to tell him to be quiet. I swallowed some more of the brandy and felt its molten heat settle in my chest. "Anyway, it can't be all that difficult to disguise one's voice sufficiently to make it un-recognizable to someone in a drugged state. But to get on with what happened . . ."

Once I got going it seemed I couldn't stop. I even told them about finding the wedding and bridesmaid dresses in the trunk in the attic. And when I mentioned the veil which I had at first thought was a mantilla and how it had been out of what had to have been its box because of the silk orange blossom circlet inside, Richard's eyes turned unmistakably thoughtful.

"What are you thinking?" I asked him.

"That it could be that someone took the veil out of the box when searching for something else and, hearing somebody coming, didn't have time to replace it for fear of being caught."

"What could the person"—I didn't say "woman," although that's what I was thinking—"have been looking for?"

"Sophia's diary."

Richard was making this up. He was trying to make a little joke to cap off my predilection for gothic romance. Undoubtedly, had I but read on I would have discovered Phoebe Phillpot had kept a diary into which she had poured out her woes while locked in her turret room and restricted to a diet of bread and water. Then my heart did a half-turn and I knew what he was going to say next.

"She started keeping it during those weeks when she hardly left her room. The ones between the time she left boarding school and finally agreed to marry William Fitzsimons. The whole situation was really quite"—he gave me a sad smile—"Victorian. None of her friends were allowed to see her, for the obvious reason that she might have used them as go-betweens in making contact with Hawthorn. That diary became her main source of company."

"You don't think Sophia found a way around her parents' restrictions to communicate with him?" I asked. "From what I've heard she sounds the resourceful sort. And surely she would have wanted him to know she was only pretending to give in to the engagement, so that he wouldn't respond by doing something wild and foolish when word leaked out." I leaned forward in my chair gripping the bowl of the brandy snifter. "I wouldn't be surprised if she had the whole thing planned out from day one, but she realized that patience was the name of the game. If she'd acceded too quickly to her parents' demands that she accept William's proposal, they would very likely have smelled a rat."

"It's what you would have done, isn't it, Richard?" Arthur grinned. "If your mum and dad had thought I wasn't good enough for you and had tried to force you into the arms of the curate?"

"You've got a remarkably short memory. Mother wasn't always as devoted to you as she is now." Richard looked at me with compelling eyes. "But I am sure, Ellie, you would appreciate my not straying too much further off the beaten path."

"It's not a particularly pleasant one." I had managed for several minutes to block out my mother's image as a faceless someone edged up behind her at Kings Cross and, under cover of an armload of shopping bags, gave her a vicious shove in the small of her back. I wasn't sure why I knew, but I could see those shopping bags as whoever it was beat a cautiously speedy retreat. "Let's get back to Sophia and how she managed to stay in touch with Hawthorn Lane, now reinvented as Sir Clifford Heath. Could it have been Edna Wilks's mother, Gladys, who smuggled their notes in and out for them? Logically, wouldn't she have been the one to take up Sophia's meals, at least during the daytime? From what I've heard of her, I can't picture Mrs. McNair trotting up- and downstairs with loaded trays of bread and water. Let alone," I added bitterly, "a cup of cocoa."

"You look even more like Sophia with that assessing look on your face." Richard stood next to my chair and laid a gentle hand on my shoulder. "I suppose it could have been Gladys. But I'd say more likely it was Edna who agreed to act as messenger. She was at the Old Rectory quite a lot at that time, helping her mother out on those days when Gladys was . . . under the weather. Meaning under the table. And Edna was close enough to Sophia in age to probably be thrilled to bits at playing a pivotal role in an exciting romance being thwarted by parental insensitivity. Besides, she was in love herself, or thought she was, with the late Ted."

"I think she really was," I said.

"There's no accounting for what one person sees in another." Arthur leaned back on the sofa and propped his large boots on the coffee table.

"I saw their engagement photo," I said, "at her cousin Gwen Fiddler's house, and there was this radiance in Edna's eyes, in her whole face, that took her from being pretty to beautiful. Yesterday it was clear from the way she talked that despite the difficult life she'd had with Ted she hadn't taken off the rose-colored glasses. We'll never know, will we, if it would have stayed that way for Sophia and Hawthorn Lane?"

"I believe it would," Richard joined Arthur on the sofa. "It's a cliché, but they were two halves of one person."

"The diary?" I prompted. "Did she tell you she had been keeping one?"

"I knew nothing about it until Rosemary brought it to me the day after your mother's accident."

"How did Rosemary come to have the diary?"

"It turned up in an attic trunk," said Richard. "I'm not sure whether it was Rosemary or one of the other two who found it. And I don't think it was the trunk containing the bridal gown, bridesmaid dresses, and veil. Rosemary said it contained possessions of Sophia's that William Fitzsimons must have brought back with him from the Belgian Congo when he returned with Mina. It was the sort of thing he would have relished, putting what little what was left of her in another coffin."

"I wonder if it was in the trunk that's now at the foot of the bed in the room where I'm sleeping? Nothing was in it when I looked but a pair of children's ballet slippers."

Lines that hadn't shown before cut into Richard's thin cheeks. "Rosemary told me that in addition to the diary there were Sophia's wedding ring and the marriage certificate. Other than those things, nothing but clothes, a handbag, handkerchiefs. Oh, and a bottle of perfume . . ."

"So he could ceremonially bury the very essence of her," Arthur added in a surprisingly angry tone.

"Rosemary said she had opened the lid of the trunk when she first moved into the Old Rectory but had closed it immediately when she saw it contained Sophia's things. She couldn't bring herself to go through it then and put it out of her mind until years later when she, Thora, and Jane took some chairs that they were no longer using up to the attic. And the three of them decided it was time to go through the trunk."

"And that was how long before my mother's death?"

"A matter of weeks—perhaps days."

"Did they read the diary?"

"Rosemary said they didn't. They agreed it would be a violation of Sophia's privacy." Richard's brow furrowed.

"But you think one of them may have done so?"

"It points that way, doesn't it?" Arthur still sat, looking powerfully muscular and set of jaw.

"What he means," said Richard, "is that Rosemary told me that she and the others determined the appropriate course of action was to give the diary to your mother. She said she telephoned Mina on the morning of the day it was found and arranged to meet her in the railway cafeteria at Kings Cross, because Mina did not want her to come to your flat. My guess is that she didn't want to prolong a meeting that would add a painful dimension to old memories."

"Yes, I'm sure that was it." My fingers tightened around the brandy snifter, and I eyed the amber liquid as if it contained some vital but unfathomable message. "Did the meeting take place? If Mother fell going down those steps, she had to have been entering the station."

Neither man looked at me as if I were stupid for stating the obvious. "According to Rosemary," Richard said gently, "her train arrived early—five or ten minutes before the appointed meeting time, and she continued to sit over a cup of coffee for an hour after Mina should have shown up.

When she finally left the cafeteria, questioning whether she had somehow muddled the arrangements, she heard people talking about a woman who had been injured falling down the steps."

"There's something wrong here." I put down the brandy. "There aren't any steps into the mainline station where the cafeteria would be. And we were told at the time that the fall took place at the underground. That means someone had to have been waiting for her as she came up from the exit." The picture was forming in my mind in all its stark horror. "Someone must have known she would take the tube from St. John's Wood rather than the bus—that had probably all been discussed on the phone. And if that person was someone Mother knew, they might even have exchanged an embrace." I drew a quivering breath. "And that embrace could have turned into a powerful shove. One that couldn't be expected to kill her but would have prevented her from getting to Rosemary and the diary."

"Which would seem to put Rosemary in the clear," Arthur interjected.

"If she was telling the truth and had the diary with her." My voice was every bit as cold as I felt inside.

"If she didn't, why did she come to me with the story?" Richard closed his eyes for a moment. "And then, of course, we come to the big question, don't we? What did someone know or fear Sophia might have put down on paper that would place them in sufficient danger, it was worth taking the risk of being seen pushing Mina down those steps? Of course, she could have claimed it was an accident. But that might still have opened up a wasp nest of questions."

"But can we be sure it was a woman?" Arthur got up and ambled around the sofa. "What about Ted? He was a nasty customer if ever there was one. I can't come up with a motive off the top of my head, other than that he might have been blackmailing Sophia, threatening to inform her parents that she was plotting to run off and marry Hawthorn

Lane. Edna, not recognizing him for the snake he was, could have told him in the strictest of confidence that she was taking messages back and forth."

"But now Ted's dead." My words echoed inside my head. "Perhaps he was blackmailing someone else. That parrot of the bridesmaids—Polly's got a vicious tongue and does a lot of nasty name-calling. But the phrase that sticks with me, because it is the most chilling, is: 'I'm telling! I'm telling!' Surely Polly must have heard it more than once to repeat it. I remember now! The wretched bird said it, in perfect mimicry of Ted's cackling voice when Edna came into the conservatory with news of his accident. An accident which she said several times didn't make sense, because it would have seemed more likely he'd have fallen with the blades of the pruning shears pointing away from him if he didn't drop them in the process. I made the assumption, and I supposed Rosemary, Thora, and Jane did, too, that he had swung them back towards him as he fell. Why didn't Edna think the same, if she thought about it at all? Was she dazed with grief? Was there something that she had heard or seen that had stirred a feeling of uncertainty? Not enough to make her sure, just enough to make her wonder?"

"I concluded he'd been murdered." Richard poured himself a brandy. "I was just glad it wasn't you, but I suppose rubbing you out the moment you crossed the threshold of the Old Rectory might have seemed precipitate."

"But you didn't come into my room last night to try and scare me away? Or leave a trail of confetti on the first landing and stand hidden somewhere singing a nasty version of 'Here Comes the Bride' as a warning that I was liable to meet with a tragic end, equal to Sophia's?"

Richard didn't ask me to explain this last part; he was patently preoccupied. "No, Ellie, but I don't want you to go back to that house, not even to collect your things. I'll do that for you, or Arthur will, later."

"But I have to go back," I protested, sounding more courageous than I felt. "We've nothing to take to the police to encourage them to take another look into my mother's death. Which means that they're not likely to take seriously our suspicions that Ted was murdered, not unless they already have questions in that regard, which they probably don't. He was old, he was tottery, and he should never have been climbing up ladders propped up against trees. He wasn't a rich patriarch with heirs swooping in like vultures for the first pickings from his will. He wasn't Sir Clifford Heath, out to destroy lives with a vengeful business scheme. The local squad won't be calling in Scotland Yard on the double. They'll write me off as a woman who's read too many gothic novels and tell me to get a life."

"We'd like you to keep the one you have." Arthur looked as though he would also have liked to tuck me into bed with a hot-water bottle, read me a bedtime story, and leave me to sleep with a night-light on. But I wasn't a little girl; I was a woman who was determined to find out who had murdered her mother. At that moment I wasn't thinking that I had children of my own who needed me, or that my husband wasn't eager to become a widower. I was thinking with my head wrapped in a towel, deaf to any voice other than that of my emotions.

"I've got a friend not far from here that I could go and stay with." I looked unflinchingly at the two men. I didn't add that her name was Mrs. Malloy and that she was staying with Edna Wilks's cousin Gwen. That might not have sounded too reassuring, given the fact that my whereabouts could so easily leak back to the wrong quarter. Nor did I say that, while I could stay there, I had no intention of doing so.

"You promise?" Richard eyed me intently.

"Yes," I lied without feeling my color rise.

"Then I'll give you Sophia's diary." He crossed to the wall behind the sofa, took down an abstract painting composed of interlocking circles of black, taupe, and gray, and pressed a finger against a spot in the white paneling. A square opening appeared from which he produced a thin brown leather book. It looked very much like the book Thora had lent me last night. Had someone thought it was the diary when they saw Thora bring it into the house? Were they afraid that she had managed to find it and was intent on showing it to me? Had they seen her slip it in among the other volumes in the bookcase, imagined that she had concluded that the best hiding place was the one in plain view, and searched for it along the shelves only to find that it wasn't the diary after all? Was that why Thora hadn't been able to find *Secrets of the Crypt* quickly, because it wasn't where she'd thought she'd put it? Or had she been playing a devilish game of her own devising?

"Rosemary brought me the diary that day when she came to talk to me." Richard handed it to me as he spoke. "Her explanation was that she didn't want to destroy it, but she didn't want it to remain in the house, because just knowing it was there would have brought Mina's ghost into the Old Rectory to join the ones that were already there. She said she was already depressed and was afraid of a recurrence of the nervous breakdown that had forced her to leave her job and persuaded her against the stress of taking another one."

"So that's what Thora meant in saying something to the effect that Rosemary could be vulnerable and why she and Jane at times seem protective of her even though in the main she seems so in charge. But what can I really believe about any of them?" The diary felt like a living object in my hands. "Did you read it?"

Richard studied my face. "I didn't look at it until I heard you had been invited to the Old Rectory. I had the same scruples that Rosemary claimed about not invading Sophia's privacy. Also, I'm a coward. I don't think I wanted to know what she might have written that had reaped such devastating results for her daughter. Best to let sleeping dogs lie. But they're not always willing to play dead, are they?"

"Did you read anything that struck you as something a person might be desperate not to have come out in the open?"

"Nothing." Richard's smile was wistful. "Sophia had her own way of putting her thoughts down on paper. The only thing that seemed of possible significance was that a couple of pages had been torn out."

"But that doesn't make sense." Arthur cocked his ponytailed head on one side and squinted through half-closed eyes. "Because if what mattered had been removed, what harm would be done if Ellie's mother was given the diary? And the time it took to rip out those pages would have been better spent throwing the whole thing on the fire or hiding it until it could be properly disposed of."

"It could be that we're dealing with someone who doesn't make sense because she's mad as a hatter behind the mask she presents to the world." I stood up. "And I'm not singling out Rosemary. Lots of people have nervous breakdowns. I've sometimes thought I was about to have one myself. I'm talking about the sort of madness that grows out of evil until it forces a body completely over the edge. And I really don't see that it could be Rosemary, not when it was she who gave you the diary, Richard. There may have been someone in the house who at one time or another thought that it was still there and went around looking for it, and while doing so, took the veil out of the bag where it had been with the wedding dress." I was suddenly feeling terribly tired, which wasn't surprising given my broken night's sleep. And Richard, seeing this, escorted me, with Arthur making up the rear, back down to the studio, where he took down the photo of the Old Mill from the wall and went with it over to the crescent-shaped counter.

"I'll wrap this in tissue paper for you," he said. "It'll be a happier reminder of Sophia. As I told you, she loved to paint that scene. And if you'll give me the diary, I'll wrap that, too, and put them both in a box. That way, if someone should happen to see you leave here, someone you would prefer wasn't watching, they'll think you made a purchase or I've given you a present. Which is what I am doing."

"Wouldn't it make more sense to put the diary in my handbag?"

"Just what I was thinking," agreed Arthur.

"But that's what this someone would expect you to do." Richard now sounded as tired as I was. "Either way"—he handed me the box—"look both ways when you go out the door, Ellie. And when you cross the street. Then go to your friend's. You'll not have second thoughts about that?"

"I'm going there right now," I told him, "cross my heart."

# CHAPTER TWELVE

I WASN'T TELLING a bald-faced lie, I thought as I went out into the High Street. I was providing an edited version of the truth. It had been my intention on leaving the house that morning to go and see Mrs. Malloy at Gwen's. And that's exactly what I was going to do. All I had failed to tell Richard Barttle and Arthur Henshaw was that I wasn't going to seek refuge there. At least not for more than a couple of hours. And I wouldn't stay even that long if Gwen or her obsequious husband, Barney, remained on the scene, making it impossible for me to tell Mrs. M. to button her butterfly lips while I skimmed through Sophia's diary. Then I would impose on her sense of loyalty to get her to hide it under her mattress. Needless to say, she would mention the hope of an increase in her wages when we returned to Merlin's Court. Along with my promise to leave her the grandfather clock in case I was foolish enough to get myself murdered.

There were quite a number of people about, bustling along with shopping bags, pushing babies in prams, trotting dogs beside them on leads, going in or out of shops, or just pausing to look in windows. It was Wednesday, I reminded myself, which probably meant early-closing day, so it wasn't surprising that there was a lot of morning activity. I had been grateful when the phone rang in the photography studio before Richard or Arthur could ask me where my friend lived and how I planned to get there. Luckily it had been a customer calling with some question that had sent Arthur into the back room while Richard returned the receiver to his ear. So I had mouthed across the room to him that I would be in touch as I nipped out the door.

So many emotions were running through me. Grief, rage, and a desperate desire to know what Sophia might have written in the diary that had impelled someone to murder my beloved mother. Fear had taken a while to rear its head. Now I had to fight the urge to keep from repeatedly looking over my shoulder. I paused in front of the greengrocer's and while pretending to be looking at the bunches of flowers in the wooden crates outside, I casually glanced around without spotting a familiar figure amongst the throng. So I moved on, intending to take the first side street I came to that would lead me back to Hawthorn Lane. From where I could retrace my steps to the Old Mill. And with any luck be able to figure out Thora's instructions on how to cut across the fields by using the footpaths and somehow end in Upper Thaxstead. But with each step I became increasingly sure that I was being followed. There was nothing to substantiate the feeling, because when I gave in to the urge to turn around, while drawing level with the bus stop, I still couldn't see anyone who looked suspicious. Even so, the prickling down my spine grew and I clutched the box containing the photograph and the diary to my middle. I wished that a bus would appear. It didn't matter where it was bound. Timbuktu would have done just fine. I would have been on board.

I was moving on at a quickened pace when a vehicle, a white van with black lettering on its side, came to an abrupt stop alongside me, and before I had finished leaping in the air, the window rolled down and a bristly head of brown hair stuck itself out the window.

"Mrs. Haskell?" The voice was curt, bordering on pugnacious—a good match for the face that could have belonged to a boxer bouncing around the ring. His gloved mitts pounding the air as he waited for the bell to ring. Actually his hands were on the steering wheel and he was smiling. "It's me, Tom, from up the lane. One of them that gave you such a hard time yesterday. Want a lift somewhere?"

I would have agreed to elope with him if he'd asked me. Instead I nodded, climbed in alongside him, and drew a deep breath. There was something a bit fishy here, but only in the literal sense, and on leaning back in the seat I allowed my grip on the cardboard box to relax ever so slightly.

"Just delivered some nice haddock to the Old Rectory." Tom looked at me before returning his eyes to the road as he drove on. "I hear Edna made one of her fish pies with the cod I brought last time. A great cook, Edna."

"Yes, we had it for lunch yesterday." I also gazed straight ahead, resolutely so. Someone had been following me. Maybe it had been Leonard Skinner, hoping I would lead him to Mrs. Malloy. But my mind refused to settle for that one. I remembered how Jane had encouraged me to visit Richard Barttle. Could that be because when he had rung up to speak to me last night and she had taken the call, she had leaped to the conclusion that he planned on giving me the diary? And then there was Rosemary who had taken it to him in the first place, which would seem to put her in the clear. Or was I giving her a pass too easily? Was this but an example of her diabolical cunning? Had she looked ahead to the possibility, remote though it might have seemed, that my mother's accident would be questioned? And after tearing out the pages from the diary that might incriminate her, toddled along to Richard? My mind didn't leap ahead to Thora. It wormed its way in circles about the question: What secret, revealed in Sophia's handwriting, had to be protected at all costs?

"Where can I take you?" Tom asked me.

"I want to get to Upper Thaxstead, but there's no need for you to drive me the whole way." I tried to sound cheerfully relaxed. "I was going to walk. It's a lovely morning. So different from yesterday, when it drizzled on and off. But it cleared up in the evening, didn't it? The sky was blue until really late, and the sun was still coming in the window when I went up to bed. I had to close the curtains tightly to keep it out."

He gave me a sideways grin. "You're still worried, aren't you, Mrs. Haskell?"

"What about?" His words struck me as decidedly menacing. Was he in the pay of one of the bridesmaids? He had turned onto a country road with only a smattering of houses, set far apart. He was pulling off at the grass verge and reaching into his jacket pocket. For what? A length of twine with which to strangle me? Trying to make as little noise and movement as possible I attempted with fumbling finger to undo my safety belt.

"About how me and the other neighbors carried on at you yesterday. Must have given you one hell of a scare."

"You could say that." My heart continued to pound so hard that my vision blurred and I had to blink several times before being able to see that he was holding a sheet of paper which he unfolded and studied, before responding.

"I know we apologized at the time, but that hardly seems enough, does it?"

Not if you're getting ready to bump me off, I thought, while mumbling something unintelligible.

"It wasn't just me that felt bad. Frank, Susan, and Irene all said they didn't know what had come over them, not taking time to find out that you was you—if you get me, and not that woman that works for Sir What's-his-face."

"Clifford Heath." I was sitting bolt-upright in my seat, my hands on my undone safety belt, the box in my lap—looking as though it were waiting to be snatched away from me.

"That's him." Tom replaced the paper in his pocket.

"There's times I've thought I could cheerfully strangle him with my bare hands"—he clenched them as he spoke and I saw the hairs on the backs of them bristle—"but the wife wasn't for the idea."

"Sensible woman."

"She says we've got to pin our hopes on the old ladies making enough difficulties about selling that he'll give up on Knells. Treating you nice at the Old Rectory, are they?"

"Couldn't be more welcoming."

"That's good. But can't be expected you're having a pleasant time of it, not with what happened to Ted." Tom grimaced. "And there was me saying only yesterday as it wouldn't be long before someone did away with the miserable bugger. Then look what happens! He does the job himself. There's none I knows that will shed many tears for him, not even the crocodile sort. But Edna's different. We all feel sorry for her. I was glad I was able to be with her at the hospital till she got word, and bring her back afterwards. Just as well you didn't see him, a right bloody mess he was. Gave me the nightmare it did. Don't know how those doctors deal with sights like that day in and day out. Didn't take long with Ted, that's one thing; gone before he got there, is what I gather." Tom turned the key in the ignition and drove on. "Sorry to have to stop like that, Mrs. Haskell, but I've got this new house on my route and couldn't remember if it was number nineteen or twenty-nine. Ah, here we are."

He pulled up, bounded out of the van, retreated around the back and reemerged a moment or so later with a white paper-wrapped parcel in one hand. "I'll just pop this into the customer's place and I'll be back to take you to Upper Thaxstead. Won't take more than ten minutes to get you there. Glad to do it even if there hadn't been that business yesterday."

It's amazing how quickly one can become extremely fond of a man when it becomes clear he isn't about to murder one's favorite self. When we continued on our way to Upper Thaxstead he asked me if Amelia Chambers had shown up yesterday.

"Yes, latish in the afternoon."

"How did the old ladies stand up to her?"

"They refused to come to terms. I believe they're hoping for another meeting in London with Sir Clifford."

"Got to give Miss Maywood credit for fighting every inch of the way. Not that it'll probably do any good. Now"—Tom slowed the car down—"where's this house I'm taking you to?"

I told him. And after proceeding on for a hundred yards he parked outside the Fiddlers' residence. "A pleasure," he said shaking my hand, "and if there's ever anything I can do, anything at all, to help you out by way of making up for yesterday, you've only got to say the word."

"Actually there is something."

"Good!"

"It's going to sound a bit peculiar," I looked at the self-important-looking house with its plethora of chimney pots. On the way here it had come to me with a return of the prickling fear that had assailed me in the High Street that it might not be such a wise idea to take the box containing the diary, along with the photograph, into Edna's cousin's home. It was no use telling myself that I was being stupidly panicky. I told myself it was unlikely, but I wasn't about to place Mrs. Malloy and the Fiddlers in danger if the penny dropped as to where I had left the diary. I'd just have to wait to read it until I was somewhere safe.

"Out with it, love," Tom prodded,

"Would you be willing to keep this for me?" I held out the box. "And put it away until I can take it back, which could be tomorrow? I know you must think I'm nuts not wanting to take it back with me to the Old Rectory, and the thing is, I can't explain." My voice petered out.

Tom's face unexpectedly brightened. "You don't have to. I can guess. It's got something to do with this business of

Sir Clifford wanting to turn Knells into one of his damn
Memory Lanes holiday camps. Some papers or documents
that the old ladies have dug up that'll keep Miss Maywood
from having to sell him the Old Rectory. And you're afraid
that if you take it there he'll send those goons of his down
to ransack the place before they're ready to show it to him."

Whatever I had thought of Amelia Chambers, I wouldn't
have categorized her as a goon, but Tom was well away.

"I expect Miss Maywood wants her solicitor to take a
look at this." He tapped the box. "Just to be sure she's on
firm ground. Don't worry, I won't look inside, you have my
word on it. I won't even breathe a word to the wife, let
alone anyone else. Can't risk one wagging tongue, and human nature being what it is, that's what would happen.
People would start walking around Knells looking all cheerful and optimistic and the game would be up. I'll hide it
somewhere the devil himself wouldn't think to look. You
can bank on that, love."

Looking like a man who has just won the heavyweight
championship of the world, Tom drove off and I went up
the path to the Fiddlers' front door wondering if I had just
made the worst mistake of my life. Ten minutes ago, I'd
been afraid he was going to murder me, now I had en-
trusted him with my life. But I had to put my faith in someone, didn't I? And who better than a virtual stranger?

Gwen opened the door before the bell had stopped ringing. She stepped aside and beckoned me into the oppres-
sively overdecorated hall with its portrait of the first Mrs.
Fiddler staring myopically down from the wall. Gwen didn't
look too pleased to see me. But I decided she wouldn't have
been thrilled even had I been one of her Cambridge-educated
stepchildren. I doubted that this unsmiling woman with a
platinum topknot, wearing tighter black pants and an even
skimpier sweater than when I had seen her yesterday,
would have noticed had I come in carrying the box. She
probably would not have noticed had I brought in John the

Baptist's head on a silver platter, except to remark that she had a server just like it, except that hers was an antique.

"How nice of you to come by." Her lips stretched into a flamingo-pink smile, but she simply wasn't up to gushing. "Dear Roxie will be so pleased to see you, Ellie. You did say I could call you that? As you must know, we've had my cousin Edna overnight." She lowered her voice to a whisper. "And it hasn't been easy—not that I'm complaining— she's suffered a loss. These things happen; they can't be helped. But she was in such a state I had to have her in bed with me all night, which meant turning poor Fiddler out. And he hates sleeping in any of the guest rooms. I kept stressing that he was welcome to choose any one of the six that he liked. Except the blue one, because I really can't have that bedspread rumpled. It's velvet and has to go to the cleaners. And of course he couldn't sleep in the rose room because that's where I'd put dear Roxie."

"Life does get difficult," I said.

Gwen pressed a hand to her brow and I watched her grow skinnier and more wan with every breath she drew. "The whole thing has me stressed to the point where I can't put my mind to getting a three-course lunch on the table." She swayed on her high heels. "We'll just have to make do with a madras lamb curry and saffron rice followed by a fresh fruit salad and perhaps some of the Florentine biscuits I get at Harrods."

"Please don't think I came expecting to be invited for lunch." I followed her past one hideous monstrosity of furniture after another down the hall.

"Oh, that is good of you, Ellie. Because I'm just not up to laying another place. I felt exhausted spreading the Irish linen cloth on the dining-room table. Fiddler had to take over for me."

"Perhaps you can have a nap this afternoon," I suggested. "And what about Edna. How is she doing today?"

"Still talking about how wonderful Ted was. But it's early

days yet." Gwen turned the knob on the drawing-room door and pushed it open. "Perhaps by tomorrow she'll remember what a truly horrible man he was, and what a pity it was that she didn't marry one of her other boyfriends. I remember there was a young man named Frank that Edna was rather keen on; she was quite upset when he got engaged to someone else. I can't say if Edna was married to Ted then or not. It was before I moved here and we didn't write all that often. But she mentioned quite recently that he's now a widower. So who knows? Love can bloom at any age, so they say. Now you won't mind if I don't come in with you, Ellie? I just have to have a few moments to myself, now that Edna's gone."

"Back to her own house?" I asked.

"No, to the Old Rectory. She left for the bus about ten minutes ago, so if she isn't there yet she soon will be. Whatever else she isn't, Edna's a good reliable worker." On these words Gwen vanished like a black moth and I found myself in the drawing room where Mrs. Malloy sat hunched in the chair where she had sat yesterday, her feet on the footstool, her hands folded in her lap.

"Hello," I said, crossing the carpet to sit down opposite her.

"Oh, it's you, Mrs. H." She raised her head and I saw purple shadows under her eyes that matched the powdered ones on her upper lids. "It's good of you to take the time to come and visit me. I feel like one of those sad little old ladies dropped off at a nursing home when they're told they're being taken shopping."

She could keep right on talking in that lachrymose voice but it wouldn't alter the fact that I was glad to see her. I felt stronger in the face of her disapproval, more ready to do battle with the forces of evil. "Rubbish," I told her, "you seemed quite happy when I left yesterday. You had Barney Fiddler fawning all over you and Gwen about to serve you a scrumptious lunch. But let's forget them for the moment.

I've come to tell you that Leonard showed up at the Old Rectory last night and he took some getting rid of. I couldn't quite convince him that I wasn't hiding you under my bed upstairs or in the jam cupboard."

"Is there one?" she inquired listlessly.

"One what?"

"A jam cupboard."

"I don't know, it was just a figure of speech." I was beginning to feel just the least bit exasperated, which was a good thing, much better than allowing my thoughts to take dark turns down tortuous paths.

"And which Leonard are we talking about?"

"Leonard Skinner. Your Leonard. The one who went out to buy the pound and a half of stewing steak and didn't come back until now."

"Oh, that one, Mrs. H." The annoying woman rested her head against the back of her chair and closed her eyes. "It's hard to think about mundane things like husbands when you're living in a house filled with terrible secrets."

After all I'd gone through in the space of the twenty-four hours since we had last seen each other, I was now rapidly losing patience. "What secrets, Mrs. Malloy? Does Barney Fiddler wear Gwen's nighties to bed?"

"I can't say, I'm sure," she replied primly, "but I wish he'd think about wearing socks. I don't know as when I've felt anything as cold on my back as his feet when he got into bed with me last night."

"He did what?"

"Well, he couldn't sleep with Gwen because she had that cousin Edna in with her. A sad time that woman's had from the sound of it." Mrs. M. roused herself to appear moderately sympathetic. "Pruning shears! Imagine having to read that on your hubby's death certificate. Doesn't sound nearly as nice as pneumonia, does it? Heart failure's good, too. Always sounds to me like an admission of product liability and that they'll be a rebate coming in the post."

"What did you do when Barney Fiddler got into bed with you?" I had never before used that stern a voice with her.

"I told him if he kept his feet on me like that I'd end up with lumbago."

"Then? This is your dear friend's husband we're talking about."

"Then I picked up the clock radio and told him I'd smash it over his head if he didn't bugger off."

"Exactly right, Mrs. Malloy!" My breathing slowed. "Did he depart immediately with his tail between his legs?"

"No need to be vulgar, Mrs. H." She was back to being prim. "I didn't take so much as a peek. Once he was out the door I got up and locked it. But as soon as that was done I felt trapped inside that room with roses climbing all over the wallpaper like they'd been fed too much plant food. A prey," she added in hollow accents, "to me terrible thoughts."

"You would have liked Barney to make love to you?" I stopped picturing myself pinning medals to her black taffeta front.

"Not likely!" She shuddered, and in doing so came fully back to life. "Of course I can't say for certain, Mrs. H., that he was in it with Gwen in murdering his first wife. But if he's daft enough to have the wool pulled over his eyes, then he's guilty in my court of law."

"Hold on a minute," I said, squeezing out a word at a time, "I know that you hate to be left out of things. Somehow you've managed to feel slighted that you weren't at the Old Rectory when Ted met his end and you've worked it out in your mind that it wasn't an accident, which means it had to be murder. And because"—I was making a great effort to keep my voice down—"I don't get to have a murder if you don't have one, you are making up this nonsense about a woman who was an invalid for years."

"All the more reason to get rid of her."

"That's a terrible thing to say!"

"I'm speaking from the point of view of Gwen." Mrs.

Malloy was way up on her high horse. "She could tell herself the first Mrs. Fiddler was suffering, that the poor soul couldn't be a wife to her husband or a mother to her dear little children, and was aching for someone to put something in her bedtime milky drink, and make her go night-night forever."

This was not funny. Especially when I pictured myself unsuspectingly drinking last night's cocoa. What I also saw was that Mrs. Malloy, for all her dramatizing, was in earnest.

Unfair, I thought. I'd just found out that my mother had in all probability been murdered, as had Ted. And that Richard Barttle and Arthur Henshaw were seriously concerned that I wasn't long for this world. Now any desire I had to share my troubles with Mrs. Malloy vanished.

"What makes you so sure that Gwen killed the first wife?" I asked.

"She told me so."

"What?" I gaped at her, not one of my more attractive expressions, but this was no time to worry about how I looked.

"Well, not in precise words," Mrs. Malloy conceded, "but close enough so there was no mistaking what she was getting at." Pressing a finger to her lips, she rose onto her stiletto heels, took a look though the archway into the formidably overfurnished dining room, put an ear to the drawing-room door, and returned to her chair. "It was like this, you see. Gwen and I was sitting in here talking while Barney was off in what they call the parlor watching the telly— dirty movies is my guess, but the point is, he was out of the way. It was round about nine in the evening, not late, as you might say, but before that cousin Edna arrived. God rest her husband's miserable soul! And it was right after getting the phone call that Gwen came over all queer and quiet like."

"What phone call?"

"The one from Edna, letting her know Ted was being measured for his last suit. Before that Gwen had talked me ears off. One brag after another about those bloody whiz-brain stepkids of hers. And asking me cheeky personal questions, like how much money I have to live on each year. I had to give meself two increases in the wages you pay me, but I won't hold you to them, Mrs. H. Worse was when she presumed to ask how much I weigh these days, with that kind little smile on her face when she followed it up with saying I'd never looked better. And that it's so much easier to find clothes in the larger sizes. Bloody cheek!"

"Could we speed this up, Mrs. Malloy? I'd like to get back to enjoying my own problems."

"If you're going to take that tone!" She heaved a sigh that threatened to send her black taffeta bosom into orbit. "Like I said, Gwen wasn't herself from when she got that phone call; or I should say, she went back to being more like her old self. The one that was under her parents' thumbs at age thirty-five and afraid to say 'boo' to her own shadow. I don't know that Barney noticed. He was too busy making sure I was comfortable, as he called it. Making sheep eyes and trying to put his hands where he shouldn't is more my take. But like I said, if you was listening, Mrs. H., he finally took himself off to watch the telly and Gwen and me got to be on our own."

"Aren't you afraid she'll come into the dining room?" I stared over her head at the velvet-draped archway. "And hear what you're saying?"

"I haven't got to the juicy bits yet. And anyway she'd come in through this door. She doesn't use the other one, because it means stepping on a strip of two-hundred-year-old carpeting. Time it went is what I'd say." Mrs. Malloy, who replaced the front-room carpet in her terraced house on Herring Street once a year, looked momentarily smug. "Well, there we was around nine last night, sitting just like the two of us is now, Mrs. H., and Gwen trying to look chirpy as a robin. Only her face kept creasing up like she was going to need another face-lift before morning. She was trying not to tear up and she was fidgeting like one of them windup toys, so I says to her that maybe we could both do with a stiff gin. It was as plain as the redesigned nose on her face that she was up to her eyebrows in some sort of trouble."

"Perhaps she was upset over the way Barney had been making up to you."

"Could have been that, Mrs. H." She paused to consider this point. "Only I knew it wasn't. Gwen had that same look on her face that she used to get when she knew her class-work was about to be checked and the teacher was going to find out she'd been cribbing off the girl sitting next to her. And after we'd had a couple of gins, she sort of broke down and blurted out all this stuff about Barney's first wife."

"What sort of stuff?"

"Oh, about how much the poor woman had suffered and how at times it seemed it would be a kindness to put her out of her misery. It was just like Gwen was a kid again and needed me to do her sums for her. Only this time she needed me to add things up so that she wouldn't feel so bad about herself. So I told her that most people have thought about killing someone at one time or another. And how I'd once been tempted to shove Leonard down the stairs when I found out he'd been with another woman."

"Please!" I said.

Mrs. Malloy looked unusually abashed. "Sorry, Mrs. H., I'd forgotten for the moment about your mum. But I couldn't skip that part, because Gwen seemed all relieved for a moment, like she wasn't a six-year-old kiddie all alone in the world no more. Then she told me how she used to hide the first Mrs. Fiddler's glasses, hoping she'd take a tumble down the staircase when she was up fumbling her way to the loo. Remember how Barney said yesterday that she was always losing her specs? Well, now we know why, don't we, Mrs. H.?"

"But the woman didn't die from a fall." I also had a memory for what had been said. "She had a bad heart. And it gave out."

"That's how it was made to look."

"That's what Gwen said?"

"She got to rambling, after her third gin. Her voice got all slurred and she stumbled over words but the gist was clear. She talked about how she'd heard that some plant or herb would cause the wife to have a massive heart attack, that'd look like it had happened natural. Better than trying an overdose of tablets."

"Thora, one of the bridesmaids, has an herb garden."

"Is that so?"

"What else did Gwen tell you?" I asked, no longer feeling impatient or resentful of her hogging stage front. There had to be a connection between the melodrama that had been enacted here and the one that was still being staged at the Old Rectory.

"Not much else." Mrs. M. frowned judiciously. "She'd got to snuffling by then. All I could halfway make out was that someone had been blackmailing her for years."

"Gwen must have meant Ted. For some reason she must have exploded yesterday and killed him, after bottling up her rage for years. Although my guess is she'd taken some of it out on her cousin in the interim." I was now pacing the floor heedless of wearing out the pattern on the antique carpet. "One of the bridesmaids said Edna always came back to the Old Rectory all upset after seeing Gwen."

"Thanks for filling me in, Mrs. H., right before Gwen's about to serve me lunch." Mrs. Malloy looked genuinely worried. Then her face brightened. "We're both thinking daft, Mrs. H., it couldn't have been her. She was with me the whole afternoon."

"Ted was injured right after I arrived at the Old Rectory."
I sat back down. "Are you sure she didn't sneak out of the
house soon after I left? I was a bit delayed getting there because my car ended up in a ditch."

Mrs. Malloy pursed her butterfly lips. "Gwen and Barney
did leave me to have a bit of a nap before lunch. And I think
I dozed off, although it couldn't have been for more than a
few minutes, because I remember looking at the clock and
thinking it hadn't budged much. And then Gwen came in
and said the first course, some kind of thin brown soup
with one of them highfalutin foreign names, was on the
table. So there's no way it could have been her. My guess,
and it's only that, is that it was Edna that killed him because she found out he'd been blackmailing her very own
cousin! That's not the sort of thing any decent woman could
overlook. Makes Leonard's disappearing act pale in com-
parison. But don't get to worrying, with everything else
that's going on, that I'm going to weaken and take him
back. Barney getting into bed with me like he did last night
reminded me that Leonard also had the most wickedly cold
feet. It was the one thing I didn't find attractive about him."

Before she could continue on that subject, Gwen came
into the room to announce that she was ready to get lunch
on the table. Mrs. Malloy said she would see me out and
scooted after me to the front door.

"You can't leave me here. Not if you've a feeling bone in
your body." She drew the door behind her and stood with
me on the front step. "What if Gwen wasn't as drunk as I
thought she was and she remembers what she told me? Do
you want to come back here to find she's murdered me just
like she did the first Mrs. Fiddler? We both need to get into
your car and drive as fast as we can back to Merlin's
Court."

"I didn't come here in the car."

"Then we'll take Gwen's bicycle and you can ride with
me on the handlebars!"

"Mrs. Malloy"—I laid a hand on her arm—"I've got to go back to the Old Rectory. What happened to Ted, and I'm sure that he was murdered even if Gwen didn't do it, well, that's just the tip of the iceberg. I can't take you back there. Pack up your things and leave. Get a taxi to a pub and see if it provides overnight accommodation. If it doesn't, ask for suggestions where you can stay." It was hard to walk away and leave her to go back into that house, but I made myself do it and began the long walk back to Knells.

# CHAPTER THIRTEEN

As I ENTERED the Old Rectory around the back way through the conservatory door, I was hoping that the bridesmaids would be in the sitting room and I would have some time to regroup before facing them. It was important that I not show that anything had dramatically changed since my visit to the photography studio. I was in luck. There was no sign of Rosemary, Thora, or Jane, and even Polly the appalling parrot refrained from making any rude remarks as I side-stepped the plants on my way to the kitchen, where I found Edna stirring something in a saucepan on the cooker.

"There you are, Miss Ellie." She looked round and smiled at me. She appeared much better today. Her cheeks were pink and her pretty hair neatly combed. Her foot was band-aged and she still limped as she came over and pulled out a chair for me at the kitchen table, but her voice was steady and there were no signs of tears. "You look tired," she said.

"It was quite a walk, but I enjoyed it. How are you, Edna? That's what's important."

"Not so bad, thanks for asking." She wiped her hands on her apron front. "I got a good night's sleep at my cousin Gwen's. She had me with her in bed. But we didn't do much talking. She was down in the dumps herself, not really to do with Ted; she gets that way sometimes, as if there's something always on her mind. It could be her husband. He fancies himself as God's gift to women. Has to be trying for Gwen. But I shouldn't be saying anything. Not with the woman that does your housework staying there. Anyway I'd rather talk about your mother." Edna sat down in the chair across from the one which I had taken. "She was a lovely girl was Miss Mina, quiet, and preferred her own company, but that was her upbringing. It quite broke me up when I heard she'd died. But I can see"—she closed a hand over mine—"that you'd rather not talk about it."

"It's been a long time," I managed to say calmly, "and I have a wonderful husband and healthy children. And I think my father's finally going to marry again. What I'd like is for you to tell me about my grandmother. What sort of a girl would you say Sophia was? You must have seen something of her." I had to be careful not to give away anything Richard Barttle had told me about her possible role as a messenger when Sophia was confined to her room.

"She looked very much like you do, Miss Ellie, but the ladies must already have told you that. She was a happy girl and kind with it, but you could say she was strong-willed. And that wasn't how young ladies were supposed to be in our young days." Edna sat looking reflective. "I've got to be honest. I never could quite see what she fancied so much about Hawthorn Lane, for all he was handsome. I suppose he just wasn't my type. I saw a cruel streak in him that's come out now. Well, you know how's he's been hounding Miss Maywood to get her to sell." She again smoothed her hands on her apron. "But I had to have been one of the few female heads he didn't manage to turn hereabouts. Not that I'm naming any names," she added quickly, "I'm just trying to say that Miss Sophia wasn't the only one that was ready to follow him to the ends of the earth. And even though I didn't much like him, I could understand . . ." Edna's voice faltered.

"Because you were in love yourself at the time," I prodded gently.

"That . . . and because most people couldn't understand what I saw in Ted." She wiped at her eyes with the back of her hand. "It made us kind of close—Miss Sophia and me—us both being in the same sort of boat. I wasn't working here regular at the time. My mother did that. But I was in and out quite a bit helping her when she was under the weather. If you haven't heard already, she had a problem with drink and wasn't always up to getting the jobs done. And I'd left school at fifteen and was already cleaning other places, but not enough to keep me busy every day, so I quite looked forward to coming here. The year before Miss Sophia left school, Miss Maywood was staying here and quite often the other two girls—Miss Dobson and Mrs. Pettinger, as she now is—would come down for the afternoon or the day and there'd be a bit of life about the place. It was fun listening to them talk about young men and what ones they found attractive." Edna got up and went over to the cooker to stir her saucepan. "And about their tennis parties and such. But I'm talking too much, Miss Ellie; it's to keep my mind off Ted. You should be upstairs on your bed having a rest before the séance business that's going to take place tonight. That's what the ladies are doing. They're all taking naps. Even Miss Dobson, who never sleeps in the day. But I don't suppose she got a good night's rest."

"It was terrible what happened to your husband."

"I don't think I'll ever get over it, not properly, but as of this moment I'm kind of numb. It doesn't seem real. Not like it did yesterday. And I can tell myself that at least I got to wed the man I loved. Not like poor Miss Sophia being forced into a marriage with a man she couldn't stand. It was terrible what her parents did to her, locking her in her room until she gave in. They wouldn't let her have any books to read or any writing paper for fear she'd somehow manage to smuggle out notes to Hawthorn Lane. I was the one that knew what she was going through, more than any-one, because I was the one that took her meals up to her on the days that I was here."

"Really?" I said, hoping I sounded as if this were the first I had heard of this.

"And I did more than carry trays up and down." Edna kept stirring whatever was in the saucepan. "I'm not ashamed to say it; I did pass notes between the two of them. I think the reason Reverend and Mrs. McNair never suspected was be-cause they didn't think I would risk costing me or my mother our jobs. People were surprised she was kept on when it was known she drank. And I could never figure that out, either. But I do know that my helping out Miss Sophia would have been the final straw."

I could have told Edna why Reverend McNair hadn't given her mother the sack after she was found passed-out on the sofa, but I prudently kept my mouth shut. "Did you take Sophia the writing paper?" I asked her.

"No." She turned around, wooden spoon in hand, to give me a puzzled look. "Why do you ask, Miss Ellie?"

"Because you said that she wasn't allowed any in her room, which leaves the question—where did she get it?"

"That's a good point." Edna sat back down. "Silly of me, but it never occurred to me before. But I don't see how it matters much, not after all this time. It can't do, can it?" Feeling like a first-class liar, I said that of course it couldn't. I'd just been talking to help keep her mind off Ted. I was so uncomfortable, so eager to get out of the kitchen that I de-clined her offer of tea and said that I thought I would have a lie-down and perhaps read my book.

"You do that, Miss Ellie; I'm sure if you fall asleep, one of the ladies will wake you in time for the séance. I'm not one for dabbling in such things at the best of times, and with Ted just having passed on, it's something I don't even want to think about. But I'll be out of here as soon as I've got din-ner on the table." Edna again wiped her hands on her apron—a nervous gesture this time, I thought. And with a pang of pity for her, along with that mounting sense of being swept into a maelstrom, I went upstairs, only sparing one glance for the photo of Sophia at much the same age as I was when I lost my mother. It was ridiculous but I wanted something back from her. Some sense of communication that would give me courage. Her blood was in my veins, and, as I remembered unwillingly, so was that of William Fitzsimons. Reaching the first landing, I told myself that I was in this situation on my own. Sophia was a face imprisoned in a frame on a wall, just as she had once been a prisoner for weeks in her room. The only hope to be gained from her might be in the diary, and I didn't have that with me, for which I felt grateful as I hurried across that landing beset by the creepy memory of the sprinkled confetti and the whispered singing of "Here Comes the Bride."

It was a relief to reach my room and to know, if Thora had been telling the truth, that it hadn't been Sophia's. I was tired. And didn't want to think anymore. I didn't want to wonder, amidst all the other horrors, whether there was any person in this house who wasn't lying about something. Now even I was doing it. I had lied to Richard and Arthur. And I'd done it to Edna just now. Everything that posed a question, anything that might form a piece of the puzzle, had to matter if I was ever to find out who had murdered my mother. The only thing I was sure of was that it all went back to Sophia and . . . I stopped in my tracks . . . that she had used the pages torn from the diary to write her notes to Hawthorn Lane. And somehow . . . I didn't know why . . . that should be telling me something.

I sat down on the edge of the bed. But my mind wouldn't un-fog. Overwhelmed by exhaustion, I climbed under the bedclothes and closed my eyes. At first I was afraid to sleep in case there should be a return of the hatefully whispering visitor. What was the point of locking my door when she had managed to get in despite that barrier last night? I would just lie still and try to relax. But after five or ten minutes when my nerves were still stretched as tight as the strings of a harp, I reached under my pillow for *Secrets of the Crypt*. Joining Phoebe on her journey through Cragstone Castle seemed preferable to staying trapped on my own dark page, so I flipped through until I found the place where I had left off.

Lord Rothbourne had again invited her to join him in the withdrawing room and was explaining to her that she must under no circumstances attempt to get past the black dog guarding the entrance to the tower room. There was nothing inside but his hunting trophies, he told her, looking fiendishly handsome despite the livid scar (which I didn't remember being mentioned earlier) trammeling his left cheek. And, he conceded, there was also a stack of slashed portraits of his deranged wife. She had claimed that they gave her the vapors and had attempted to overdose on her smelling salts. But that was all of minor import. His main purpose in summoning Phoebe was to commend her on her plain face and mouse-like demeanor and to invite her to take a spin with him out into the gardens in his wheelchair.

Once ensconced in the gazebo overlooking the lake where his twin brother had drowned himself in a fit of pique after losing at a game of snap with their grandmother, Lord Rothbourne ordered Phoebe to attend the annual masked ball. His housekeeper would have suggestions as to a costume. Perhaps one modeled after the one worn by his ancestress, the first Lady Rothbourne, whose portrait hung in the portrait gallery and who had laid a curse on all future governesses. Seemingly, she had been ticked off by the one who had seduced her husband, a gentleman who had previously claimed to have been reduced to a pathetic shadow of his formerly lascivious self by an injury received in the Napoleonic wars. The complete details of the curse had been lost in the folds of time but Lord

Rothbourne was able to relate the part which demanded that any woman hired to provide instruction to the young at Cragstone Castle must attain fluency in Latin and Greek. Phoebe was explaining that she already spoke both, in addition to fourteen other languages, including Arabic, Swahili, and Gaelic. And that while they were having this little chat she would like to request an afternoon off so that she could march for women's rights, practice her hospital bandaging, and learn to ride a horse. At which point Lord Rothbourne winced at the memory of his hunting accident that hadn't been mentioned in several pages and my eyes drifted shut.

I tried to stay awake or at least get up and lock the door, on the premise that a stable half-bolted was better than nothing, but I heard the book slide to the floor and felt my hand reach under the pillow. This time for my mother's ballet slippers, and holding them close, I slept. There were no dreams this time, at least none that I remembered when I came back up to the surface after what seemed like hours. And the clock on the bedside table agreed with me. It was almost five. Instead of waking feeling warm and snuggly as I always did at Merlin's Court, I was shivering with cold, and when I sat up and rubbed my arms, my teeth started to chatter.

A glance out the window showed that the sky had turned overcast and I was sure that rain would soon be pelting the windows. What I needed was to curl up under an extra blanket or two. It occurred to me that the coffin-sized chest in the bathroom might serve a purpose other than to reduce the remaining space to the barest minimum. So I climbed out of bed and went through the doorway to snap on the light. It had darkened considerably in the last few minutes as the rain had indeed started coming down, accompanied by rumbles of thunder. After removing my sponge bag I raised the pink lid decorated with butterflies. My heart stopped beating as I stared down in bewilderment. There were no blankets inside. There was nothing inside. What was revealed was a flight of rough-hewn stone steps enclosed by a wall that looked as though it might have been whitewashed a century and a half ago. So this was how my nocturnal visitor had gained entry! I was halfway down those steps before I realized I had moved my feet. The light from above provided sufficient illumination, so I wasn't in danger of stumbling. When I reached the bottom I was in an empty cellar. Who would store anything in such a dank place? I could see an archway opening onto another staircase. It had to be the one leading up to the hall—the one I'd found when I was looking for the downstairs loo yesterday. And there was another door that I knew, even before I went and checked it out, must open onto the back garden. When I turned the knob, I met with a grunt of resistance but soon I was standing outside getting splattered with rain.

I went back up the stone steps faster than I had gone down them, closed the lid of the blanket chest, and peeled off my damp clothes. This staircase, I reflected, must have been put in so that the maids carrying up coal or firewood to the top floors wouldn't have to haul their buckets through the hall. My discovery of the door into the garden didn't add much, I told myself as I got into the shower, because all one of the bridesmaids had to do was take the stairs from the hall down to the cellar and the other ones up here. If my invader had been anyone else, Leonard Skinner for instance, that would have been a different matter. But why hadn't it been locked? An oversight? The cellar wasn't a place to invite frequent visits. While toweling off, I decided that tonight before going to sleep I would drag the trunk from the foot of the bed into the bathroom and put it on top of the blanket chest. That should put paid to another nighttime visit.

My thoughts refused to go further. I brushed my teeth, did my hair, decided against bothering with makeup, and got dressed in the first thing I could grab out of my case. I had just finished buttoning the front of the olive-green dress that the saleswoman had said was supposed to have a creased look, when a tap sounded at the door and Jane's voice informed me that dinner would be ready in fifteen minutes.

"Thank you," I called back and spent several of those minutes longing for the feel of Ben's arms around me. It was time. I couldn't put off going downstairs any longer.

Rosemary was waiting for me in the hall. At least I didn't feel underdressed. Her skirt, blouse, and cardigan were the ones she had worn earlier in the day. It struck me that her hair was not as neatly combed as usual and that her octagonal glasses could have done with a polish.

"You look nice, Ellie. Green suits you, as it did your grandmother." She led the way into the dining room with its pleasantly old-fashioned rose-patterned wallpaper and well-polished furniture. Jane and Thora were already seated across from each other at the long table. It was laid with a linen tablecloth that might well have turned Gwen Fiddler green with envy. The bone china dinner service was of a pleasing, fairly modern design but the solid silver cutlery looked old. In the center were a pair of Georgian candelabras, with their candles unlit.

"I thought we'd wait to light them until Edna has cleared away and Hope arrives." Rosemary pulled out a chair for me next to Thora before taking her place beside Jane. "I imagine she will want us grouped around a table."

"The trouble is that this one is so big," Jane demurred, "we'll have to stand up and lean across it to hold hands in a circle if we're to create the necessary emanations."

"You and your emanations!" Thora grunted, her eyes startlingly dark this evening against her snow-white crop of hair.

"I can't help the fact that I'm more in tune with the invisible forces than you are," flared Jane.

"Cod's wallop!" was the response she drew.

"Please, girls, no squabbling!" Rosemary pressed a hand to her brow. "Whatever will Ellie think of you?"

"It's quite all right," I said, staring down at my plate. "This is a stressful situation."

"Oh, I don't know." Thora's dimples appeared fleetingly. "I'm rather hoping that Ted puts in an appearance along with Sophia, so that I can tell him just how little he's going to be missed."

"You do say the most obnoxious things!" Rosemary's voice sounded depleted.

"I call it refusing to hide behind a load of sentimental claptrap."

"He's probably up there listening to every word you're saying and plotting ways to get even." Jane shivered and the black bow slid further down her neck. "Listen to that thunder! It doesn't sound normal. It's Ted, I tell you. Any minute now the windowpanes are going to crack from top to bottom and huge shards of glass are going to come hurtling into the room and we'll be sliced to ribbons."

"If Ted should put in an appearance we could ask him how the accident happened," I said as casually as I could manage.

Rosemary pressed a finger to her lips, and with good reason. Before she could lower it, Edna entered the room with a couple of serving dishes to add to the ones already lined up on the sideboard. As if aware of the charged atmosphere, she went silently back and forth setting them on the table, placed a serving spoon beside each one and disappeared back into the kitchen. After that, apart from someone's asking to have this or that passed, not more than the odd word or two was spoken during the course of the meal. It looked to be an excellent one of braised beef in a rich gravy, served with plenty of vegetables. But I for one was hardly aware of what I was eating. Nor did I manage more than a few mouthfuls of the treacle tart and custard that followed.

"Everything was excellent," Rosemary told Edna when she returned with the coffeepot. "And it was good of you to stay late. Jane and Ellie can take their cups and saucers into the sitting room; Thora and I will join them after we've helped you clear away."

"I'd as soon do it on my own," Edna replied. "I need to keep busy and I'm always best left to myself. It goes quicker that way, Miss Maywood. More elbow room in the kitchen, but thanks for offering."

"If you're quite sure?" Rosemary got to her feet and Thora, Jane, and I followed her into the sitting room, where we sat in silence listening to the ticking clock. It was half past six. At ten minutes to seven Edna, in coat and hat, stuck her head through the doorway to say that the washing-up was done, except for one saucepan that she'd had to leave soaking in the sink. She said she would be off now and we all bade her goodnight before turning our eyes back to the clock. As it began to strike seven, the doorbell rang. Rosemary went out into the hall and returned, before the rest of us could finish exchanging glances, with Hope. The witch woman with the wild black and orange hair and the incredible green eyes.

"I've come," she said, "but I don't think I can go through with the séance. Not tonight. As I was coming up the path, before I had even set foot over the threshold, I felt that the emanations are not right."

"Oh, but they are," Jane exclaimed, "and now that you're here I sense Sophia's presence even more strongly. It's as though she's right here in this room waiting to step through the veil separating us from the great divide."

"I don't disagree with you, Mrs. Pettinger." Hope hadn't moved from where she stood just inside the doorway. "But there are other forces at work here. Deadly, diabolical ones, and I cannot risk ignoring them. The consequences might be too dreadful and irreversible. Something has changed in this house since I was last here. The darkness has returned."

"It's my patience that's in peril at this minute." Thora's voice deepened into a growl. "I came round to this séance thing. Thought if nothing else it would make Rosemary feel she had done everything possible to prevent Sir Clifford from turning us out of this house. And, I've got to say, I was halfway convinced that you did have the sight or whatever it's called. Now I'm wondering if you aren't playing games with us. Hoping that if we have to beg and plead with you to go ahead you'll hear a voice inaudible to the rest of us. One telling you that the only way you can safely call upon Sophia to make an appearance is if you extract a sizable sum of money from us. Cash up front. No checks. No credit cards."

"Oh, Thora." Jane was practically sobbing.

"Of course Hope senses something different in this house." Rosemary's voice lacked all expression. "A man bled to death outside in the garden yesterday afternoon."

"Not the case," responded an unabashed Thora. "He waited to draw his last breath until he reached the hospital. One of the few thoughtful things he did in his life."

"I heard about it." Hope fixed those impossibly green eyes on my face. "And not from Ted Wilks himself the moment he set foot on the other side. But that's neither here nor there. The dark forces I speak of do not emanate from beyond the grave. This evil lives and breathes and it is directed against Mrs. Haskell."

"But that's impossible! It's also wicked. I'm glad now that dear Thora was rude to you." Jane's glasses looked ready to take flight on their black wings. "Why would any one of us wish to hurt Ellie?" There were tears in her pale eyes as she looked at me. "She's the granddaughter of our precious Sophia. She's Mina's daughter."

"I could be wrong." Hope pushed back her wild mane of

hair. "I did tell you from the outset that I am not a professional psychic. Just a woman with a possibly overdeveloped sense of intuition, who, if Mrs. Haskell should have the misfortune to meet with an accident, as did Ted Wilks, would consider it her duty to go straight to the police. You may pass that word along to anyone you think might be interested, because—you understand—I am not making a direct accusation, just wishing to be neighborly." Leaving a heavy silence in her wake, she brushed past Rosemary on her way out into the hall, where a scratching could be heard at the front door. When she opened it the lean gray dog bounded inside. And after making his way into the sitting room and weaving around Thora's and Jane's legs, he skidded to a panting halt in front of me, rose up to place his front paws on my chest, and gazed soulfully into my eyes.

"They do say dogs know things, don't they?" Hope's smile did not reach her green eyes. "Come, Shadow! I think it's safe for us to leave Mrs. Haskell." She patted her thigh. He whimpered, but reluctantly dropped back down and with several backward glances at me wove his way back around the legs that hadn't moved to join her with drooping head at the door. "Oh, I do have one message from Sophia." Hope addressed Rosemary, who looked ready to crumple to the floor.

"Yes."

"It's for Mrs. Haskell."

"What is it?" I moved forward on what felt like wooden legs that hadn't been properly fitted.

"She wants you to know that she didn't kill her father." With that, Hope and Shadow went out the door. And I stood staring at the bridesmaids, too stunned to consider what had transpired before that shocking statement.

"What did she mean?"

"Come back into the sitting room and we'll all have a glass of elderberry wine." Thora had materialized at my side and was marshaling me towards the closest armchair.

"What an appalling woman. Should be struck off the register, if they have such things for psychics. I'd like to write a letter myself requesting an official inquiry."

"But she never claimed to be a professional," Jane pointed out tearfully. "We've got to be fair about that, despite her wicked implications."

"Accusations!" was Thora's brusque retort. Rosemary had yet to move from where she stood rooted in the hall, let alone to speak.

"I don't want anything to drink," I said.

"Of course you don't." Jane stood wringing her hands over me. "You're afraid it would be poisoned or, at the very least, drugged."

I almost mentioned last night's cocoa, but thought better of it. "Someone has to tell me," I said. "It's clear from the looks on all your faces, especially Rosemary's, that you know what that message from Sophia was about."

"But, Ellie, why would you believe anything we have to say after hearing what that malevolent woman said about the three of us being the dark forces of evil intent on doing you harm?" Jane slumped down on the sofa, the black bow dislodged and her hair hanging down her back now. "And now that I think about it, I'm sure she was suggesting that we might have had something to do with Ted's accident. Only it wouldn't have been an accident in that case, would it?"

"Got to pull ourselves together." Thora handed her a glass of wine and did the same for Rosemary, who had haltingly made her way to a chair. "Whatever we said yesterday, that woman has to be in Sir Clifford's pay. The man's out to unhinge us by whatever means. Amelia Chambers went back last night and reported that she hadn't got anywhere with Rosemary. He doesn't have all the legal cards up his sleeve as she claimed. So this is his next move."

Rosemary finally spoke. "That is a possibility. But what about Sophia's message?"

"That is the part even I find puzzling." Thora sat down

and sipped at her glass of wine. "How could Hope know about that? Sophia impressed on all of us that she wasn't going to tell Hawthorn. And she made the three of us swear that we wouldn't either. She was afraid if he knew, he would try to talk her out of her decision to marry William Fitzsimons. She said that was the penance she had to pay for what she had done."

"And what had she done?"

"Put sleeping tablets in her father's tea." Fortified by two swallows of alcohol, Jane now looked a little less woebegone. "Gladys, or sometimes Edna if she was there, always took a cup into his study after Sunday lunch. After she had agreed to marry William, Sophia saw that time as her one opportunity to get out of house and meet Hawthorn. We knew about that, but not about the tablets. She didn't tell us about that until after he was found dead, slumped across his desk. Rosemary, Thora, and I were all in the house that day. We were there to try on our bridesmaid frocks. We were actually wearing them when Sophia came running upstairs to tell us. She'd come back from seeing Thorn, as she called him, and gone into her father's study. And that's when she told us everything. Her mother, Mrs. McNair, hadn't presented a problem because she always went out to choir practice on Sunday afternoon. It was her father who was the difficulty. And Sophia decided to get round that with the sleeping tablets. But the week before, she'd had a scare. He'd been awake when she got back, and in a towering rage demanded to know where she'd been. She told him she'd gone for a walk in the garden and he appeared to believe her, but she was afraid of the same thing happening again, so on the Sunday he died, she'd doubled the dose."

"Where did she get the tablets?" I wanted to know.

"They were her mother's. She started taking them when Sophia was refusing to marry William," Thora said. "But Mrs. McNair didn't want word getting around Knells that the vicar's wife needed sleeping tablets. Wouldn't have done at all! She had Rosemary get them from the chemist's where she was training." Thora chortled without amusement. "Such a fuss! She refused to take them with a sip of water, because she said Gladys had almost died after taking some when she was drinking!"

"But surely Sophia couldn't seriously have thought she'd killed her father by putting a couple of tablets in a cup of tea?" I protested.

"Not at first. But afterwards there was no getting her to believe otherwise, even though the doctor had said it was a heart attack." Thora shook her head. "Her feelings of guilt completely swamped her common sense. I don't think that even a postmortem would have convinced her she wasn't to blame. Isn't that right, Rosemary?"

She received no reply. The woman who had spoken barely a word since Hope's departure got up from her chair and walked out of the room. And because my mind was in such a muddle, the only thought that worked its way to the surface was that the first Mrs. Fiddler's death had been written off as a heart attack too, and, if Mrs. Malloy had understood Gwen correctly, that hadn't been the case.

# CHAPTER FOURTEEN

THE BRIDESMAIDS HAD sounded so convincing that I'd found myself believing that Sophia's father, Reverend McNair, had died as befitted a man of the cloth, from natural causes. And perhaps two out of the three had been speaking what they believed to be the truth. Had Rosemary left the room because she was stricken by remorse? Or because she knew that one or another had to be lying? Now, sitting on my bed a half hour later, I felt as though my mind had turned into a bog of the sort that Phoebe might have decided to amble across on her day off. But a few conclusions bubbled their way to the surface.

Someone had murdered Reverend McNair. That person had wanted Sophia to assume the burden of guilt, and had also known that the vicar was a secret imbiber. I had a flash of memory: of Frank standing in the lane with his walking stick, talking about his boyhood prank of looking in the vicar's study window on Sunday afternoons and seeing Reverend McNair empty his teacup into a plant pot. Not all that puzzling a circumstance if Edna's mother couldn't make a decent brew. Even less so if there was a bottle of cherry brandy secreted in the study. It wouldn't have mattered how many pills Sophia put in his tea, other than to put the plant to sleep for a week. Probably the reason her father had been awake when she arrived on the Sunday afternoon prior to the one in question was that something, perhaps a visit from his son-in-law-to-be, had prevented him from getting into the booze. Or he might have discovered that Gladys had failed to replenish his supply, which would account for his bad temper. What mattered was that the killer knew that the prescribed dosage of pills was not to be taken with alcohol. Making it almost a certainty that a large quantity ground to powder and mixed in with the cherry brandy was likely to prove fatal. If the killer was as clever as I thought, the thing to have done was to make sure that there was only one bottle of brandy in the vicar's hiding place and that it was just sufficiently full to get the job done. No point in diluting the effect of the pills.

I could see a shadow in my mind's eye of someone keeping watch to make sure no one else went into the study before the empty bottle could be retrieved. But from the sound of it, that risk would have been small. Mrs. McNair was out at choir practice. It would have been unlikely that the two other bridesmaids would have interrupted Sophia's father in his study. And Gladys or Edna, whichever one of them had served lunch that day, would have finished the washing-up and gone home. Or would they? I got up and began prowling the bedroom.

Had I been wrong in so readily concluding that one of the bridesmaids was the villain of the piece? What if Reverend McNair had caved in to William Fitzsimons's insistence that he give Gladys the sack because of her drinking? Or that he'd found out that Edna had been Sophia's accomplice in communicating with Hawthorn Lane and had in a towering rage given mother and daughter the boot? I sat down on the trunk at the foot of the bed.

Was finding oneself out of a job sufficient reason for murder? Perhaps—if there was no other money coming in. But Edna had told me that she was doing housework for other people at the time. And even if that wasn't true, or if it hadn't made any difference to her or her mother's venomous feelings towards Reverend McNair, I couldn't get past the feeling that the killer had wanted Sophia to take the blame for her father's death. And what would be the reason in this particular scenario? Far better for Edna or Gladys that no suspicions were raised at all.

I got up and began prowling again. Of course, the doctor at the death scene must have known Reverend McNair had been drinking. He would have smelled it on his breath and not been gullible enough to think that the man had been sucking on cherry-flavored cough drops. But he was unlikely to be shocked, or to mention the fact to the grieving widow or the daughter, who was about to marry a man known to have strong views on the subject. The clergy, with the possible exception of William Fitzsimons, are human after all. The doctor would have seen the teacup with the dribble of cherry brandy inside and probably smiled. The cup of course wouldn't be the one Reverend McNair had used, and the brandy would contain no residue of the pills. Oh, yes! I was sure the killer had been craftily careful about such details. Unless the object had been to get the daughter charged with her father's murder. Was it too far-fetched to believe that either Gladys or Edna, for the motive I had ascribed to them, was so consumed with rage that she would have wanted to take it out on Sophia to the extent of seeing her imprisoned for life? Or—worse yet—hanged? So what had the killer wished to happen to Sophia? I had to be tired to pose that question. It had been answered in the sitting room this evening. To end her relationship with Hawthorn Lane, by convincing her that she now had no alternative but to marry William Fitzsimons.

It was all about Hawthorn—the handsome scoundrel named for the road where he had been abandoned as a baby. The sort of young man from whose clutches every right-thinking parent would fight tooth and nail to keep a daughter. Arrogant, willful, heedless of what people, especially in those days, would regard as the proprieties. And the young women had found him irresistible. Which one of the bridesmaids had been in love with him? Which one had hoped that with Sophia well out the way in the Belgian Congo he would turn to her? As perhaps he had previously turned while Sophia was completing her last year at boarding school? That hope hadn't been realized and then, years later, Sophia's diary had turned up in a trunk and someone, an innocent party, with nothing to hide, had insisted that it be taken to my mother. And that was something the killer could not—would not—risk. Either she had read it and come upon an entry that pointed to her involvement in Reverend McNair's death, or her guilty conscience had driven her into a blind panic.

She may not have intended to kill again, but that didn't alter the fact that my mother was dead. Even so, she had again been lucky. No one came forward. No one claimed to have seen her push my mother down those steps at Kings Cross. Life went on until the past again reared its head. Sir Clifford Heath proved to be Hawthorn Lane and I was invited to the Old Rectory. But why use scare tactics to drive me away? I could understand Richard Barttle's doing so. He feared for my life. But why would the killer want to stir up what was safest laid to rest? I shivered and realized I was even more chilled than I had been when I'd woken from my nap and gone looking for a blanket in that chest—which wasn't really a chest at all. And I remembered my determination to put the trunk on top of it before I got into bed.

It wasn't an easy task, even accustomed as I was to moving around furniture at Merlin's Court, but I had just finished the job and was standing panting in the archway between the bathroom and the bedroom when I heard a tap at the door. Before I could squeeze out enough breath to ask who was there, Rosemary came in.

"I've got to talk to you," she said without preamble.

"All right." I looked around for something to cosh her with if she got too close.

"I'm sure that when you saw Richard Barttle this morning he gave you Sophia's diary." She stood with her arms at her sides. And it struck me that she looked like a headmistress immune to understanding how anyone could hate gym while at the same resembling a defensive schoolgirl. "He'll have given you the details of when I took it to him."

I waited for her to demand that I fetch it and hand it to her, but instead she sat down on the edge of the bed and looked up at me through those rimless octagonal glasses of hers, with bleary eyes. Then she said something that I found puzzling: "I'd hoped that in taking it to Mina I'd be making some small reparation for destroying her mother's life." She continued, "I didn't know what was in the diary. Jane and Thora agreed with me that we had no right to pry into Sophia's private thoughts even at that late date."

"Really?" I continued standing in the archway.

"We didn't know that she'd ever kept a diary. She'd never seemed much of a girl for writing. Except when it came to her letters to Hawthorn. And she once told me laughingly that he complained they were too short. She said she could put her thoughts down far better in her drawing and painting than she ever could in words."

"So you telephoned my mother at our flat to ask her to meet you at Kings Cross?"

"She suggested the place. I don't think she wanted to spend much time with me. Not because she disliked me, at least I don't think so. It was more, I think, that she didn't want to be reminded of the Old Rectory. But she did say that she would like the diary. And in addition to giving it to her I wanted to tell her the whole story. But I didn't say anything about that to Thora and Jane. They were against my taking the diary in the first place. They thought it might contain information that would be upsetting to Mina.

Things about the way her father had treated her mother. But my belief was that she already knew what sort of a man he was and it couldn't make too much difference under the circumstances."

"What circumstances?"

Rosemary didn't appear to hear me. "Looking back I realize it was a mistake and that I was acting out of my own selfish compulsion to lift the burden that had haunted me through the years and still does. That's why I was of two minds about having you here. Part of me dreaded the idea, the rest hoped that at long last I could make some sort of amends."

"How?" I asked, while telling myself that I mustn't allow myself to be taken in by her pitiful demeanor.

"By telling you what I intended to tell Mina. That she wasn't William Fitzsimons's daughter. She was Hawthorn Lane's child. Sophia didn't tell me, and I'm sure she didn't know she was pregnant when she married William. If she'd had even a suspicion she would never have gone through with it. And I never heard from her after she left for the Belgian Congo. I told you she wasn't one to write, but I don't think she would have kept in touch anyway, not with me. It was William who told me Mina wasn't his daughter, she'd been born barely seven months after the wedding, and that was the reason he did not intend to leave her the house."

"You never said a word about this to my mother when she brought me here that day?"

Rosemary shook her head. "I'd lived so long trying to block out all memories of Sophia, which is undoubtedly why I suffered a severe nervous breakdown that forced me to give up my job. But when I found the diary it seemed like a sign from Sophia, as if she were reaching out to me from beyond the grave. And I had the same sort of feeling when this business with Hawthorn—Sir Clifford—came up. I would have sold out to him if it hadn't been that I would have been letting down the other villagers, when here was my opportunity to try and do something decent. There was also the fact that I'd have had to explain to Thora and Jane why I was willing to give in without a fight. They never knew, you see, about the role I'd played in persuading Sophia that she had killed her father."

"And what role was that?" I no longer felt chilled. I was numb.

"Thora was right." Rosemary hadn't shifted her position. "At first Sophia wasn't convinced he had died because she'd put those sleeping tablets in his tea. Even though she had doubled the dose. But she was in a very agitated state of mind. She had been through so much in recent weeks and had such conflicting feelings about her father. He wasn't an ogre. He could be very kind, as he and Aunt Agatha both were in allowing me to live here while I was in training at the chemist's. Sophia wanted to put her mind at rest by talking to the doctor and telling him what she had done. Just so she wouldn't always wonder about it. She told me what she was going to do. With our being cousins she was closer to me than she was to Thora or Jane. Until that moment I hadn't known anything about what she had been up to. Not even that she had been slipping out on Sunday afternoons to meet Hawthorn. I was usually away from the house at those times playing tennis, sometimes with Thora and Jane if they were down for the weekend but more often with Richard Barttle. I had rather a crush on him. No, that's not strong enough—I was in love with him, or thought I was, not realizing he couldn't reciprocate. When Sophia confided in me on the evening of her father's death, it came as a dreadful shock—the part about her planning to talk to Dr. Gibson. Because she also told me that he hadn't refilled her mother's prescription. And, as she had known I also occasionally took a sleeping tablet, she had taken the tablets for her father the last couple of times from the bottle in my room. What she didn't know was that I didn't have a prescription for them. I'd been feeling depressed for months over Richard's not showing any romantic interest, so I'd gone to see Dr. Gibson and told him I wasn't sleeping. But he said that all I needed was to get plenty of exercise and drink a cup of hot milk at bedtime. So I took some from work. Just a few at a time, so I wouldn't get caught, at least that's what I told myself. I couldn't have got away with it for very long."

"And you were afraid that if Sophia told Dr. Gibson she had used your tablets you would find yourself in terrible trouble," I said.

"At the very least"—Rosemary sat rubbing her arms—"I would never have been allowed to work as a dispenser again. My parents would have to be told, but it was worse than that. At that moment when I was talking with Sophia I really thought I would be sent to prison. I was afraid that if I asked her not to go to Dr. Gibson's on my account she might refuse, saying that I was exaggerating the possible consequences to myself. And wasn't it every bit as important that she not have to go through life wondering if she had contributed to her father's death? I felt I couldn't risk telling her the truth, so I said that my sleeping tablets weren't the same as her mother's. They couldn't be taken by anyone with the least possibility of a bad heart, so were only prescribed for young people. And seeing that Dr. Gibson hadn't even suggested a postmortem, he must have believed from examining her father on prior occasions that there was a heart problem."

"How did Sophia react?"

"She became hysterical. She said she would never forgive herself. That there was nothing she could ever do to make up for his death. And if what she had done were to come out and she were charged with his murder, it would kill her mother. So I told her that the only way that was likely to happen was if people began talking about how his dying so suddenly had solved the problem of her being forced to marry William. And how very convenient that was. Making it highly possible that in a matter of time someone would be suggesting his body be exhumed."

"Which you didn't want to happen for your own sake." I wasn't allowing myself to think. I couldn't let myself feel sorry for her or to blame the doctor for not providing her with the help that would have averted the tragedy.

"So now I've told you." Rosemary stood up. "I should feel better, but I don't. Sophia's dead and Mina's dead. And I killed them both. Because if your mother hadn't been on her way to meet me she wouldn't have fallen down those steps. I heard someone who had been on the scene right after the accident talking about how she'd heard your mother—she called her 'that poor woman who broke her leg'—say that somebody pushed her just as she reached the top of the underground steps. And for a while I had an awful feeling that someone had done it on purpose. I don't know why I felt so sure about that. Or felt compelled to take the diary to Richard and ask him to keep it hidden. It must have been my illness. I had another breakdown. That's why Thora and Jane didn't go to the funeral. They were afraid to leave me. I'm so sorry for it all, Ellie, and I don't ask you to forgive me."

"I'm sorry, too," I said. I believed her. I couldn't at that moment think of any reason for her to make up such a harrowing story. I might even have gone back to believing that my mother's death had been accidental and that Reverend McNair had really died from heart problems, if it hadn't been for the frightening events of the past two days.

"What are you going to do, Ellie?"

"I don't know," I told her. But I did. I was going to see my grandfather, Sir Clifford Heath, and give him Sophia's diary. Because if Richard Barttle, who had been her dear friend, hadn't been able to find anything revealing within its pages, it was unlikely I would either. But the man who had loved her might.

When Rosemary left without either of us saying another word, I locked the door and leaned against it for several moments until my thoughts stopped whirling and settled in a ball in the middle of my stomach. I should leave this madhouse right now. All I had to do was throw everything back into my suitcase. I didn't even have to take the staircase down to the hall and risk being heard by someone lying awake and alert in her bedroom. I could use the one that descended from the blanket chest. This meant heaving the trunk back onto the floor. But five minutes later I had my raincoat on over the green dress that now looked and felt as though I had slept in it for days, its having creased every bit as successfully as the saleswoman had promised me it would. And with handbag and case in hand was making my cautious way down those rough-hewn steps. All I needed was to trip and be found helpless and just waiting to be finished off at the bottom. When I looked down, my eyes had spots in front of them. Tiny, pastel-colored . . . confetti-sized ones. I hadn't noticed them on my previous venture into the cellar. I had been thinking only that I had discovered how the nocturnal visitor had got into my room. My earlier fright had been blocked from my mind.

Now I shivered and with each step remembered the scent of orange blossom while my heart thudded out the tune to "Here Comes the Bride." I pictured, in the black and white of the photographs hanging on the walls of Richard Barttle and Arthur Henshaw's studio, my illwisher squinting through the partially raised lid of the blanket chest to make sure no one was in the room, before tiptoeing to the door, opening it a crack, and chanting that twisted version of the song. But what if one or more of the bridesmaids had come upstairs with me and seen the confetti sprinkled in that trail across the landing? The orange blossom could have been explained away as air freshener. Hadn't Jane said she had smelled it on several occasions? The rest wouldn't have been so easy to dismiss. Had someone deliberately created her emanations, as she called them? So that if need be it would be thought that Jane was so determined to believe in her fantasies for the sake of the drama it added to her life that she was prepared to bring them to life? I had reached the bottom steps. If Jane along with Rosemary was in the clear, that left Thora. The woman who might not have needed to come up with a supply of powdered sleeping tablets to dose Reverend McNair's cherry brandy because she already knew her plants and herbs so well.

I was now in the dank-smelling cellar. In addition to the electric light coming down from my bedroom there was some of the natural sort sifting in through the narrow window set in the front wall of the house. But even though it was a large space and empty, with not so much as a broom handle to hide behind, I kept glancing over my shoulder, expecting a figure to rise up larger than life and prevent my reaching the door. Or that I would find it locked this time and the key still gone. Neither of these terrors came to pass and I sped along the path that led through the vine-covered archway into the front garden and out through the gate to where my car was parked at the curb.

I set the suitcase down and was wondering, between panting breaths, if Tom and his wife would be particularly chuffed when I knocked on their door at this late hour. To ask for the return of the box containing the diary and the photograph of the Old Mill. I had to fish deep in my handbag for my keys, and the moment I had them in my hand I dropped them. When bending to pick them up, I saw that both the front and the back tires were completely flat. It was a pointless exercise, but I went round to check the other side. Those two were fine. But I knew I wasn't going anywhere tonight unless I walked to the closest railway station, which was undoubtedly miles from Knells. I glanced at my watch and saw that it was going on ten—no buses would be running at this hour. Not in such a small village. It didn't make sense, I thought as I picked up my suitcase and crept back around the house and reentered the cellar. Why would the person who was so anxious to get rid of me make it impossible for me to drive away in my car? Standing in the doorway I stared back over my shoulder towards the garden shed and the tree that overhung it, and remembered the shadowy figure of a man who might have been Leonard that I had glimpsed when I closed the curtains last night. I went back up the stone steps.

When I had returned the trunk, hardly aware of its weight this time, onto the lid of the blanket chest and locked the bedroom door, I lay down, still in my raincoat, on top of the patchwork quilt. I didn't want to risk getting too warm and comfortable in case I fell into a deep sleep. I couldn't banish the fear that even with the precautions I had taken my fiendish aggressor would find some Houdini-like means of gaining entry and I would wake up dead, as Mrs. Malloy might have put it. I made myself think about Ben and the children and how much I loved them. I wondered what he would have to say when I told him my grandfather owned Memory Lanes. I wondered and wondered and dozed and woke and then dozed again. And when I opened my eyes I saw, on looking at the clock on the bedside chest, that it was morning. To be precise it was seven-thirty. Leaping up with all the energy of someone who had slept for a week, I grabbed my handbag and case and headed downstairs. I took the stairs to the hall this time. Daylight had brought a return of courage. Should someone try to stop me walking out the front door, they would get a punch in the nose at the very least.

Rosemary came out from the sitting room as I reached the bottom, looking as though she hadn't slept a wink and couldn't have withstood my breathing in her direction.

"You're leaving," she said. "There's nothing I can do to stop you?"

"Other than flattening my other two tires, nothing." I didn't like the sound of my voice, it sounded so hard.

"I don't know what you're talking about, Ellie." She wasn't wearing her glasses, which made her look extra-vulnerable. And despite everything I found myself wanting to put my arms around her. "Too soft by half, that's you, Mrs. H.!" I could hear Mrs. Malloy saying. And, stiffening my spine, I walked through the front door and out onto the lane, where I turned towards the cottages at the top and suddenly found myself knocking on Tom's door. He opened up within seconds and gave me a beaming smile that incongruously made his face look more pugnacious than ever. He invited me inside as I hurriedly told him that I was leaving by train because my car wasn't working. And, after fetching the box—which he assured me, as if standing with his hand on a stack of Bibles, he had not peeked at—he offered to drive me to the station.

"On a mission for the ladies, one connected with this Memory Lanes business?" Tom asked as we drove along in the van from which he delivered his fish.

"Well, I guess you could say that," I answered, and he said he was proud as Punch to help out in any way he could, even if it meant putting his life at stake. I told him that this was unlikely to be necessary, but thanks very much. And in great good cheer he parked outside the station, which turned out to be in Rilling, accompanied me to the ticket office, offered to pay my fare, and then waited with me on the platform until my train arrived some five minutes later.

There were plenty of empty seats and I chose one with no one occupying either side of the dividing table. Having stowed my case in the overhead bin, I sat down next to the window just as the train started up again. And with my handbag at my side, I opened the box and unwrapped the diary from its sheets of tissue paper. But I couldn't bring myself to open it at once. Instead I stared out at the buildings and houses flashing by until green fields replaced them, some with sheep grazing in them as if posing while

Constable painted them. The children loved to look for animals in fields when Ben and I took them on outings. There were always squabbles between Abbey and Tam over who had spotted the first cow and whether in fact it was a cow. Which always ended up with my suggesting that we look for dragons instead.

I opened the brown leather-bound book with "Diary" embossed on the front and, after leafing through it, saw what Richard had meant when telling me Sophia had her own way of putting her thoughts down on paper. There was nothing written on any of the lined pages, apart from the date printed halfway down each page, providing limited space from day to day in which to pour out one's heart in words. Sophia had poured hers out in drawings. Some in ink, but most of them in pencil. There were several of the Old Mill and of St. John's churchyard and of cottages and houses—one of them I was sure I had seen when walking down Hawthorn Lane yesterday. It had a particularly beautiful tree in the garden. Sophia showed it casting a graceful shadow over the lawn.

But mostly they were drawings of people. Some full-length, in varying poses. Others were headshots. Many in profile, but a number full-face. I came across vividly recognizable likenesses of the bridesmaids. The fact that they were elderly now and had been girls when these were drawn didn't matter. Not only had Sophia rendered them accurately, she had captured their expressions. Ones that were a part of their personal landscape. Others that I'd seen flit across their features or show in their eyes a moment and be gone the next—as in the case of sturdy Thora, when she had talked about her relationship with Michael, the man who had finally gone back to his wife. More than that, Sophia seemed to have captured some inner essence of all three. It was amazing, the power of those drawings. I came across ones of a man and a woman—elderly, rather than middle-aged. I knew they had to be her parents. Far from being drawn with malice, there was a certain, possibly reluctant tenderness in their rendition. Reverend McNair was depicted down to his clerical collar and had an irascible look about him, as if he could have benefited from being put in the corner until he learned to behave as nice vicars should. Mrs. McNair was wearing the black hat I had found in the wardrobe. She appeared to be just as described to me—the sort of woman who bustles about, sorting out other people's lives for them until they find themselves again. I came across the missing page that Richard had mentioned—in addition to the ones torn from the back of the diary. Then leafed through a few more drawings of the Old Mill and came to a woman wearing an apron and an unmistakable hangover. Who from a faint resemblance to Edna had to be her mother, Gladys.

But the vast majority—pages and pages—were of a young man who could be none other than Hawthorn Lane. He was every bit as handsome as I had imagined him. But there was none of the arrogance and surly resentment of the disadvantages dealt him that I had pictured. There were drawings of him with mischievous laughter brimming in his eyes. Others showed his face in repose, and if such a masculine face could be called beautiful, his was. A particularly evocative full-length drawing showed him leaning against that tree in the garden of the house I'd thought I recognized and there was sorrow mingled with a great yearning on his shadowed face. Something stirred in me. A remembrance of those early days with Ben, when I wanted time to stand still long enough for me to etch every beloved detail of him on my heart.

The train pulled up to a platform, a surge of people got on—one of them an earnest-looking young man who sat down beside me, opened up his laptop computer, and began clicking away at the keys. I closed the diary. I had been impressed by the drawings, curiously moved by the ones of Hawthorn Lane. But I was also deflated. Richard had been right. I had come across nothing to suggest why anyone would have been desperate to prevent Rosemary from giving it to my mother. Not one of those drawings cried out to be titled "Murderer!" There wasn't a wicked-looking face or figure amongst the group. And the only thing that could be said to strike any incongruity was those printed dates showing through what I believed to be truly gifted miniature works of art. Sophia could have had a great future, instead of a tragically curtailed one.

The soft clicking of the computer keys, along with the murmur of voices coming to me from nearby seats, formed a musical rhythm that entered my head. To lull me, within minutes of the ticket inspector's stopping at my seat, into a doze. When I roused, it was to a stampede of movement in the aisle. We had arrived at Kings Cross. I staggered up, put the diary back in the box with the photograph, took down my case, put the box inside, picked up my handbag, and got off the train to join the herd heading for the barrier. I felt hemmed in and for the first time wondered if I had been followed. But I determinedly shook off the feeling. No one other than myself and five or six strangers had got on the train at Rilling. And I didn't have that prickling down my spine that I'd felt when leaving the photography studio.

I joined the taxi queue outside. It was fairly short. Not one of those that coil around as though belonging on a board of Snakes and Ladders. Less than five minutes later I was giving my driver directions to Sir Clifford Heath's office building. Tom had given me the address, not seeming surprised that the bridesmaids hadn't done so, saying that he should remember it after all the letters he'd written in conjunction with the other villagers. The taxi plowed through the heart of London, then wove its way amidst a maze of side streets with pricey-looking restaurants, understatedly elegant boutiques, and rows of Georgian houses, to draw up before what appeared to be a converted carriage house. I looked and to my surprise saw that the address was correct. I had been expecting a multi-storied, glass-and-steel building. Could Tom have made a mistake and sent me to Sir Clifford's private residence? I wondered as I paid the driver and got out. But a brass plate beside the door indicated that this was indeed Heath Enterprises.

Ringing the bell, I waited with a fast-beating heart. Why hadn't I planned out word for word what I was going to say to this stranger who was my grandfather and didn't know it? I rather expected an impeccably clad butler with a suitably disdainful expression and a permanently raised eyebrow to open the door. It was that sort of place. But instead I was ushered inside by a woman of uncertain age who might have been the housekeeper—of the sort that ruled the roost at Cragstone Castle, except that she wore a pleasant expression.

"My name is Ellie Haskell," I informed her. "I'm here to see Sir Clifford Heath."

"Do you have an appointment?"

"No, but it's a matter of urgency."

"In what regard?" We were standing in a graciously furnished hall, a far cry from other office vestibules I'd seen. There was a rose-and-blue-patterned silk rug that put Gwen's precious antique to shame, on the cherry-wood floor. Pictures—mainly landscapes that looked as though they had been purchased at auction for sums of money that would have left even the well-to-do spluttering. And a graceful staircase curving its way up to the first floor.

"It's in connection with his desire to purchase the Old Rectory in the village of Knells," I told her.

"He's in a meeting. One that's likely to last all morning. Possibly into the afternoon. And it's more than I would dare to interrupt him," she responded in a still affable voice. "If Ms. Chambers, his personal assistant, were here, you could see her. I do know that he has been awaiting word on the matter to which you refer. The meeting presently taking place is with Sir Clifford's team of architects in regard to the Knells project. I really don't know what to tell you." She stood looking perplexed, as if wondering where to find the silver soup ladle that should have been on the top shelf of the butler's pantry.

"I'd like to wait."

"If you're sure you won't mind sitting for what could be hours, that would perhaps be best. He's really not a difficult man, but he has his rules. I'm the guard dog. Suitably named Mrs. Rover." She smiled and led me past the staircase, which she told me was for Sir Clifford's and Ms. Chambers's use, down the hall into an addition to the building that made up, she told me, the main office space.

"Sir Clifford's architects designed it so that the exterior of the house would retain its Georgian facade." She continued past several glass doors with names and job titles on them and around a corner. We now went up a plain white staircase to a gallery that had been converted into a waiting room with a Chippendale table on which reposed a telephone and other desktop accoutrements. The rest of the considerable space was furnished with comfortable-looking leather sofas and chairs, several glass-enclosed bookcases placed between the row of doors, and a number of side tables on which were set vases of flowers, or magazines and books.

"The powder room is in there." Mrs. Rover pointed to the door closest to us. "There's a brass plate on it, just as there is on the others, so you can't mistake it. Now you relax and I'll be back shortly with a cup of coffee for you."

As soon had she disappeared down the stairs, I undid my case and took out the box. What was to stop me from walking in on Sir Clifford and handing it to him? Nothing, apart from the fact that he might well refuse to take it and order me out the door before I could get out two words of explanation as to why I had come. I looked over at that Chippendale table that served as a desk. A moment later I was sitting behind it with the box close to hand, pulling a pad of paper towards me and picking up the pen that reposed in the crystal tray. Unlike Sophia, I didn't mind writing. I sat organizing my thoughts before getting started. I had completed two pages by the time Mrs. Rover returned with coffee and a plate of biscuits that had almost certainly come from Fortnum & Mason. She didn't reprimand me for making free with the desk and told me, before going back downstairs, that Ms. Chambers had telephoned to say that she would be in within the next couple of hours. That bit of news didn't thrill me. But I didn't let it stop me from filling up another three pages. I had just finished signing my name when I looked up to see her standing over me.

"Just what do you think you're doing, Mrs. Haskell?" Even with the steam coming out of her nostrils she remained the epitome of elegant good looks. Today she was wearing an exquisitely simple black dress with a single row of pearls at her throat to match her earrings, except that they were circled in diamonds.

"I'm writing to Sir Clifford." My smile was genuine. Now I knew why she had looked at me with such dislike the other afternoon. Amelia Chambers knew, had perhaps known for years, probably having been told by her mother, about Sir Clifford's relationship with Sophia. And Amelia had seen something in me, perhaps just a passing expression, that had convinced her I was Sir Clifford's granddaughter. And she had been afraid that if he should ever see me, he might realize it also. And now here I was, just a closed door away from him.

"Very well, he's in a meeting, as Mrs. Rover informed you, but if you give your letter to me I'll take it into him and perhaps he will agree to step out here and see you for a few moments."

"I'll wait to give it to him myself."

She turned on her elegant heels and walked to the door farthest from the stairway, tapped on it and went in. I knew what would happen next. She would come back out and tell me Sir Clifford couldn't see me. I could either give her my letter or take it with me. She wouldn't of course have told him anything about me. She'd come up with another excuse, possibly a legitimate one, for not interrupting the meeting. I was on my feet with the letter and box in my hands and across the floor in a flash. Without consciousness of having reopened the door I found myself standing in a room that was a gentleman's library in all but the enormous table. Seated around it were a dozen or so men and women and there were large sheets of paper scattered the length and breadth of its mahogany surface. Only Amelia Chambers and Sir Clifford were standing. He was instantly recognizable from Sophia's drawings and still a strikingly handsome man, despite his seventy-odd years. His dark hair was sprinkled heavily with silver and there were lines on his hawklike face, but I didn't have a doubt in the world that many women, even some much younger ones, would still find him dangerously attractive. Amelia was frozen in place beside him and he was staring at me as if he had seen a ghost.

"Here," I said, crossing the room to stand in front of him. "These are for you. There's a letter and Sophia's diary—only it's filled with her drawings, and oh, yes—there's a photograph that may remind you that there was a special place in Knells that she loved. It's a place that shows up in several of the drawings. Could it be because it was one of the places where you and she used to meet? If you should ever want to see me, I'm sure a man of your brilliance will be able to figure out where to find me." I emptied my hands into his and without looking up into his face ran out of the room. I was halfway down the stairs, suitcase and handbag in hand, when I heard someone cross the gallery. But the footsteps stopped and I kept going. Let him read what I had written; let him look at what was in the box before we talked.

I didn't see Mrs. Rover when I passed through the hall. I went out the door and hailed a taxi.

"Where to, lady?"

"Kings Cross." I had to take the train back to Rilling. I couldn't leave Mrs. Malloy abandoned, either still at Gwen's or at some bed and breakfast. I'd pick her up, arrange to have my car towed to a garage, and when the tires were repaired drive with her back to Merlin's Court. I got out of the taxi and headed for the underground. I wasn't thinking about my mother, not even when I reached the steps going down. Not until I felt that prickling down my spine and I became frozen, unable to inch my head around to see who was there. I was seven or eight years old again and someone was coming up behind me before bending over to kiss my cheek. And suddenly I knew who that person was. I realized that today was Thursday and that I should have known from what Jane had said that it all hinged on the third bridesmaid. Now all the pieces were falling into place.

A hand took a firm grip of my arm and Hope's voice spoke in my ear.

# CHAPTER FIFTEEN

WE DIDN'T SPEAK much on the train back to Rilling. Hope and I had spent an emotional couple of hours in a cafe near Kings Cross Station. I had told her all that had happened since my arrival at the Old Rectory. Detailing how'd I'd heard that rendition of "Here Comes the Bride," had woken to hear the evil voice, and my subsequent discovery of the secret staircase. She then explained that she had also decided to go and see Sir Clifford and had arrived in a taxi just as I was leaving in mine. And some compulsion had led to tell her driver to follow that cab. I'd told her how I had stood frozen at the top of those steps, certain that someone was about to push me down them, just as had happened to my mother. But that person must have hesitated a moment too long before catching sight of Hope.

And now there we were, Hope and I, in that cafe. For the time being, safe and sound. I told her I was certain I had figured out who the person was who wanted me dead—laying out my reasons. After which she explained to me who she really was and why she had disguised herself as best she could with the wild hair and colored lenses and gone to Knells. To say that it was a shock was putting it mildly. It was this more than everything else we had discussed that I sat mulling over on the train. I knew now why I had experienced that sense of recognition on first meeting Hope in the lane—why her perfume had made me think of the violets my mother had grown on the windowsills of the flat in St. John's Wood. Hope was my mother's twin sister. Hadn't one of the bridesmaids said when we were talking about Abbey and Tam that twins tended to crop up in families?

Sophia had given birth to two baby girls out in the Belgian Congo. Having contracted a fever after a difficult delivery she had been too ill to name them. William Fitzsimons, having done his sums, as Mrs. Malloy would say, and realizing that they were Hawthorn Lane's children, had refused to do so. So the caring black midwife (hadn't I dreamt about her?) had named one baby girl Sophia after her mother and the other Wilhelmina after her presumed father. For second names she had chosen Hope and Faith.

My immediate question was how had the babies come to be separated? Hope had grown misty-eyed in the telling. When Sophia had regained her health sufficiently to leave William, who had grown increasingly angry and punitive, she had been seriously injured in the car accident, as had Hope, while Wilhelmina had been lucky—suffering only mild abrasions and bruises. When William showed up at the hospital, he had informed a barely conscious Sophia that he was taking the healthy baby home; what became of the other one, or of Sophia herself, he did not care. He must have considered this to be his final act of vengeance.

"But you lived," I said to Hope. "Who brought you up?"

She had looked at me for a long moment. "My mother."

It was almost more than I could take in.

"Not only didn't she die in that car accident, Ellie. She is still alive."

"Then why didn't she go to William"—my voice broke—"and demand that he give her Wilhelmina?"

"He was the legal father. And he told my mother that if she did not disappear with me, never to return, he would report her to the authorities for murdering her father, Reverend Hugo McNair. Something she had revealed while in the throes of that fever after giving birth."

"But why, after the passage of time, after William was dead, didn't she attempt to get in touch with my mother?"

"She was afraid he would have poisoned Wilhelmina's mind against her, and that in making contact she might do far more harm than good. It may be hard to understand, Ellie, but my mother was so emotionally shattered that she couldn't work her way out of the nightmare to think clearly about any of it. The best she could do was try to block it out."

"Did you grow up knowing that you had a twin sister?"

Hope had sat in that cafe, her coffee cup, like mine, sitting in front of her untouched. "I didn't know any of this until recently, when my mother was found to have a growth on the spine and thought she was dying. And all the barriers she had built up over the years came crashing down. And after she had told me I persuaded her to talk to one of her doctors, a wonderfully kind, sympathetic man who assured her that she couldn't have killed her father with those sleeping tablets. The idea was preposterous."

"And she realized that Rosemary had lied to her."

"That's why I came to Knells." Hope's eyes flashed in anger. "My mother was out of the woods. The growth wasn't malignant, as had been assumed. And after leaving the hospital she was sent to a convalescent home for rehabilitation of her right leg, which had lost all feeling. I wanted to find out why Rosemary had done what she did. I wore green contact lenses and the wild hair hoping that people—in particular the bridesmaids, as you call them, Ellie—would miss the resemblance to my father, which my mother had told me was strong. The idea of pretending to have psychic powers came to me the first day I was invited to the Old Rectory. I later proposed a séance seeing it as a means of frightening the truth out of Rosemary. Then

Memory Lanes entered the picture and when the brides-maids suggested that Sophia might wish to make contact with you, I couldn't do anything but agree, without raising their suspicions that I wasn't the genuine article. Besides which I was so eager to meet you. I never thought I might be placing you in danger because it never occurred to me that Reverend McNair had died from anything but natural causes, which Rosemary had played upon for her own ends."

"Then why didn't you go through with the séance last night?" I asked.

"It's strange." Hope shivered. "Because, as I've said, I don't consider myself to have any psychic ability. But from the moment you arrived I became increasingly alarmed that you were the target of a resurrected malevolence. I was afraid that if I were to confront you with my fears you might well think them far-fetched. All I could come up with was to unnerve you sufficiently to get you out of that house, or at the very least frighten your ill-wisher into leaving you alone until I could come up with a better solution."

"Which is why you went to see Sir Clifford, hoping to find out if he had an ounce of gallantry left in him."

"But that's all right, Ellie; you were there ahead of me."

"He still doesn't know the whole story."

"Perhaps it's best he doesn't." Hope frowned. "We still have to figure out what we are going to do. But why don't we talk about ourselves for a little while. We've so much to catch up on."

So I talked to her about Ben and the children. I told her of my mother's happy marriage, of her dancing, her win-some nature, and the wonderful childhood she had given me. She told me that she was married, with two grown sons, and that her husband had been in Canada on busi-ness for the past couple of months.

"It was strange how Shadow took to you right away. Almost as though he knew. He's been missing Mummy dreadfully," said Hope.

Then, after we had sat holding hands across the table, I told her of the idea that had taken root in my mind. The one I hoped would succeed in exposing a three-time murderer. And she added her suggestions. One of which occupied much of my thinking on the journey back to Rilling.

When we got off the train, Hope took my arm and as we headed for the exit asked me if I was sure I wanted to go through with our plan.

"Are you?" I asked her.

"Of course, but you're the one who has to go back to that house, Ellie. Alone, because I have to make the arrangements we talked about."

"I'll only be there for a few hours before you arrive, and being forewarned I'll be quite safe. Don't worry, I really can take care of myself."

"But do you think the bridesmaids, as I'm now beginning to think of them, will agree to a full-scale séance after the scene I made last night?"

"I'll tell them you were in the grip of such powerful forces that you were confused, or deliberately misled, into thinking that the darkness came from an earthly source. After all her talk about her desperation to make amends, Rosemary will have to agree to a reenactment of the day Reverend McNair died, and persuade the others. It would be difficult for Jane to refuse after all her talk of emanations. And I don't think Thora will." We were now standing outside the station under overcast skies.

"I really was afraid you wouldn't believe me if I told you who I was." Hope put up an umbrella as the rain came down. "You might well have thought I was working undercover for Sir Clifford." Her lips formed a half smile. "Well, there's no point in thinking about that now. We've got to concentrate on this evening and pray that nothing goes wrong. You'll be sure to have Richard Barttle and Edna there?"

"Try not to worry." I signaled to a taxi and got in. "See you at seven."

Talk, of course, was easy. By the time I found myself standing outside the Old Rectory gate, I felt more than a little sick and wouldn't have been at all surprised to see Ted waving at me with a pair of pruning shears while blood dripped down his neck and he cackled, in a perfect imitation of the parrot: "I'm telling! I'm telling!"

Before I could quake myself to death and join him on the other side of the earthly fence, the door opened and Rosemary came out, looking relieved to see me. So I gave my legs their marching orders and she and I went into the house together.

"Let's go into the sitting room," she said, taking my suitcase from me and depositing it by the stairs. "Thora's out in the garden and Jane's in her room. Both of them are quite upset. I told them about the talk I had with you last night. And it was a shock to them. Although they both tried hard not to show it or to condemn me. They weren't surprised you had left."

"But I've come back," I said when we were both seated. "I've spent a good part of my time away talking to Hope. And I'd like you to listen to what I have to say."

She did so. Sometimes adjusting her glasses. Sometimes unbuttoning her cardigan only to do it up again within moments. When I was finished she agreed to the proposed scheme without quibble.

"If you think this is what it will take to restore harmony between the living and the dead I will do my utmost to make sure that all is as you ask, Ellie. Perhaps if I had taken Jane's emanations more seriously you would have been spared the awful visitations you have described. It must be me"—Rosemary trembled visibly—"with whom Sophia has been attempting to make contact. But my guilt must have formed an impenetrable barrier."

"You do understand how important it is that we re-create everything as nearly as possible?" I asked, unsure how often her mind had wandered.

"Yes, Ellie." She twisted her hands in her lap. "Jane, Thora, and I are to wear our bridesmaid dresses. And we are to gather at seven in the conservatory. Although I don't quite understand why we should not be in the bedroom where we tried them on that day."

"Don't worry about that now. You'll understand when the time comes."

"Very well."

"And you can persuade Thora and Jane?"

"No question." Rosemary appeared to be brightening. "And I will also arrange for Richard and Edna to be here. They weren't in the house that day. At least Richard wasn't; but I do see that as such a dear friend of Sophia's his presence could be an added inducement in summoning forth her spirit. And, of course, there is the link, as you mentioned, that he was the best man at her wedding. And now I come to think of it, Edna could have been here filling in for her mother. Some parts of that day are so clear and others very vague." Rosemary got up. "If only I could believe that I have the opportunity to finally make peace between Sophia and myself."

"We can try."

"Exactly." She squared her shoulders. "Thank you for coming back, Ellie. Now, why don't you go and rest."

"What I'd like to do is move some of the plants in the conservatory out into the garden if you wouldn't mind, to allow for more space, especially the ones around the staircase."

"I'll have Thora see to that."

"And the candles?" I asked.

"Jane will set them out and light them just before seven."

"Not too many," I said, "just sufficient to create the mood. And there mustn't be any outside light coming in."

"The lack of curtains in the conservatory will not present a problem." Rosemary looked as if she were making a mental list of all the things to be done. "I'll hang sheets at the windows."

"Then, if you don't mind, I will lie down for a little while."

"What about something to eat first?"

I told her I wasn't hungry and that I shouldn't be expected down when Hope arrived. Because I wasn't one of those immediately connected with the day of Reverend McNair's death, she had asked me to remain out of sight until summoned. Rosemary accepted this readily, saying she would come up for the bridesmaid dresses shortly. Once in my room, I set my suitcase and handbag beside the bed and took off my raincoat. Then I went up the spiral staircase into the attic and returned with an armload of material. After hanging Sophia's wedding dress, veil, and circlet of orange blossom in the wardrobe, I laid the bridesmaid dresses on the bed. Next I checked to make sure that the trunk that had been at the foot of the bed was still on the blanket chest. Finally, having locked the door, I sat down to wait. I wasn't in any mood to lie down, nor was I about to risk falling asleep. It was now four o'clock. In two hours I would start getting ready.

I picked up *Secrets of the Crypt*, but after only a few paragraphs I was sick of Phoebe and her undaunted courage in the face of the unspeakably gruesome creature of the black bog and I wondered if I should take my shower now. I was about to get undressed when Rosemary tapped at the door and said that she hadn't come up only to collect the bridesmaid dresses; there was a Mrs. Malloy in the hall wanting to speak to me.

Bother! But as I headed downstairs in Rosemary's wake,

I grew worried. Had something worse than a visit from Leonard befallen Mrs. M.? With all that had happened since I last saw her, I hadn't given much thought to her suspicions of Gwen. I couldn't remember whether I had mentioned them to Hope. There had been so much else to say. Had a row erupted? Had Mrs. Malloy been forced to flee that terrifyingly overfurnished house?

"About time, Mrs. H.!" She glowered at me as Rosemary disappeared down the hall. "The time it took you to get down here, you could have flown in from Japan. And me with nerves all shot to pieces and worn to the bone lugging them cases in and out of the taxi."

"Where are they?"

"Out on the doorstep. That old girl that opened up didn't seem to notice them, along offer to bring them inside."

"She's got a lot on her mind. We're having a séance tonight!"

"Well, if that isn't something." Mrs. Malloy looked ready to cut herself in half with the belt of her cherry-red raincoat—the European equivalent, I imagined, of committing hara-kiri. "A séance and me not invited! After all the times I've told you I'd give up going to bingo if I could attend one of them things just once in my life. Never know who you'll end up holding hands with at a séance. Could be me very own Prince Charming."

"It won't be tonight," I told her. "The only man who'll be here has his own Prince Charming at home."

"That's no excuse for not inviting me. And you still haven't asked why I'm here," Mrs. Malloy huffed. "But I suppose you'll go trying to make it up to me by bringing them suitcases inside and carrying them upstairs for me."

"I'll take two," I told her. "You'll have to manage the other one. I can't grow an extra arm at the drop of a hat, you know. And I'm not about to make an extra trip."

"Oh, well, if that's the way it's got to be, Mrs. H., and don't go thinking I'm thrilled out of my noggin at having to share your room; but I don't suppose the old ladies thought to get one ready for me. And, truth be told, I don't expect to get a wink of sleep and you won't either when you hear what I've got to tell you." She was still talking when she reached the bedroom.

"I've got a good idea what it entails," I said.

"There you go, showing off—using them fancy words. And this time you didn't even get it right. Entails is what they took out of them poor sods they used to draw and quarter back in the days when just telling the king he took a bad photo got you hauled off to the Tower."

"That was the first clue." I put down my two cases and added hers to the group.

"What was?"

"The photograph. But your story first, Mrs. Malloy."

"It's not a pretty one, but then murder and blackmail rarely is." She took off her raincoat and tossed it on the bed as if it were one more burden too heavy to bear. Then she sat down and told me everything Gwen had told her. Pausing every now and then with just the right amount of melodramatic emphasis to incur my exclamations of horror. Which weren't up to snuff because I'd already figured out the gist of it. "So what do you think of them apple dumplings?" she finally asked.

"Let me fill you in on what I uncovered at this end."

She listened attentively but I began to sense by the time I was halfway through that she was a bit miffed that not only did I have the bulk of the story, but my experiences at the Old Rectory had been more harrowing than hers at the Fiddler residence.

"Well, that's life!" She crossed her legs in their black fishnet stockings and tapped a high-heeled foot, but then her finer feelings emerged and she said it was terrible about my dear mother as well as not having been much of a treat for Reverend McNair. And she didn't know what she could have been thinking to have contemplated spending a night in this house. "It was just that I know how obstinate you can be, Mrs. H., about seeing things through and I couldn't go leaving you here unprotected. But now it's as clear as a pikestaff up the bum—as Leonard would say in that common way of his—that we need to forget all about this séance business and get in your car and be off to Merlin's Court before someone slashes the tires."

"That's already been done." I was pleased to note that this time away from home seemed to have cooled her fond memories of Leonard and spent the next five minutes talking her around to the fact we couldn't bunk off, leaving a murderer plotting the next move. "And talking about moving, that's what I need to be doing if I'm to be ready in time. Would you help me get the trunk off the blanket chest and back at the foot of the bed?"

"Why not leave it where it is?"

I explained and she began to grow visibly into her role of conspirator. Her bust grew at least three inches, which mine hadn't done since I was ten.

"Well, I'll have to take off me shoes for fear of breaking me neck. But as I'm always telling you, mostly around Christmas time and me birthday, no sacrifice is too small. But why don't we wait till you've got yourself all fixed and ready before moving the thing. Just to be on the safe side. You go ahead and take your shower while I lie back and think what I'm going to wear. Wish I'd got one of them black shawls with the tassels. I don't suppose you thought to bring one, Mrs. H.?"

I apologized for the oversight and suggested that she get ready first. It was now close to six and I would—no offense intended—move more quickly once she had gone downstairs. She agreed to this without demur, saying she understood I would need solitude in which to think myself into my role. She only hoped it wouldn't prove to be my swan song. With unaccustomed speed she completed a change of outfit, from one back taffeta frock to another, redid her makeup, helped me move the trunk, and, stepping back into her shoes, headed for the door.

"But don't expect me to come off chummy, Mrs. H., I'll keep to meself and not accept so much as a thimbleful of gin, unless of course it's forced down me throat."

"Just tell Rosemary I asked you to stay, let her introduce you to the others, and then pretend you've lost your voice."

As soon as I had the room to myself I began feverishly to get ready. The water trickled out of the showerhead, the skimpy towels wouldn't dry me fast enough, and my hair didn't want to stay in its coil, so that my head ended up feeling like a pincushion. Luckily I didn't have to bother with makeup. The more washed-out I looked, the better, I thought, as I pulled Sophia's wedding dress over my head. The doorbell had rung several times. I had lost count by the time I had put on the veil so that it covered my face, and added the circlet of orange blossom. Then I looked at the clock, noted the time, and waited for ten minutes, as arranged with Hope. Now! I drew a deep breath and went down the steps to the lower landing, past Rosemary's and Jane's rooms and the bathroom, towards the plant-screened balcony leading to the spiral staircase that descended to the conservatory. I stood looking down into a room of shadows, the forms and faces of those grouped there palely illuminated by the sparse scattering of candles. Hope was the only person standing and I could hear the muttering of her incantations. They grew steadily in volume until she cried out the words for which I had been waiting.

"Sophia, we await your return! Cross over, Sophia! There are none but friends here!"

I heard Mrs. Malloy pipe up that she couldn't go so far as to claim that sort of acquaintance, but she was sending the right sort of vibes and would be pleased as Punch to make her acquaintance. When she stopped talking, possibly because someone had poked her in the ribs, I felt a presence behind me and froze as I had done at the entrance to the underground steps. But a moment later I was stepping slowly down the spiral rungs. A series of gasps drifted up to me but they were instantly blocked out by the voice that wasn't mine.

"Yes, it is I, Sophia. I have come to name my father's murderer."

It wasn't my voice speaking. It was that of my grandmother, whom Hope had promised to fetch from the convalescent home after leaving me in Rilling. She had been due to leave in a couple of days anyway, the function of her leg being fully restored. It was her presence I had just now felt behind me. And her voice continued to float down from the balcony where she was screened from view by the foliage.

"I have come to name the one who added those sleeping tablets to my father's cherry brandy. Not because she hated him"—her voice grew in power—"but because she wanted the man I loved for her own. She wanted me to take the guilt upon myself so that I would see no other option than to marry William Fitzsimons. She pretended to be my friend. She alone knew I kept a diary because she saw me tear the pages from the back of it to write the notes that she agreed to deliver for me. And when I drew a picture of her that showed something not quite so nice lurking behind that pretty smiling face of hers, she tore it out. But even then I never thought, not even after Father was found dead, that she was evil. Year by year, she has come, mask in place, to this house, hating the man she had married, hating my daughter so much that she killed her rather than let her have those drawings of the man she had never stopped wanting. No one was going to have any part of him, if you could help it. Isn't that so, Edna?"

The scream that erupted almost sent me toppling down the remaining stairs. There was a lot of scurrying about and suddenly the lights went on. The conservatory looked almost vulgarly naked without its foliage. I could see Rosemary,

Jane, and Thora sitting as if turned to stone. Richard Barttle and Mrs. Malloy were standing so close together that they seemed to merge into one person. Hope was coming towards me, but I knew she would go on past me up those stairs to her mother. I couldn't bring myself to look at Edna; instead, my eyes finally fixed on Sir Clifford Heath. He was staring upwards, his face alight with wonder and disbelieving joy. My grandmother had stepped out from the balcony. She was standing on the top rung. And it was as though the years fell away and there were no silver in his hair. No lines on his face. He looked twenty again and the woman now coming down the stairs looked about seventeen.

"Sophia," he whispered as he went to her.

"Thorn," she breathed as she went into his arms.

"Well, I'd say that was a bit of all right," said Mrs. Malloy.

"Sophia, we thought you were dead!" The bridesmaids were falling over themselves, all babbling at once.

"Thank God!" Rosemary cried.

"We don't understand," Jane sobbed, "but it doesn't matter!"

"Just so long as we've got you back!" That was Thora. And there might have been a consensus of agreement if Edna hadn't straightened up and dragged a knife out of her apron pocket.

"Everyone stay away." She brandished the knife in my direction. "I should have killed you when I had the chance that night in your room. Scaring you wasn't good enough. You were too stupid to leave. And then some other busybody went and slashed your tires."

"Edna, I'm shocked," Jane gasped. "But not cross, because it's clear Ted's death has unhinged you."

"I had to kill him"—Edna's face was now a mask of maniacal glee—"the louse had seen me push your mother down those steps. He'd followed me that time, like he was always doing on Thursdays—them being my days off. Always thinking I was sneaking away to see another man! Well, he found out different that time, didn't he?"

"That's right," Richard said kindly, "get it off your chest. We all understand that the man got what he deserved."

"When he heard Mina's daughter was coming, he kept on saying it—'I'm telling! I'm telling!' Couldn't let that happen, could I? And it was exciting playing out the role of the grieving widow. Pretending to sprain my foot running in with the bad news. Saying it was an odd sort of accident, so that if suspicions were raised it would be remembered how I'd said it and how I'd always loved my dear hubby to the point of distraction. They'd probably have thought it was you." She now brandished the knife in Thora's direction. "Had a row with him over the garden that morning, didn't you?"

"Edna, dear, do be careful!" Jane quavered. "You could cut yourself, and we wouldn't want that. It would spoil Sophia's homecoming."

Edna ignored her. "Oh, I did have a good laugh when Miss Dobson put that poultice on my bruise that was made up with food coloring. Think you're Miss Medicine Woman, don't you?" She now swiveled the knife in Rosemary's direction. "Or it could have been you that was suspected. So sad her having those nervous breakdowns, I would have said. Never been quite right since; and then there's you!" The blade was now pointed at Jane. "A woman that sees and hears things that aren't there. Of course that was all my doing. So that if one or both of the other two dear ladies had gone upstairs with Sophia's look-alike granddaughter when she arrived, and had smelled the orange blossom and seen the confetti, they would have thought you'd done it to convince them you were potty after all. You all thought I was still at the hospital." She now addressed all three bridesmaids. "Weeping buckets for my precious hubby, but I had Tom bring me back as soon as you two left." Eyeing Thora and Jane: "The doctors had already told me Ted was dead. But I'd kept that to myself. I came in through the cellar door and saw you"—hatred glowed in her eyes as she looked at me—"open the one at the top of the stairs. I tiptoed to the top after you closed it and watched you go up the hall stairs. And quick as lightning I went up the ones to the blanket chest and sang you that pretty song."

"Edna"—Sir Clifford released Sophia and took a couple of steps towards her—"give me the knife and let me get help for you. It will be the very best that's available." She did not look at him.

"You can't know"—she eyed the bridesmaids venomously—"how good it feels to have the whiphand after all these years of being at your beck and call. Seeing how you pitied me for being married to Ted and never having the sort of life where I went out to tennis parties."

Everyone in the room stood transfixed in position as if participating in a tableau. Sir Clifford again had his arms around Sophia. And Hope stood close to them. It was Mrs. Malloy who suddenly moved.

"You're a disgrace, Edna Wilks, that's what you are to charwomen everywhere. A proud profession like ours. It doesn't bear thinking about. And doing what you did to your own cousin. Encouraging her to bump off Mr. Fiddler's first wife. Telling Gwen that if hiding her glasses so she'd fall down the stairs didn't work, it would be a snap to give her some herb that would do the trick. And when the poor woman died right after, without Gwen having the heart to do it, you blackmailed her all these years."

"I never could squeeze much money out of Gwen, not with her having to account to Barney Fiddler for every damn penny, but it made our little visits interesting." She chewed on her lip. "Even so, I'd always go home properly ticked off. She'd become such a snob." Edna smirked. "But she had her uses. Like my going over to stay there that night and getting her to say I'd slept in bed with her so that I'd have a nice tight alibi. Never suspected it was me, did you?" She waved everyone back towards the wall before moving closer to me, the knife steady in her hand.

"No," I admitted, "not until I was standing at the top of the underground steps this morning and I remembered how I'd felt when I came here as a child and someone came up behind me and bent to give me a kiss. Someone who was chanting a nasty little rhyme that I afterwards thought I'd made up. I had always pictured three bridesmaids, as my mother called them, and it came to me that Jane had said she wasn't here then, so the third woman had to have been you. I also realized that today is Thursday, and that my mother's accident happened on a Thursday, your day off. When no one would question your whereabouts."

"And what else do you have on your little mind?"

"You said yesterday that you didn't know where Sophia got the paper to write to Hawthorn, when you had to have known it was taken from her diary. The printed dates alone would have told you that."

"Oh, aren't we smart, Miss Ellie! Tuck any other clues up your sleeve?"

"Your engagement photo that's on Gwen's piano. You looked so in love. And so you were . . . with the man who *took* the photograph. Hawthorn Lane."

She finally looked at him. "You're an old man," she said. "That wasn't supposed to happen. If I couldn't have you with me through the years, then I wanted you to stay as you were in my mind and in those drawings of Sophia's. Mina wasn't going to have them. I'd already had enough taken away from me."

"That wasn't why you killed Sophia's and my daughter." Sir Clifford's eyes glittered with grief and rage. "You were afraid that not only would she bring those drawings to me, she would tell me what Rosemary had confessed and the past would be torn open. I haven't forgotten your screaming rage when I refused to take up with you after Sophia's marriage. And I've often wondered why you agreed to carry those notes back and forth when she was kept in her room. If Mina had come to me, I would finally have seen the light—that you had schemed to win my gratitude so that when you had accomplished your diabolical scheme, and I was left heartbroken, you'd be the woman to console me."

"And so I should have been. I was prettier than your darling Sophia. I was prettier than the whole lot of them!" Edna flashed the knife at the bridesmaids. "I just didn't get to wear the expensive frocks and had a mother that was a drunk."

"Merciful heavens! I do feel my emanations failed me where Edna was concerned," said Jane plaintively to the rest of us.

"Cod's wallop!" Thora put an arm around her, and another around Rosemary. "Anyone could have been deceived."

"We all get duped once in a while," responded Richard sadly.

"Shut up! Everyone into that corner!" Edna began backing out into the hall the instant her order was obeyed. And it is impossible to know what would have happened next, if the cellar door hadn't opened and Leonard Skinner hadn't spoken from behind her.

"The game's up!" His voice radiated triumph. "I know my little Roxie's here! I saw her arrive in a taxi. Knew if I kept watching the place I'd get lucky."

"Who is this idiot?" inquired Sir Clifford.

"Don't everyone look at me," Mrs. Malloy bridled, "I married him, it's true, but I didn't give birth to him."

"Now, then, Roxie, me darling!" Leonard wagged a remonstrative finger. "It's not all been fun and games. I had to slash that Mrs. Haskell's tires," he added piteously, "so she'd have to go on foot or by bus and I'd have a better chance of keeping up with her. But I lost her yesterday when that chap in the fish van gave her a lift."

"And you all think *I'm* mad!" complained Edna.

"Leonard, you're embarrassing me in front of me new chums. I don't like that new way you've done your hair." Mrs. M. glowered at him from under neon-coated lids.

"So this is the thanks I get." He was beginning to look the least bit offended by the lack of welcome on all sides. He had yet to be offered a cup of tea. "Sleeping in the garden shed isn't yours truly's idea of posh, but it did prove useful when I spotted you, dearie"—he placed an arm around Edna's shoulders—"coming and going through that cellar door and found you'd kindly left it unlocked. That way I didn't have to worry about not being allowed in the front. But now I'm here, is anyone going to ask me to join the party? It's not like I've come empty-handed. I'd have been here sooner if I hadn't gone off—after I saw Roxie— to get that pound and a half of stewing steak that seems to be all that's standing in the way of our beautiful reunion."

"You think that's all it'll take to get me back!" Undaunted by the possibility of having her bosom deflated by a plunge of Edna's knife, Mrs. Malloy lunged out of the conservatory at him. "Me, a woman that's forged a career for herself with the granddaughter of a peer of the realm!"

Edna came back to life—I suppose even murderers become discombobulated at times. She pulled away from Leonard, seemingly uncertain whether to stab him or Mrs. Malloy first. Leonard toppled forward in a faint and knocked Edna off balance. Mrs. M. grabbed up the package of stewing steak and hit her over the head with it. There followed a stampede of footsteps mingled with a lot of shouting, which was suddenly reduced to a murmur when the conservatory door, which apparently no one had thought to lock, burst open. And the neighbors—Tom, Irene, and Frank, led by the inappropriately named, massively built Susan—burst in upon the scene. It turned out later that they had seen Sir Clifford's car draw up and had been waiting outside at the front listening for sounds of trouble, before they thought to go around the back.

After that, things calmed down considerably. The police were phoned and after a brief interrogation Edna was taken away. Rosemary, Thora, Jane, and Richard agreed to go down to the station and give statements. Leonard departed, saying the fall had brought back his amnesia, and Mrs. Malloy, after tossing the package of stewing steak out the door after him, said that she thought she would go upstairs and read a nice scary book. I recommended *Secrets of the Crypt*. In a moment I would join my grandfather and grandmother and my mother's twin sister in the sitting room. But I thought they needed just a little time of its being just the three of them. And I needed time to absorb these new additions to my family. So I went into the kitchen and sat at the table. My mother would be so happy for me, I thought. And feeling as though I had finally laid her to rest, I went back into the hall and peeked into the sitting room. Hope sat watching her reunited parents holding hands. The illusion in the conservatory had passed. They were two elderly, if still good-looking, people, but the expressions on their faces were more beautiful than youth. It was, I thought, eternal. And even though, like Hope, I didn't claim to have any extrasensory gift, I felt my mother's presence. I could picture her sitting there with them, not outside the circle but at its core. As I was about to go in and join them, the telephone rang and I went to pick it up. When I heard Ben's voice I felt my world become complete.

"Don't say anything," I said, "just let me hear you breathe. The redecorating can wait—for fifty years if it has to. I'm coming to join you and the children tomorrow. I want to talk to you about Memory Lanes."